Fractured Eden

Steven Gossington

Developmental Editor - Andrea Hurst

Copy Editor - Marie de Haan

Cover design by Natasha Brown

Marketing by 2Market Books

Author photograph by Portrait Innovations Professional Studios

ISBN-13: 978-1518804236

ISBN-10: 1518804233

Library of Congress Control Number: 2015919091
CreateSpace Independent Publishing Platform, North Charleston, SC

Acknowledgements

I wish to thank several of my friends, Bill Damm and Paul, for their invaluable help with portions of this story, and Dennis and Carole Wazaney for their amazing advice and encouragement.

When we remember we are all mad, the mysteries disappear and life stands explained.

Mark Twain

Prologue

Something's not right, Aaron thought.

He touched the bandage taped to his lower jaw and then eased open the door to the chief of staff's office.

Aaron Rovsing, MD peeked around the office door into an anteroom, and a wide-eyed secretary shot up from behind a desk.

"I'll show you right in. They've been waiting for you."

"Do you know what this is about?" Aaron said.

She shook her head. "It's not for me to say."

Aaron stepped past her and glanced around the inner meeting room. Three medical staff members sat flanking the chief of staff at the far end of a polished rectangular mahogany table.

"Sit down," the chief said.

Aaron sat on the edge of a chair.

"I'll get to the point. We're all here to inform you of some complaints against you."

"Complaints?" Aaron squeaked out the words. "About what? Who's complaining?"

"Some of the medical staff have questioned your clinical decisions recently, and—"

"My clinical . . ." Aaron gulped.

"Complaints about your medical judgment, including a charge of patient endangerment—"

"Endangerment?" Aaron whispered the word again. "Endangerment?"

"And that patient of yours that overdosed and died because of what you prescribed." The chief leaned forward and pointed at him. "That was the last straw."

Aaron's body stiffened.

The chief's eyes glinted at him. "We recommend that you resign."

Aaron's legs wobbled as he struggled upright, his mouth gaping. The chief of staff slid a paper toward him. "Sign this paper, indicating that we had this discussion and that you understand—"

Aaron scribbled his name with shaky fingers.

The chief looked around the room with his hand poised above the table, and the other three men nodded in turn. He slapped the table and growled at Aaron. "This meeting is over."

Aaron stumbled out of the room, striking his shoulder on the doorjamb.

As he hurried down the hall, Reuben, a doctor friend of his, hailed and approached him.

"Did something happen? You look pale as a ghost," Reuben said.

Aaron sputtered, his eyes wide. "The chief just asked me to resign." He turned to the wall as two nurses clattered by, their giggles echoing down the glistening hallway.

Reuben leaned toward Aaron. "Wow. That's serious."

"It doesn't seem real."

"Are you going to fight it?"

"You mean like appeal it?"

"Sure."

Aaron looked down. "I don't know."

Floating before his eyes was an image of the chief, a muscular and athletic man whose eyes gloated over everyone, a man with a commanding presence in any room.

I don't think I could stand up to the chief, he thought.

"You're not just giving up, are you?"

"He said I was incompetent." Aaron looked at Reuben. "Be honest with me. You think I'm a competent doctor, don't you?"

"Well—"

"You hesitated."

"No, Aaron, don't get the wrong idea. I don't work with you directly. I'm not in a position to answer that question, but I imagine you're competent enough. Why not stand your ground and challenge it?"

Aaron dropped his head and walked away, avoiding eye contact with anyone else. *What will my wife say?*

Outside in the late winter chill, he pulled his coat tight around him and walked to his car in the hospital parking lot. *Lauren will help me. We can get through this together.*

"Damn it. I'll start a new practice." He hammered the dashboard with his fist. "How could that asshole do this to me?"

His hands squeezed the steering wheel. *I wonder if I should fight back. The overdose was not my fault. That could've happened to any doctor.*

I'll ask Lauren.

3

Even with the car heater blasting, he shivered during his drive home.

Aaron unlocked the door to his house. "Hello, honey?" he said. "I've got some bad news." He heard no noise. "Lauren?"

He switched on lights and scanned the front rooms and kitchen. Sensing no movement, he hurried to the master bedroom. "Lauren?"

Aaron stood by their bed and scratched his cheek. He was alone. *Did she have an emergency? She has been acting different lately, like she's stressed over something.*

In the kitchen, he spotted a yellow post-it note on an otherwise bare counter.

His hand trembled as he read the message: "I've left you. I'm in love with someone else."

Uncaring, foul words that blurred into black blobs on the paper.

What is happening?

Aaron's body buckled. As he slumped to his knees, the bandage slipped off his jaw and fluttered to the floor.

Chapter 1

Something is different out there, Aaron thought as he stared out the windshield of his car.

With the air conditioner near the maximum setting, he drove along the two-lane country road at dusk, 1500 miles from his previous life. He'd scoped out this area a few months before, but now that he was moving here, he paid more attention to details.

Looking toward the sky, he saw pine trees swaying over the road. *These trees are taller than the ones a few miles back.*

After finding a country music station on the car radio, he cranked up the volume.

I've got to give country music a chance.

Aaron swayed in time with the melody. It was a song about feeling crazy over a hopeless love. " 'Crazy,' by Patsy Cline," the DJ said.

He glanced at his shoes and slapped his knee. "And I need to get some boots, real cowboy boots."

As his mind wandered to his recent divorce, he shut his eyes and shook his head.

I don't want to go there.

His eyes opened.

"What the . . ." He jammed the brake pedal and jerked the steering wheel to avoid something—a figure—darting across the road in front of his car. Screeching and sliding in a 180-degree oval, the car came to rest on the shoulder at the opposite side of the road. Aaron gasped for breath and his heart pounded. His knuckles were white on the steering wheel.

Easing his grip, he looked in the direction of the figure.

What the hell was that?

After turning the car off, Aaron stepped out onto unsteady legs and examined the front bumper and the road nearby. No other headlights were in sight. A smell of burnt rubber permeated the muggy air.

Standing still, he scanned the nearby trees and listened. *Soft footsteps in the trees?*

He walked around and studied the pavement and the grass beside the road.

Well, whatever the hell it was, at least I didn't hit it. Maybe it was a deer.

After several minutes, his breathing slowed and his jitters eased. He started the car, punched the radio off, and made a U-turn, squinting for any sign of motion.

A hazy image of a frowning, bald man popped into his mind.

Surely that wasn't him I almost hit: the guy with the machete?

After several miles, Aaron slowed to a stop in his driveway. He gazed at the front of his new home and sighed.

I can't believe it. I'm finally here.

He unlocked the front door, switched on a light inside and surveyed the empty rooms.

So it starts, he thought. *A new chapter.*

"Should I even be here?" he said, slapping the wall.

He sighed and walked outside to the street in front of his house. *They're chintzy on the streetlights. Maybe the Texas moon gives off enough light.*

"Yikes." He threw up his arms and ducked as a bird flapped by just over his head. He looked up but didn't see anything.

His house was at the end of a row of one-story homes, and across the street was fenced-in land that sloped up to a mansion.

I guess someone owns all that property. Maybe it goes with that huge house on the hill.

As Aaron carried in bags and boxes from his car, an owl hooted from a grove of trees nearby.

After emptying his car, he wiped the sweat off his forehead and plopped down on top of a sleeping bag. He closed his eyes.

No, get something to eat first.

He forced himself to walk outside, and he took a deep breath of fresh evening air and looked up at the stars.

Aaron cupped his hands around his mouth. "I'm here now and I'm not going back."

After pushing his car air conditioner to the max, he consulted a restaurant guide and some map pages scattered over the front seat and planned a route to a nearby diner.

Several miles and a few turns later, he spotted the diner's sign and saw lights inside the restaurant. *Good, it's open.*

He parked and walked inside to an aroma of cinnamon and apples. *Mmm, apple pie.*

"Let's put you right over here," a waitress said as she led him to a booth. "How are you tonight?"

"Hungry," Aaron said as he gazed at her. *Mid to late forties, I'd guess.* She was tall and pudgy, with jet-black hair.

Her eyes were wary. "I'm Wanda. Are you traveling through?"

"No, I just moved here."

She stepped back. "You're the new doctor?"

"Yes. I'm Aaron Rovsing."

"I heard you'd checked us out, and we all hoped you'd come. Where're you from?"

"The Northeast, Connecticut."

"Welcome to our little piece of paradise. It's quite a bit hotter here in East Texas, especially now in late summer."

"I think I'm okay with that."

"Is anyone else joining you tonight?"

Aaron followed her eyes to his bare left ring finger. "No."

She cocked her head. "I'll give you a few minutes to look at the menu."

Wanda stopped by a table with two occupants and motioned toward Aaron. A woman and child stood from the table and followed Wanda to his booth.

"This is Dr. Rovsing, our new doctor in town," Wanda said to the woman.

Aaron stood and they shook hands.

She's got quite a grip.

"Nice to meet you. I'm Marley." She had short blond hair and stood a few inches shorter than Aaron's five feet ten.

I might like this town after all, he thought.

The child peeked out from behind Marley and pointed at Aaron. "Mommy, what's wrong with his face?"

Marley looked down. "Now Cristal, that's not nice."

Aaron touched his left lower jaw. "It's all right. It's just a battle wound."

"You were in the military?" Marley said.

"No, a different kind of battle."

"I'm sorry."

Aaron smiled. "No worries."

"It's good to meet you. I hope you like it here," Marley said.

Aaron waved at Cristal as she and Marley walked away.

He snorted and touched his face again. "Damned scar."

Aaron polished off a decent meal of coleslaw, a turkey sandwich, and a slice of apple pie with ice cream. Everything, even the tomatoes on the sandwich, tasted fresh.

At one point, he glanced up and caught Wanda staring at him. She turned her head away.

That was an odd look in her eyes.

When he paid the bill, Wanda's eyes were back to normal. She was all smiles.

Back at his house, all was quiet, except for an occasional hoot from an owl. In less than a minute, he was asleep on a sheet on top of his sleeping bag.

Aaron woke up in a pool of sweat. Bright red numbers on the alarm clock showed 3:00 a.m. In the bathroom, he toweled off and dried his short dripping hair.

He recalled fragments of a dream. A young woman with a headache sat on the floor. "Hydrocodone is what I need." She wore sunglasses and held her temples, crying, rocking back and forth. She swallowed all the Vicodin at once and collapsed right in front of him. He shook her, but she didn't respond. Two muscular men dragged him into a courtroom, in front of a judge with white hair and a black gown. Her sunglasses still on, the dead woman was stretched out on the floor at Aaron's side. While pointing down at her, the judge yelled something at Aaron . . .

Part of the dream, the fatal Vicodin overdose, had happened in real life over six months ago, but he hadn't been summoned to court yet.

Aaron sighed and gazed at his blue eyes in the mirror. *I don't remember what her eyes were like.*

He dried his sleeping bag with a towel and stretched out over it, and stared at the ceiling until sunrise.

At 8:00 a.m., a moving van rumbled to a stop in front of Aaron's house. For the rest of the morning, Aaron directed the two men with their payloads of furniture and boxes. They took frequent breaks to drink water and cool off.

His long, dark wood desk just fit through the door of the office room. Next, the men heaved into the office boxes labeled with "college stuff" and "medical school stuff."

"What's in these boxes?" one of the men asked.

"Those are old school papers. I can't seem to part with them."

"Oh, yeah, I know what that's like," the man said with a nod. "I still have boxes from high school. I have a hard time throwing anything away. Drives my wife crazy."

Near noon, Aaron blotted his forehead with a paper towel and turned to the men. "It's hard to move around in here now. I didn't remember that I had so much stuff."

"We hear that all the time," one of them said. "Sometimes, there isn't room for it all."

During one of their breaks, Aaron overheard part of a conversation from the front yard.

"I sure can smell the livestock around here."

"These country folks are used to it. They probably don't smell a thing."

Aaron walked to his back yard. *What are all these cows doing at my house?*

A tightly grouped herd of brown cattle lingered near his fence. Some of the cows looked at him. Aaron shrugged. "All the animals around here are checking me out."

He stopped at the fence. "Hello. I'm your new neighbor."

One of the cows mooed back at him.

Aaron laughed. "Thanks. I'll take that as a 'welcome to our town.' " He watched the herd for several minutes. *They don't seem afraid of me.*

Resting on the sturdy, flawless fence, he looked beyond the cattle at an undulating green pasture that spread out as far as he could see, to a faint line of trees in the distance. Groups of trees scattered around the pasture provided the cows welcome shade from the midday sun. A cool breeze lifted his hair and ruffled the cows' fur.

He turned in a circle, scanning the horizon. *Even the sky seems bigger in Texas.*

In the late afternoon after the moving van had gone, Aaron stood in his front yard and studied the house. Its light coral paint job was holding up.

Good. No missing shingles.

He strolled around the property, admiring the grassy lawn and azalea bushes that surrounded the house, and stepped into the street. *Wow. I can see the heat rising from the asphalt.*

Including his, four houses stood in the block, separated from each other by groves of pine trees.

Sweat ran down the sides of his face. He toweled off and drove to a nearby store to buy supplies. Along the way, he listened to a few country music songs on the radio.

After a savory, spicy barbecue dinner at a restaurant not far away, Aaron busied himself with opening boxes and arranging his closet. On his bedroom wall, he hung a framed painting, which featured a dirt footpath winding through the forest. Shoe prints and footprints were imprinted in the dirt. Among the trees at the far end of the path were hazy figures that appeared to be watching.

Aaron positioned the painting so he could see it from his bed.

Chapter 2

Am I really up for this? Aaron thought.

He stepped into his white Volvo sedan and lowered the driver side window. Out in the street, he filled his lungs with fresh air. It was Monday morning, the first day at his new job.

He shook his head. *I can hardly believe I'm here, in Hicksville, in the middle of nowhere.*

A smell of pine trees piqued his nose as he rolled to the end of his street and turned right onto the road that led to his family practice clinic.

Aaron squeezed the steering wheel with both hands, his knuckles white. "Who was the son of a bitch that complained about me back in Connecticut?" He sighed. "Surely I'm as good as any other family doc—"

"Geez," he shouted as he stomped his brakes. His tires squealed to a stop just short of a large green turtle plodding across the road.

Gasping for air, he glanced in the rearview mirror. No car was behind him.

"My tires . . . might not . . . last long around here."

He slowed his breathing, got out, and walked to the front of the car.

Safe and sound at the side of the road, the turtle looked back at Aaron.

"Turtle dude, you look mighty pleased with yourself." Aaron stared into the turtle's eyes. "I think this has happened to you before. Maybe you like the smell of burnt rubber?"

Aaron eased the car past the turtle and drove the short remaining distance to his office. He pulled into a parking space in front of the clinic at 7:30 a.m.

He sat and studied the building through the windshield. *It's just as I remembered. The outer walls are made of brick, so this place could be here for a long time.* He glanced up at the sky. *I wonder when the last tornado came through here.* Aaron's heart skipped a beat as he unlocked and opened the front door of the clinic.

He turned to look as two other cars entered the parking area.

One of them must be Stella. He'd learned of her from the owner of the clinic building. She was the office nurse of the previous doctor, and Aaron had spoken with her by phone. "Yes, I'm available," she'd said. She'd been making ends meet by providing in-home nursing care for patients who could afford it.

Aaron held the door for an attractive black woman. "Stella?"

"That's me."

"Good morning. It's lucky for me to work with someone with experience here."

"I'm glad to be back."

Another woman walked toward the door, and Stella motioned with her hand. "This is Juliana, our receptionist and billing expert."

"Good. Someone to make sure we all make a living and pay the rent," Aaron said.

Juliana laughed. "That's what I'm good at."

She and Aaron followed Stella into the clinic. Standing in the middle of the waiting room, Stella smiled at Aaron. "It'll be good to see this place alive with patients again. Come along and I'll show you how I set up everything."

Aaron followed Stella on a tour of the waiting room, four treatment rooms, the doctor's office, and a small lounge in the back with a refrigerator and coffee maker.

"I know it smells kind of musty in here," Stella said. "This place hasn't been used for a while, so I came in yesterday to tidy up what I could. I put in new light bulbs, and I've ordered supplies."

At the rear of the clinic, Aaron stood in the doorway of his office. Light from the morning sun streaked in through partially opened window blinds.

He settled into his office chair and explored the desk drawers, then strolled around the room and flipped through a few medical books from two wall shelves.

I guess the last doctor didn't want these books. Maybe he or she left in a hurry.

An hour later, he walked into a patient room and saw a woman in tears. He closed the door behind him.

"I'm Dr. Rovsing. How can I help you?"

"I'm falling apart. I can't sleep," the woman said between sobs. "I cry all the time." She held a tissue to her eyes. "Maybe if I could just get some sleep."

"Has this happened to you before?"

She took a deep breath. "No. My daughter disappeared two weeks ago. She's sixteen. Everyone thinks she just ran away, but I know she wouldn't do that."

"The police are looking into it?"

"Yes, along with all my friends and neighbors." She sobbed into the tissue.

Aaron waited as she composed herself. She looked up at him. "I'm sorry. It's so hard for me to talk about this."

Aaron examined her pupils, heart, and lungs, and prescribed a mild sedative. "I hope this helps you, and I pray you find her."

Just after noon, Aaron dabbed his forehead with a handkerchief and adjusted the thermostat a few degrees cooler until the air conditioner was blasting arctic air. He stood under a vent for several minutes to cool off and then followed the aroma of coffee to the lounge and poured himself a cup. He sat with Stella and Juliana at a small table and studied them while they talked. Stella was a bit overweight; Juliana was slender. They were about the same height: Aaron guessed about five feet seven. Stella had a jolly face, and appeared to be mid-forties and about twenty years or so older than Juliana, who had smooth Hispanic facial features.

"Did you bring family with you?" Stella said to Aaron.

"No family, no kids. I divorced a few months ago."

"Well, I think you picked a good place to start over."

"I hope you're right. How long have you lived here?"

"A long time, over twenty years," Stella said.

"Only three years for me," Juliana said.

Aaron looked at Stella. "You probably know everyone in town."

"Oh, yeah. I can help you with medical histories, for sure." She raised an eyebrow. "You can bet most everybody for miles around knows about the new doctor. I expect many folks will drop by this week just to check you out."

"No problem. I'll get to know everyone sooner or later."

Stella shook her head. "Maybe not everyone."

Aaron put his cup down. "Why do you say that?"

"I'm thinking of the Taggetts. Wanda Taggett used to take her husband, Sid, to nearby hospitals every few months. He'd often go by ambulance. She takes care of him in their home when he's not in the hospital. For the last few months, I don't think he even gets out of bed much."

"I met a Wanda in the diner down the road. Is that her?" Aaron said.

"That's her, Wanda Taggett."

"What's wrong with her husband?"

"I heard it was some kind of neurologic disease. Wanda says no one can figure out exactly what his problem is. I think they recently ran out of money for a lot of medical visits and tests. They don't come here to the clinic anymore."

"Surely she'll let me examine him at home," Aaron said.

"Good luck with that. She hasn't let any visitors inside that house and Sid hasn't been back to the hospital since the state tried to remove her husband and son from the home a few months ago. She fought back, and husband and son are still with her in the house."

"That's serious. Someone must've complained about her."

"We figured the hospital did. I think they were worried she was unfit as a caregiver."

"She seemed a reasonable person when I talked with her in the diner."

"Away from her home, she can be as normal as you or me."

Aaron smiled. "You don't know me that well yet."

Stella laughed. "That's all we need. Another strange person in this town."

Late afternoon, as Aaron approached a patient room, Stella walked up to him and whispered in his ear. "He's got a loud voice, so I like to put him away from other patients. You know, for privacy reasons."

Aaron nodded and entered the room. A large man in a cowboy shirt and boots stood and extended a thick, weather-beaten hand. "I'm Grant Belkin. Welcome to our town."

"Glad to be here," Aaron said. *I finally meet a real cowboy.*

"I need my blood pressure medicine refilled, and I wanted to meet you. I run the ranch behind your house." His words echoed around the room.

"So those are your cattle. They're a fine looking bunch."

"Sometimes they make a lot of noise. I hope they don't bother you."

Aaron smiled. "I don't think that will be a problem."

"Good." Grant put his hands in the pockets of his jeans and looked down. "Anyway, they've been quiet lately."

"Maybe they're content?"

"Nope. When they're quiet, I get worried."

"Worried about what?"

Grant raised his head and started to say something, then he closed his mouth and smiled. "I guess I just worry more than most people."

Aaron put the stethoscope to his ears and listened to Grant's heart and lungs, and then completed a thorough physical examination. He handed Grant a prescription and watched as he walked out of the clinic.

Aaron's brow was furrowed. *That was a strange light in his eyes.*

That evening, Aaron sat in his home office at the computer and typed in key words for an internet search. *I need to find a good happy hour place. Got to have my evening wine.*

After reading about several local bars, he decided on a nearby restaurant. He found a space for his car in the crowded parking lot and strolled into the lounge. Most of the bar chairs were occupied with chatty drinkers, but he spotted an empty space near one end around a corner of the bar. As he nestled into his chair, he nodded at the people around him. He looked twice at the man to his right, in the last bar chair against the wall.

That man turned to Aaron. "Howdy. I'm Red."

Aaron glanced at the sparse hair at the sides of his head, and the man smiled. "It's short for Redmond. I never had red hair."

"I'm Aaron. I'm new around here."

"Good to hear that. You're not just traveling through."

He must be well over eighty, maybe in his nineties, Aaron thought.

Aaron ordered a cabernet wine with clam chowder and Caesar salad. He leaned toward Red. "So you've lived here a while?"

"Many years. I stopped counting, and I'm too old to live anywhere else. Not that I want to."

"I guess you're well-adapted to the heat by now."

"I'm careful. Like most everyone else, I try to find someplace cool in the middle of the day. Do that, and you'll be fine."

"What do you do for entertainment?"

"Entertainment? I walk my dog, watch my vegetables grow, and …" He looked at Aaron and smiled. "I come here."

"This area seems to be a safe place to live, compared to the big cities that I'm used to."

"It's safe enough, but we've got our share of criminals and crazies, just like everywhere else."

After more small talk and two glasses of wine for Aaron, Red looked down at his pocket watch and pushed his chair back. "It's time for me to go. I've got to tend to my dog."

Aaron paid his bill, and the bartender brought back change. "I see you met Red Relford."

"Interesting guy."

"He's been coming in here for a long time, most nights every week. He sits in that same chair and has two snifters of brandy."

"Do you know how old he is?"

"He won't say."

"I'll bet he's got stories to tell."

"You might get lucky there. He won't talk to most folks."

Back home, Aaron plopped down on the carpeted floor of his office and grinned at times as he rummaged through the boxes of school memorabilia. He studied photos of college parties and happy people in colorful clothes and outlandish poses.

Here I am, drunk on beer, marching right over a VW Beetle, from back to front. Someone snapped a photo of me stepping off the hood.

He picked up a photo of a beaming couple in graduation outfits. *They didn't make it. Like me, married and divorced.*

Aaron frowned when he came across a photo of his ex-wife. He stared at Lauren's photo for a minute or so, then returned it to the pile, upside down.

From another box, he retrieved a photo of his graduating medical school class and a later photo of a class reunion. Several of his med school classmates weren't at the reunion. One had committed suicide. Aaron looked up toward the ceiling.

One thing I hadn't realized in med school: how prevalent mental illness is.

He paced around the room. *I wonder if I'll go crazy someday.*

21

Stumbling over a box on the floor, he threw his hands in the air. "Hell, maybe moving here was a crazy idea."

He opened the box and unwrapped a photograph of his parents. He propped the framed photo on one side of his desk, then sat and studied their smiling faces.

I sure do miss you two.

His eyes filled with tears as the memory of that night flooded back. A knock on his front door. "Are you Aaron Rovsing?" a policeman said. "Your parents have been shot by a robber who broke into their house. A neighbor heard the shooting and called us. We have the shooter in custody. We believe he's hopped up on drugs."

Aaron's voice was raspy. "My parents, shot? Are they okay?"

The policeman shook his head. "I'm afraid not. I need you to come with me . . ."

Aaron lay in bed later that night, listening to rain pounding his roof and thunder shaking his walls, the windows lit up every few seconds by lightning. After half an hour or so, the lightning and noise subsided, and he drifted off to sleep.

Thunder was replaced by a booming voice. A man appeared out of a mist. "My daughter OD'd. You killed her," the man shouted at Aaron. "It's time to even the score, you bastard," he said and swung a machete at him. Aaron lurched backward and raised his arm, impeding the man's forearm, but the blade struck his lower left face, opening a deep wound that spurted blood like a fountain.

Aaron sat up screaming. He turned on a bedside lamp and looked around the room, sweat dripping from his face. His hand went to his jaw and sensed wetness but no painful fresh wound; his finger traced the deep, long scar from the machete. He examined the pillow and sheets. They were wet, not bloody.

Damn nightmares.

Aaron stood against the bed until his breathing slowed, then he walked to the bathroom and studied his face in the mirror.

I hope he's still not after me. If he is, I've got to put up a better fight next time.

Chapter 3

"No, Doc. Those boots won't do."

Stella stood in Aaron's office doorway shaking her head, her hands on her hips.

Aaron glanced down at his new boots, and his face reddened. "I thought they looked okay when I bought them."

"After work, I'll take you to a decent boot store, and we'll get you some good Texas boots. You want to look like you're at home on a real ranch, not a dude ranch."

Aaron stomped his foot. "Let's do it."

"I hope you have a pair of shoes around here."

Aaron laughed. "I do. Now that you mention it, these boots aren't very comfortable anyway."

Stella snorted. "Honey, I'm surprised they're still making boots that ugly."

Aaron turned on his computer, opened up a daily medical news bulletin, and scanned a few articles.

"Shortage of physicians across the U.S. ..."

"Americans are still too obese ..."

He switched to a local news source, and the first headline read: "Local woman dies from overdose of prescription pain pills."

His stomach tightened and he clicked off the internet. He sat back in his chair and gazed out the window. After a few minutes, he sighed and walked out into the clinic.

Aaron smiled as he entered the room of his first patient of the day. "Good morning, Ms. Brighton. I met you at the restaurant a few nights ago."

"Please call me Marley, and do you remember Cristal?"

"I sure do. Is she sick today?"

"She came down with a fever last night, and sniffles, and coughing."

Aaron examined the five-year-old Cristal. She smiled at him as he listened to her chest with his bright yellow stethoscope.

"That looks like a toy," she said, pointing at the stethoscope.

"It works well enough for me, though. Now breathe deep in and out." He completed a physical exam.

"I don't find anything serious. I think she picked up a virus. Kids need to work their way through viral infections, you know. It helps strengthen their immune systems." Marley helped Cristal down off the examination table.

Aaron sat at a computer terminal in the room and printed out a prescription for a medication. "This can help her congestion, if she needs it. Give her plenty of fluids and acetaminophen for fever or pain."

Cristal looked up at him. "My daddy travels a lot."

Marley stroked Cristal's hair. "She hasn't seen her father in a while."

"He's big and tall like you," Cristal said.

"Come on, little one, we have to go now." Marley took Cristal's hand.

Out in the hallway, Marley turned to Aaron. "By the way, we're neighbors. I live three houses down from you."

"I'm happy to know that. I'll try to be a good neighbor," Aaron said.

"It's a quiet neighborhood. Not much happens." She and Cristal walked away.

Sometimes after people say that, things start to happen. Aaron's forehead wrinkled. *Now what put that idea in my head?*

He and Stella stood in the front lobby. Through the window, he saw a potbellied man in a police uniform approach Marley before she opened her car door.

"That's our constable, Keller Greevy," Stella said. "He's got the hots for Marley and follows her around. Problem is, he's married."

Aaron whistled. "Oh, boy. That could be trouble."

"He thinks no one notices, but it's obvious to everybody."

"Marley's husband travels a lot?"

"Sure, he travels, with other women. Not long ago, he ran off with a sweet young thing."

Aaron's eyes widened. "He left Marley? Where did he go?"

"He and his girlfriend left town, but I heard they're not too far away. He's a creep and deserves a bad end, leaving Marley and Cristal like that."

"Those are mighty strong words."

Stella touched his shoulder. "Honey, it all comes around."

They watched as Marley shook her head at Constable Greevy and stepped into her car.

Keller swatted at insects buzzing around his head, then retreated to the front wall of the building and stood with his arms crossed as Marley backed up and drove away. When her car was out of sight, he turned and walked into the clinic.

"So you're the new doc. Welcome."

Aaron nodded.

"I'm your constable. I try to keep the peace around here."

"I'm sure that can be a tough job," Aaron said as they shook hands.

"Some days are tougher than others, just like your job."

"So there is crime in these parts."

"Sure, like everywhere else. Otherwise, I wouldn't have a job now, would I?"

Keller turned to Stella. "Have you seen Forrester?"

"No. He hasn't come around here."

"He can be a hothead. I wouldn't be surprised if he comes in here with some kind of injury." Keller returned to the front door. "See y'all later."

"Who's Forrester?" Aaron said to Stella.

"Marley's husband, the creep that ran off with the pretty young thing."

Aaron joined Stella and Juliana at the table in the lounge for lunch.

"I've been on the phone all morning," Juliana said. "Patients are calling for appointments. The word is out about you."

"You can thank me for that," Stella said. "I told the whole town you were coming."

Aaron smiled. "I appreciate that. Word of mouth still works, doesn't it. We're certainly off to a good start."

"You don't need to worry. You'll do well here," Stella said.

"How can you know that?"

Stella raised an eyebrow. "Trust me. I can tell."

"The voice of an experienced nurse. That's reassuring." He looked down. *I hope you're right.*

"Here, you two, have some black people's soul fruit." Stella held out a plate piled high with watermelon slices.

Aaron laughed and scooped some on a napkin. "I now have a new appreciation for watermelon." He swallowed the last bite of his tuna salad sandwich. "How long was the previous doctor here?"

"Less than a year," Stella said.

"That's not long."

"He was smart but a little odd, if you ask me. His interactions with patients were awkward sometimes. He wasn't always comfortable around people."

Aaron chuckled. "Maybe he'd be better suited for pathology or laboratory medicine. In those specialties, a doctor can usually avoid direct patient contact."

Stella nodded. "You may be right. Patients grumbled to us about him. 'He doesn't listen to me' was a common complaint."

"Thanks for the reminder. I'll try to always be a good listener."

"We'll let you know of any significant patient complaints."

Aaron coughed and his face flushed. A vision of the chief of the medical staff and that last meeting in Connecticut flashed into his mind.

"Is anything wrong?" Stella said.

"No, I'm fine." Aaron took several deep breaths. "By the way, is that why the last doctor left? Patient complaints?"

"I'm not sure. He seemed anxious about something the last few weeks he was here, but he didn't talk to me about it. I had the impression that something scared him. One day he said he was leaving, and the next day he was gone."

After work, Aaron followed Stella's car to a boot store in nearby Beaumont. Along the way, he dialed the radio to a station he hadn't heard yet. The DJ said he was playing some of his favorite Cajun music.

"Here's Johnny Janot with 'I'm Proud to Be a Cajun.' "

Aaron smiled as he bobbed his head to the beat. *Interesting sound,* he thought.

Aaron noticed a strong scent of leather as he stepped inside the boot store.

Stella walked up to a sales person with Aaron in tow. "This man needs a good pair of boots," she said. "Can you show us some Lucchese?"

"You got it, ma'am. Sir, just have a seat there, and we'll fix you up real good." He measured Aaron's foot. "I'll be right back."

Aaron and Stella sat down in adjoining chairs. "How do you know so much about boots?" Aaron said.

"Number one, I live in Texas. And two, I used to help my husband buy them. I have boots of my own that I wear sometimes."

After several minutes, the salesman returned with a few pairs of boots. "He might look good in these Lucchese Destroyed Leather Boots. This here is the 1883 Antique Buffalo."

"Lucchese. Isn't that a foreign name?" Aaron said.

"It's Italian, but Lucchese boots are handmade right here in good ol' Texas, since 1883. So if you called 'em Texas boots, you'd be speakin' God's honest truth."

Aaron pulled on the dark brown boots with tan side scrolls and wingtips and pranced around the store.

He stood in front of Stella. "I like the way these feel. What do you think?"

"They look good. You should get 'em."

"So, 1883," he drawled. "I could be right at home in the Old West wearing these." He clomped out of the store in his new pair of boots.

"Now you look like you rode in from the range for supper," Stella said. "You've just gone up a few notches in the eyes of Texans."

"That's great to hear." Aaron walked in a circle. "These boots are really comfortable. I feel taller and stronger, like I could kick some butt.

How about a beer? Let's you and I raise some hell in the nearest saloon."

Stella laughed. "Now don't get carried away. I have to get home."

"Okay, see you tomorrow, Annie Oakley."

Stella shook her head and smiled. "No, I'm more like Calamity Jane."

Later that evening, Aaron stretched out on his bed wearing only his boxer shorts and boots, his hands behind his head. It was the first time he'd thought about his previous house and restaurants and routine.

I haven't missed my old digs. That's got to be a good sign.

****

Constable Keller Greevy braked his patrol car to a stop in his driveway. On his way home from the police station, he'd been thinking about a missing person report. A sixteen-year-old girl from a nearby town . . . no one had seen her for two weeks.

That's the second girl gone missing in this area in the last few months, he thought.

He walked through the front door and saw that the kitchen light was on. "Hello, I'm home."

As he sat down in a chair at the dining table, his wife, Valerie, slammed down a plate of grilled chicken and green beans in front of him.

Keller lurched back. "What's the matter?"

31

"I can't take it. Everyone knows you like that hairdresser, Marley Brighton."

"It's nothing. Don't you worry about it. Your friends gossip too much."

Valerie stomped her foot. "You're my husband. I won't let another woman take you away from me."

"You're all upset about nothing. I have to watch her. Her husband, Forrester, is a loose cannon. No telling when he'll show up again."

Valerie's thin lips twitched. "You'd better stop following her, or I might have to do something to make you stop."

Keller stood up as she wheeled around and stormed out of the kitchen.

"Do what? You're crazy," he said. "Stop talking like that."

Chapter 4

Aaron strutted into the clinic the next morning, his arms held wide.

Juliana stood from her chair, looked over the registration counter at Aaron, and nodded. "*Bueno.* The boots make the man. Good choice. They look just right on you."

"Thanks. I'm walking tall this morning."

He clomped away snapping his fingers to the beat of a country song he'd just heard on his car radio.

Later in the morning, Stella stopped Aaron before he entered the patient room. "You'll get to know this guy well. He's the town drunk and lives in the trailer home just down the road. He's got some kind of bite on his arm, so he probably fell asleep again in the Big Thicket."

"The Big Thicket. That's our local forest?"

"It's more than a forest. There's nothing else like it. Lots of different animals and insects live in there, not to mention all kinds of snakes and even alligators."

Aaron opened the door and winced at the smell of cigarettes. A man in a dirty T-shirt and tattered jeans thrust his hand out. "I'm Rocky Donnigan," he said with a gravelly voice. "Glad we have a new doctor in town."

"Thanks. How can I help you today?"

Rocky pointed to his right forearm. "Something bit me here a few days ago, and it's a lot more sore and swollen today."

Aaron examined the skin lesion. "It looks like an infected insect bite. We need to get you on an antibiotic."

"That's what I figured."

Aaron continued with a general physical exam and spotted healed insect bite lesions over his arms and lower legs.

"I hope you stay, Doc."

"Why wouldn't I?"

"There's a lot of weirdness in this town. The last doc got spooked, I think."

"Weirdness, what kind of weirdness?"

"Evil people. Strange things happening. But, you know, I've lived here my whole life. Maybe all towns are like this one. Was your last town weird, too?"

Aaron's chest tightened as a vision popped into his head: idiot doctors sitting around a mahogany table demanding that Aaron resign. He nodded. "Yeah, I guess in a way it was."

On his way out, Rocky stopped at the door of the room and turned to Aaron.

"I like you, Doc. I hope you'll like us, too."

Aaron grinned. *I've made some positive impressions so far.*

After Rocky left, Aaron stood at the registration desk.

"I know it's just your first week, but how do you like it here?" Juliana said.

"So far, so good. One thing I like, no one ever seems to be in a hurry."

Stella laughed. "Only when you're being chased by a bull or by somebody with a gun."

"You mentioned Calamity Jane yesterday," Aaron said. "Are you a history buff?"

"I like to read books about history. My high school history teacher turned me on to it. And then I learned I had an ancestor that died in the Civil War, fighting for one of the 'colored' infantries."

"You traced your family tree?"

"Part of it. Some of my ancestors were slaves, and many slaves had no last names, so it's difficult. I hit a lot of dead ends."

"I can't imagine the whole slave thing. If I was given a slave, I wouldn't know how to relate."

"It's part of our American history, an ugly part of it. Even though slavery is over, the black-white relationship still has a ways to go."

Aaron cocked his head. "What do you mean? You and I are relating okay, aren't we?"

"You don't believe me? Let's go together to a restaurant and see what happens."

"You think something will happen? Blacks and whites together is common these days. What could happen?"

"Chances are, we'll get seated in the back or in a corner, away from the all-white groups."

Aaron snorted. "Are you sure you're not exaggerating?"

"One of these days, we'll go together for a meal. You'll see."

Later in the afternoon, Aaron walked up to Juliana at the copy machine.

"Where did you move from?" Aaron said.

"Not far away. Dallas."

"Ah, the southern tip of Tornado Alley."

Juliana looked off into the distance. "I saw a tornado once. *Terrible.*" She crossed her fingers. "But I'm lucky so far. I've never been hurt by one or lost anything."

"Does life seem much different out here for you?" Aaron said.

"Well, it's country life. More wilderness and wildlife."

Aaron nodded as he thought of the huge green turtle he almost hit with his car. "How about the people?"

"I think country people are different in some ways from city people. For one thing, they seem more connected with each other."

"That's got to be good."

Juliana smiled. "I believe it is."

Just before closing time, the waiting room was empty and the clinic was quiet.

A man threw open the front door and ran back to the hallway in front of the patient rooms.

"Sir," Stella shouted after him. She stood from her chair and jogged toward him, then she stopped and gasped.

The young man pointed his handgun at her. "Open your medicine cabinet, the one with narcs." His hand was shaking and his pale face was sweaty.

Stella held her hands up. "We don't have any narcotics here."

"Open the cabinet, now."

Aaron ran around the corner. "What's all the noise ..." He stopped and his eyes widened as the gun barrel swerved over to his chest.

Aaron's legs turned to jelly and he fell to his knees with his hands up. "Don't shoot."

"I need Vicodin. Give me your Vicodin."

Aaron's throat tightened and his words squeaked out. "We don't—"

"You've got to help me. The last doc had Vicodin here. I'll use this gun if I have to."

Everyone turned to look as the front door of the clinic banged open.

A tall silhouette filled the doorway. "Son, lower the gun. Don't do this."

The young man's gun quivered as he stepped toward his father. "No one will help me. I need medicine. Can't you see I'm sick?"

Stella crept up behind the man and locked him in a tight bear hug, his gun hand trapped down by his side. He struggled, but he was no match for Stella.

"Let me go. You're hurting me." He took a breath and screamed.

Aaron flinched as the high-pitched shriek stung his ears.

The man's father bounded over and extracted the gun from his hand, slid the gun into his own pocket, and looked at Stella. "I'll take him to a hospital now."

Stella squeezed the young man, who moaned and gasped for air. A few words escaped as his face turned blue. "I can't breathe."

Tears streamed down Stella's cheeks.

"I said I'll take him to a hospital now. You can let him go." He gripped Stella's wrists and forced her arms open.

Stella fell back several steps, holding her hands out. Her eyes were wide and her face flushed.

"Come with me," the father said. He supported his son as they stumbled out of the clinic to their truck.

Stella collapsed into a chair in the hallway. She was trembling and her hands were clenched. "I can't handle . . . drug addicts," she said between shallow breaths.

Aaron stood up on shaky legs. "I have a hard time with addicts, too. Let's go back to my office." He turned and watched the truck drive out of the parking lot.

Juliana helped Stella into Aaron's office and they plopped into chairs.

Stella laid her head and forearms on the desk and sobbed. "Two years ago, my son was killed during a drug deal." Tears wet her forearms. "He was my only child."

Aaron sat up in his desk chair. "I'm so sorry." He pushed a box of tissues to her.

It was a struggle for Stella to get her words out between the sobs. "I think about him all the time ... I try to forgive ... I pray about it ... I thought I was getting better, but it's so hard to control myself around those people. They killed my son."

Aaron and Juliana were silent as Stella wept. After a short while, she raised her head and took several deep breaths. "I'm sorry. I just lose control."

"I know. I have the same feelings," Aaron said.

Stella raised her eyebrows. "You do?"

"I was responsible for something." Queasiness gripped his stomach as he thought of the woman who died from the Vicodin he'd prescribed. "Something I regret."

Stella blotted her eyelids with a tissue. Aaron stood and came around the desk to her. "I know it's tough. Let's both keep trying to heal those wounds," he said.

Stella covered her eyes with the tissue and nodded.

No one spoke for several minutes.

"You saved the day," Aaron said to Stella.

"It's all a blur. The last thing I remember is looking at my hands and him walking out."

"Who were those people?"

"Brad Benningham and his son, Preston. Brad's a rich oilman. They live in the mansion on the hill," Stella said.

"That must be the big house I can see from my front door."

"That's the one."

"How long has Preston had a problem?"

"A long time, I think. He's been through rehab before. Brad tried to fix things with money, like big birthday bashes for Preston in Vegas. But we all know just throwing money at a problem doesn't do crap."

"Should we call the police?" Aaron said. "I guess that might mean our constable."

Stella shook her head. "No, I don't think it would help. They know about Preston's problem. They usually let Brad take care of it."

Aaron walked toward the office door. "In that case, let's lock up and go home. I'm exhausted."

Aaron brought creamy tomato soup and a large chicken salad home for dinner. He sat in his office and picked at the food for a while, then walked out to the front yard. An owl hooted from a nearby tree.

He looked up at the Benningham mansion. *I'm not through my first damn week, and I've already run into a drug addict.*

Listening to the owl, he tried to imagine where it was in the trees.

A shudder passed over him. *I've never had a gun pointed at me before.*

His legs felt heavy as he meandered over and kicked at a rock in the driveway. *Stella and Juliana saw me fall on my knees today. Am I that weak?*

Aaron sighed and walked back into the house.

That woman's overdose death and her father's malpractice lawsuit against me . . .
I should call my lawyer and find out about the status of the suit.

He sat on his bed, searched the contact list on his smart phone, and found his lawyer's number to leave a message.

After staring at the number for several minutes, he threw the phone down on the bed. "Oh, to hell with it."

Aaron climbed into bed several hours later. He tossed and turned all night.

Over and over, he saw in his mind the father of the dead girl with his raised machete, his bushy eyebrows scrunched together on his beet red face.

Chapter 5

Aaron heard a horse trotting behind his house.

He swallowed the last drop of home-brewed coffee and walked out the back door, his shoes slipping along the dew-moistened grass. Behind the fence, a horse and rider loomed in the early morning light.

"Hello." Grant Belkin's voice echoed around the pasture as he dismounted his horse. He strolled over to Aaron's backyard fence. "I noticed my cattle were over in this part of the pasture. I thought I'd see if you were still home."

Aaron leaned against the fence. "You're up early."

"I'm a cowboy."

"How long have you run this ranch?"

Grant looked over at his cattle. "A few years now."

"Do you have family to help you?"

"A daughter. She's married and lives in California." He rubbed his horse's face. "Cancer took my wife two years ago."

"I'm sorry to hear that."

A few of the cows mooed.

"You keep the herd healthy and then sell them?" Aaron said.

"I used to." Grant put his hands on top of the fence.

Startled, Aaron stepped back. *His eyes are like lasers,* Aaron thought.

"What are you running from, Doc?"

"What?" Aaron touched his jaw. "I ..." He sighed and looked down. "I'm not sure."

"Ever'body runs from something now and then. You're lucky. Sometimes there's no place to run to." Grant mounted his horse. "What brought you to our neck of the woods?"

"I just want to plant my roots and run a decent medical practice. I've heard a little bit about this part of the country. I'm told it's pleasant and relaxing."

"Pleasant and relaxin'?" Grant pulled on the reins and turned his horse. "It can be." He looked back at Aaron. "Stop by my place sometime, and I'll show you around the ranch."

"I will." Aaron watched him ride away. He stood by the fence until he could no longer hear Grant's horse.

Aaron shook his head. *Who is he to ask if I'm running away from something?*

"Are you okay?" Aaron said to Stella as she walked into the clinic.

"Sorry I'm late. I overslept my alarm. I didn't sleep well last night."

"Neither did I. Let's face it. We both have a neurotic problem with drug abuse patients."

Stella smiled. "So we're both neurotic. Got a pill for that, Doc?"

Aaron shook his head. "No pill. No magic wand." He pointed to his temple. "We've got to rewire our brains."

"Now, how do we do that?"

"Practice and time. It takes effort, and maybe some counseling."

Stella sighed and looked out the window. "So we have to take on the demon again, face to face."

"That's one way to look at it. We've got to stay confident. Others have overcome this. We can, too."

"I'm not looking forward to that day."

He looked down as Stella walked away. "I sound like I know what the heck I'm talking about," he said under his breath.

Later in the morning, Aaron opened the door to a patient room.

"Good morning, Cristal and Marley Brighton." *Marley is looking great today.*

Marley had one leg folded under her, so that she sat on her foot in the chair.

That is one flexible woman. I don't think my knee could ever bend like that.

"Cristal wanted to tell you that she's better," Marley said.

"I'm glad to hear that."

Cristal held up something.

"What have you got there?" Aaron said.

"Genie." Cristal hugged the light green plush character.

"That's her favorite character," Marley said. "She saw it in a children's book at her day care center."

"Interesting. Why do you like Genie?"

"He can give me a flying carpet if I want one."

Aaron nodded. "I'd like to have one of those."

"Then I could fly real high and find my daddy."

Marley stroked Cristal's hair. "She really misses her father."

"And ... and I'll save my third wish for when I grow up."

"That's smart. Have you already made your first two wishes?" Aaron said.

"Yeah. One was for my daddy to come home."

"That's a good wish. What's the second one?"

"I want to talk with the cows like Mr. Belkin does."

"Mr. Belkin talks to his cows?"

"I don't know where she got that," Marley said.

Cristal looked up at Marley. "Mommy, I've heard him talk to the cows."

Marley patted Cristal's shoulder. "It's okay. I'm sure you're right."

Cristal nestled Genie in her arms and rubbed his turban. "And sometimes they talk back."

Aaron smiled at Marley, and then looked at Cristal. "I might ask Mr. Belkin about that. I'd like to learn to talk with cows, too."

In the hallway, Marley turned to Aaron. "I don't mean to meddle, but I wonder if you could look into something?"

"Sure."

"A family lives down the street from my house. The Taggetts. You met Wanda at the diner, remember?"

Aaron nodded.

"Sid is her husband, and Race is her son. I'm worried about them. I hear that Sid is very ill, and no one seems concerned. Could you look in on them?"

"I will."

Marley smiled. "Good."

He watched Marley as she and Cristal walked out the front door of the clinic.

I have to get to know her better.

A few minutes later, Stella approached Aaron in the hall. "A drug rep is here to meet you. I know him well. He's sharp, but a little strange."

Aaron nodded and Stella returned with a well-groomed man, medium height, thin and angular.

Aaron offered a handshake, and the man responded with a fist bump.

"Hi, I'm one of your local drug reps. I cover middle East Texas." He rocked up and down on his heels.

"That's a big area."

"It sure is. I put a lot of mileage on my car, but I enjoy the job." He lifted his briefcase to the hallway counter. "It's great to have a doc around here again."

Aaron smiled. "Do you have any freebies today?"

"Sure, always." The rep laid writing pens and pads out on the counter. He aligned the pens in a level parallel row and stacked the pads in a flush pile.

He stood back and admired his work and then launched into a spiel about an antibiotic he was promoting for the treatment of sinusitis, bronchitis, and ear infections, rocking on his heels as he spoke. After he finished, he rubbed his hands with an antiseptic wipe.

"I'll keep your antibiotic in mind, when it's indicated," Aaron said. The rep handed Aaron a few drug samples and discount coupons for patients.

"Are you a runner?" he asked Aaron.

"Not now, but I need to get back into jogging."

"Great. There's a 5K run coming up soon. I'll get the information to you."

"That may be just the incentive I need."

The rep turned to Stella. "Was that Marley Brighton I saw driving away from here?"

"Yes."

"I haven't seen her in a while. I was in school with her husband, Forrester."

"Lucky you," Stella said.

He laughed and turned to leave. "See you next time."

Aaron watched the rep use hand wipes after he walked out the front door.

Stella knocked on Aaron's office door.

"Come in."

She and Juliana stepped inside.

"I called the hospital this morning," Stella said. "Preston was admitted last night. Maybe he'll kick his addiction this time."

"Some addicts recover, right?" Juliana said.

Aaron nodded. "People can overcome addiction, with the right help. It can take a long time."

After a few seconds, Aaron looked up.

"Okay, Doc, I have to know," Stella said. "Are you seeing someone?"

Aaron laughed. "Give me a break. I just got here."

"Everybody needs somebody. You should know that."

Aaron sighed. "I thought I had somebody."

"Ah. She hooked up with someone else, did she?"

Aaron's face reddened. "With her personal trainer."

Stella nodded. "I've heard that story before. What if she comes back to you?"

"It wouldn't work."

"So is that why you moved away?"

He frowned. "That's one reason. I couldn't go to work anymore. I felt like I was the butt of a joke. I had to get out of there." *And some bastard doctor complained about my patient care.*

"Well, there's a church not too far from here with a singles group. You should check it out. Or maybe there's a social club at the hospital for medical people."

"I appreciate your interest, but I'm okay for now."

Stella furrowed her brow. "I don't know about that."

Mid-afternoon, Aaron walked into a patient room. A tall, thick-chested man stood from a chair and extended his hand.

"I'm Boots McCorkindale."

Aaron shook his hand and nodded. "Mr. McCork—"

"Folks call me 'Dale.' "

Aaron stopped his handshake. "Okay, sure. Dale, how can I help you?"

"I need a refill on my medications. I'm diabetic, and it's good to have a doctor close by again."

Aaron unwound his stethoscope and listened to Dale's heart and lungs. "Are you doing well with the diabetes?"

"Yep. No problems. You from the Northeast?"

"Connecticut."

"You'll need to get into the good food around here, especially authentic Tex-Mex food and real barbecue. Makes me hungry thinking about it."

"Don't worry. I plan to sample all the restaurants."

"I don't think of some of the Tex-Mex places as restaurants. The best ones are sometimes just little hole-in-the-wall shacks. Not much on the decor, but don't let that fool you. The food will have you a-howling like a coyote."

Aaron laughed. "I guess that's good."

Dale nodded. "You'll see."

In the hallway, Dale turned to Aaron. "I run the car dealership down the road."

Great. A car salesman, Aaron thought. *I got ripped off by one of you guys once.*

"I've got a great deal on a pickup truck that would go well with your Volvo."

"I'll think about it."

"You're in Texas now. You need a pickup truck."

Aaron frowned as Dale walked away. *Can I really trust you, Mr. Car Salesman?*

Stella discharged the last patient on the day schedule, and then she closed and locked the rear door of the clinic.

Aaron walked up to her near the front door. "I think I'll drive over to Wanda's place. How do I get there?"

Stella pointed at the road in front of the clinic. "Turn left out of the parking lot and drive straight. This road dead-ends at her house, right on the edge of the Big Thicket." She looked at him. "Are you going for any special reason?"

"I'll ask if there's anything I can do to help her husband. Do you want to come with me?"

Stella shivered. "No, thanks. I steer clear of that weirdness."

There's that word again.

Stella touched his shoulder. "I mentioned her son to you before. Sometimes he's at the house. He works at the local cemetery, and as far as I can tell, he doesn't have any friends."

"You told me the husband is an invalid?"

"The word is he stays in bed most of the time. He used to be a real Casanova and played around on Wanda a lot over the years. Until six months ago or so."

"Should I call first?"

"I don't know if we have a number for them." Stella walked to the registration desk, opened a drawer, and rifled through some files. "It looks like they had a land line once, but the number's crossed out.

50

There's not a cell phone number listed. I can check the computer records, if you want."

"No. I'll just drop by."

"Good luck."

Aaron drove away from the clinic and passed by the alcoholic Rocky Donnigan's trailer home on the right. He came to the intersection with the road he lived on and glanced at Marley Brighton's house across the road to the left, then continued straight through the intersection and parallel with the Grant Belkin Ranch on the left. A house loomed into view, and he eased toward it until the road ended in a round, dirt cul-de-sac in front of the house, which was set back from the road about twenty yards. Aaron parked his car in the cul-de-sac and walked through a muggy mist up a dirt driveway, stepping over potholes.

Scraggly weeds threatened to choke off the sparse grass wilting in the yard. Broken splintered remnants of bushes lined the ground along the front of the house, which was one story with dark brown wood and opaque curtains hanging inside the windows.

Aaron climbed front steps that rose between two thick columns to a bare porch that extended across the front of the house. He pressed a doorbell but didn't hear any sound, then waited half a minute or so and knocked. Sweat streaked down beside his eyes.

"Go away," a voice said after his second knock. "We don't want anything."

"Ms. Taggett, I met you in the diner. I'm Aaron Rovsing, the new doctor in town. I just stopped by to say hello." He dabbed his face with a handkerchief.

Aaron heard a creak and a slit opening appeared in the door. He could make out part of a face in the opening. "You shouldn't have come. We don't want visitors," the face said.

I smell something from in there, like urine, he thought. "I'm available if you or your husband or son needs medical help."

"We don't need any help," she said and slammed the door.

Aaron backed away from the door and retreated down the front steps.

It sounded like her, and the face is the same face I met in the diner.

He heard running footsteps, trotted over to the corner of the house, and peered around the side. No one was in sight. From behind the house, a group of blackbirds beat their wings and scattered into the tall trees that hovered over the back yard. He crept about halfway along the side of the house and stopped as he heard a door creak open at the back and then a voice from inside the house.

"Have you been camping out all this time?" a woman said. Aaron couldn't make out the response. "You need to check in with me more often . . . Have you been to work? I want to know where you go . . . Remember, I always take care of you. Don't walk away from me." Her voice became inaudible.

She must be talking with her son, the cemetery worker, Aaron thought as he hurried back to his car. *Why is she refusing to let me examine her husband?*

Aaron drove to the happy hour bar that he'd discovered several days before.

Good, he thought as he saw an empty bar chair next to Red.

"Have a seat," Red said, swirling his brandy.

"Cabernet, right?" the bartender said.

Aaron nodded. "Good memory."

"How do you like Texas so far?" Red said.

"It's a change."

"I'm sure this place is a bit different from the big cities you came from."

"Well, for one thing, I've never before lived right next to a ranch."

"Ah, there's nothing like the scents and sounds of a ranch."

Aaron laughed. "You're right about that, but I rather like it."

"Have you traveled around much in Texas?"

"Not really."

"There's a place you should see. Terlingua."

"I've heard of it. It's south of here, right?"

"Near the border with Mexico."

"That's a long drive."

"It feels like a different world down there. You can isolate yourself if you want. There are long stretches of empty wilderness."

"Why have I heard of Terlingua?"

"Interesting folks live around there, and you can find some unique Texas art."

Aaron cocked his head. "Maybe creative people go there for the solitude."

"Yep. Some people are there to escape from their old life. Like when I was in the Caribbean some years ago. A few folks on the islands had no interest in what was going on in the rest of the world. They were there to drop out and start a new life. You can do that around Terlingua."

"I'll add it to my bucket list of places to see."

Red smiled as he talked about other sights and experiences in Texas.

"It sounds like there are plenty of places in Texas where you can drop out from the world and start over," Aaron said.

Red turned to him. "That's probably why we're both here."

His eyes. There's sadness in those eyes.

Chapter 6

Aaron clapped his hands. "Okay, Stella. It's time."

He watched Juliana drive away to run a few errands.

Stella looked up from the registration desk. "Time for what?"

"Let's go to a restaurant for lunch. My 'Thank Goodness It's Friday' treat. I'd like to test your black-white theory."

"Good idea. I know just the place to go."

Stella stepped into Aaron's car and directed him to a steak restaurant not far away.

"You check us in at the podium," Stella said before they left the car. "I'll join you when they're ready to seat us."

Aaron checked in for two with the greeter, who made a mark on a seating chart and picked up two menus just as Stella walked up.

"She's with you, sir?"

"Yes," Aaron said.

Looking back down at the seating chart, he erased his first mark and chose another booth instead.

Aaron's eyes widened as he looked at Stella.

"Honey, it's all right," Stella said.

They were led to a booth at a far corner in the back of the seating area.

"I'm amazed," Aaron said after the greeter walked away.

"That's the way it is."

"Is it just this part of the country?"

"No, it happens in many other places, too."

Aaron frowned and scratched the side of his head.

Stella touched his arm. "I don't worry about it, and neither should you. Things will change for the better as time goes by."

They studied the menu. "I know it's a steak place, but the grilled chicken is always tasty here, too," Stella said.

"Sounds good to me. I'll have the chicken with sautéed broccoli."

"I will, too." Stella put down her menu. "Did you see Wanda yesterday?" Stella said.

"I did for a second, through a small opening in her front door. She wouldn't let me in."

"I'm not surprised."

"When she opened the door, the inside smelled like a dirty hospital ward."

Stella shook her head. "That's been a nasty situation and probably still is."

After their meals were served, Aaron glanced up at Stella. "You seem down, like you've had a bad day."

"It's been a tough week. My husband is in a nursing home. The nurses complained to me several times this week about him."

"Why is he in a nursing home?"

"He's got dementia, and sometimes he's mean to the nurses."

"Dementia. How old is he?"

"Fifty. He was diagnosed with neurosyphilis a few years ago."

Aaron sat back. "Syphilis, now there's a fascinating disease. Historically, it's been a kind of punishment for a momentary lapse of reason." Aaron caught his breath and turned to Stella. "I didn't mean to imply—"

Stella chuckled and held up her hand. "It's okay. You hit the nail on the head. My husband is living proof of what you just said. He's a veteran. They said he got syphilis overseas as a young man after playing around with the ladies, but he wasn't treated for it until it was too late. Now he's confused all the time and his balance is off and he can't feel his feet, so walking is difficult. He stumbles and falls a lot."

Aaron remembered the story of her only son who was killed. He put down his fork. "You've had a really rough couple of years."

"No rougher than anyone else. It's my lot in life, so I deal with it." She smiled. "At least I don't have syphilis."

"Count your blessings, right?"

"Something like that."

"You're amazing. I don't know if I could handle all that."

Stella's eyes burned into his. "Faith and forgiveness."

"I see."

She looked down. "It's easy for me to say those words, but I have to try to renew myself every day. I worry there are some things I can never forgive."

Stella finished her meal and sat back in her chair. "It's ironic. My husband's dementia prevents him from remembering or feeling guilty about the syphilis. He doesn't even know what happened to him."

Back at the clinic, Aaron checked information on the next patient. Stella stopped him as he approached the room.

"This is one of our local psych patients with his mother. They're Cajun. He's bipolar and usually reasonable, when he takes his medicine. But be on your guard."

A man sat on the examination table, his short hair wanting to fly away. An older woman sat in a chair at the side of the room.

"I'm Tucker Boudreaux," the man said. "I heard we had a new doctor in town." His gaze returned to the ceiling.

Aaron approached the woman, who stood and shook his hand. "I'm his mama."

Aaron turned to Tucker. "I see it's your birthday."

Tucker extended his arms. "I'm thirty, and I'm happy about that, but it doesn't really matter how old I am. I feel like heaven and earth open up for me, like I can do anything, at any age, any birthday. Birthday party. Party down. *Laissez les bon temps rouler.*"

"I'm sorry?" Aaron looked at his mother.

"Oh, sometimes he speaks Cajun. He said, 'Let the good times roll.' "

"Okay." Aaron turned back to Tucker. "Any problems today?"

"No, I'm good. I'm better than ever." He rubbed his hands on his thighs.

Aaron checked his pupils and reflexes and listened to his heart and lungs. "I'm glad you're good. You seem happy."

Stella knocked on the door and walked into the room. She stopped beside Aaron and smiled at Tucker. "Did you tell the doctor who you are today?"

"What do you mean today? You know who I am, every day."

"Who are you?" Stella said.

Tucker held out his hands. "I'm an angel from God."

Aaron stepped back. "An angel—"

"I'm sent by *le Bon Dieu*." Tucker stared at Aaron. "I know things. I can see the future." He looked at Stella. "Everyone in this town knows about me."

Stella nodded. "Yes, they do."

"Just ask me anything, Doc. The answer will pop into my head. It's a special gift."

"Let me think on that."

Tucker pointed a finger at Aaron. "You don't have a dog, do you?"

Aaron shrugged his shoulders. "No."

"I can tell that you need one. You need a dog."

His mother stood up. "Doctor, tell him he has to take the lithium."

"Listen to your mom, okay? The medicine is important for you," Aaron said.

Tucker put his hands to his temples. "So everybody says."

They walked out into the hall. Tucker's mother whispered to Aaron, "He's been almost full-blown manic for a week now. He's not sleeping much. Sometimes it takes a while for him to come down when he's like this. So I see that he takes the lithium, but I think sometimes he doesn't swallow the pill on purpose."

"You're doing the best you can. Just let me know if I can help," Aaron said.

"His psychiatrist is hours away, and he won't always go with me for appointments."

Aaron whispered to Stella as he watched Tucker's mother hurry after her son. "They're not into voodoo, are they? I've heard about voodoo over in Louisiana."

Stella chuckled. "They might be, but they're Cajun. Voodoo is generally connected with African-American Creoles, who are a different group from the Cajuns."

"Isn't voodoo mostly found not far from here, in New Orleans?"

"That's true these days. Voodoo started in Africa, and it migrated to Haiti and Louisiana and other places."

"I have visions of evil spells and voodoo dolls that look like pin cushions."

"That's from the movies, and it's not completely accurate. Some folks claim voodoo is a religion for the good. They worship saints and an all-powerful god and they do good works in the community, and it's not just Creole people. Anyone can practice voodoo."

"So voodoo might be with us now, right here in East Texas?"

"Honey, you can count on it."

After closing the clinic, Aaron stopped at his car door. *I wonder if Wanda is working. She wouldn't talk to me at her house. Maybe she will at the restaurant.*

He drove to Wanda's diner and spotted her serving a customer. He waited in a corner by the check-in area.

Wanda turned and walked toward the front. She saw Aaron and stopped. "Hello, Doc. Can I seat you for dinner?"

"No, thanks. I came to your house yesterday. You told me you don't like visitors."

"As I said, we're a private family. If my husband or son needs medical help, I have to take them to a hospital where tests can be done. You understand that, don't you?"

"Sure, I understand, but just because I'm interested as a doctor, what's wrong with your husband?"

"I don't know. They think it's MS or ALS or some such alphabet soup. I have to take total care of him."

"What about your son?"

"He's not sick like my husband. He keeps to himself. I take care of him, too."

"Remember I'm available if you need help, and I won't charge for the first house call."

Wanda wagged a finger at Aaron. "Don't you concern yourself about us. We'll do just fine." She whirled around and walked away.

She won't even let me in the house. Aaron shrugged his shoulders. *Who would say no to a free house call?*

He started up the Volvo. *Maybe Wanda is just ornery, but I have a feeling there's something else. Marley Brighton is worried about them, too.*

He nodded. *I've got to find out more about that family.*

Aaron drove to Grant Belkin's ranch house. He'd called ahead of time and Grant was waiting for him.

"Come on in," a voice boomed from the front door.

Aaron stepped through the door into a vestibule with a high ceiling that led to an expansive living room, in the middle of which sat a brown couch with a small coffee table facing a fireplace. No other furniture was in the room.

"No TV," Aaron said.

"Don't need much."

Aaron noticed built-in shelves and cabinets filled with books.

Grant motioned to Aaron. "While it's still light, let me take you around the ranch."

He led Aaron to a rear door and out to the back yard.

Aaron walked up to a fence. "You've got a garden."

"My vegetables. They keep me healthy."

"This is one serious garden."

Grant pointed out the rows of plants. "My tomato plants." He moved further along the garden fence. "The peas and okra are doin' well."

"Okra. I'll have to try that."

"I'll make you some stewed okra sometime. That's good eatin'. Good for you, too."

They walked behind the long garden and climbed into Grant's pickup truck.

Aaron blotted his forehead with his handkerchief. "Will I get used to this heat?"

"You're from up north. Your blood's too thick. It'll thin out over time."

Grant started the engine. "Ever been to a rodeo?"

"Never," Aaron said.

"I've got some rodeo tickets for next Saturday. Want to come along?"

"Sure thing. Thanks."

Aaron admired the orange sunset over the horizon as they bounced along the turf away from the ranch house. He lost the border fence for five minutes or so, and then he spotted a faint line of trees approaching. They slowed and stopped before a boundary fence, beyond which a tall row of pine trees extended parallel to the fence as far as Aaron could see. A haze enshrouded the tops of the trees.

Grant turned to him. "The Big Thicket."

Aaron sat forward. "So that's the Big Thicket. I saw it on road signs when I drove down here."

"It's our own rainforest, right here in East Texas, and it goes on for miles. It's hard to walk in it because of the thick underbrush. All kinds of critters and strange plants live in there, like plants that eat bugs."

"Is that why people talk about it?"

"That and its shady history. Folks used to hide in there: outlaws, escaped prisoners, even Civil War dodgers back in the day. Anybody up to no good. Some folks went in and never came out."

A shiver passed over the back of Aaron's neck as he studied the forest. An evening breeze bent the tall pine trees toward him.

After a few minutes, Grant turned the truck around and headed back to the ranch house.

Aaron turned to Grant as they walked through the house. "Do you know the Taggetts, the family that lives just across the road from here?"

Grant sighed. "I know they need your help."

"There's something strange going on over there."

Grant touched Aaron's shoulder. "I'll help you all I can with them, but it's up to you."

"Up to me? So you believe there's a medical illness in that house that I can help with?"

Grant nodded as he escorted Aaron to the Volvo. He leaned into the driver's window. "Just look into it. You may be their last chance."

Aaron frowned as he drove away. *Last chance. What does he mean by that?*

Aaron drove a circuitous route home to pick up a to-go order of chicken quesadillas with rice and black beans. After dinner, he paced around his house. He held up jittery hands. *Maybe I had too much coffee today.*

His heart was beating faster than usual. *Okay, from now on, no caffeine after three in the afternoon for me.*

Later in bed, Aaron took deep breaths and concentrated on pleasant thoughts, like an image of Marley, but her smiling face would dissolve into the strange waving trees he'd seen earlier with Grant Belkin. He pulled the sheet up to his chin, but that didn't prevent the return of the shivers he'd felt near the Big Thicket.

****

After her shift at the diner, Wanda Taggett drove home with a beef taco meal from a local fast food restaurant. She would enjoy that for her dinner later. First, she had to feed her husband, Sid.

"Are you awake?" she asked Sid. He didn't respond.

She pushed her hand under Sid's pillow, nodding as she felt the cloth pouch containing various objects, then she walked to the kitchen to unlock a cabinet. She pulled out a box and poured some white powder from the box into a glass, taking care not to touch the powder herself. After adding milk and chocolate syrup to the glass, she stirred the liquid into a dark brown mix and placed the glass on a small table by Sid's bed. She shook Sid and shouted in his ear.

"Wake up. It's time for dinner."

Sid moaned and opened his eyes. Wanda helped him sit up in bed and handed him the glass. He began to sip the liquid.

After several swallows, he looked at her. "Tastes good."

She smiled. "Sure it does. Just give it a little more time to help."

Sid sighed. "All right. I guess you know best."

"Trust me. Everything will work out just fine."

Wanda bared her teeth as she walked away. *And, you'll never cheat on me again.*

Chapter 7

Aaron yawned and rolled out of bed Saturday morning.

"Today's the day." He pumped his fist in the air. "I start jogging again."

He donned his old running shoes, socks, shorts and shirt, and stretched out his hamstrings and calves for several minutes. After gulping down a large glass of water, he grabbed a key and locked the front door behind him.

Now start slow and work up to a decent distance over a few weeks. Don't overdo it.

He took a deep breath and broke into a gentle jog down his street. Marley was in her front yard and Aaron waved at her as he jogged by. She smiled at him and he picked up his speed, turning right at the intersection. *Slow down, she's not watching now.*

He was able to make it as far as the trailer home of his alcoholic patient Rocky Donnigan, where he turned around and walked back to his house.

That felt good. I'll have that pleasant muscle soreness later.

After throwing off his soggy shirt and showering off the sweat, Aaron drove from his house in the direction of a large hospital about forty-five minutes away. He cranked up the radio.

After a while, he smiled. "I'm beginning to recognize some of these country songs. That's 'People Are Crazy,' by Billy Currington."

He parked in the main lot at the front, walked through the entrance, and studied the directory on a wall by the front lobby elevators. After a few turns down hallways on the first floor, he came to a nursing administration office.

He knocked and a woman appeared at the door. "Are you Dr. Rovsing?" she said.

"Yes, thanks for seeing me."

"My pleasure. I'm Rachel. Please have a seat." Rachel sat down in a chair behind her desk. "You wanted some information about a patient?"

Aaron handed her a piece of paper. "I'd appreciate whatever you can tell me about this patient. He lives near my clinic, and I'd like to find out if I can help him in any way."

She smiled at him. "You're not from around here, are you?"

"I just moved here from the Northeast."

"Well then, welcome to Texas."

"I imagine I'll pick up a little of the Southern drawl over time."

"Most people do."

Rachel typed on her computer keyboard and studied the monitor. "Sid Taggett. He was admitted three times over the last six months or so. The doctors suspected a neurologic disease of some sort, but no specific diagnosis was given. They considered amyotrophic lateral sclerosis, ALS."

"Some neurologic diseases can be difficult to pinpoint, and it may take time. If you don't think of an unusual diagnosis, you may not order the right tests."

Rachel looked up. "How's he doing now?"

"He's mostly bedridden. His wife takes care of him."

She opened more records on the computer screen. "There's something else here, an interesting note in the past medical history from one of the doctors."

She summarized the report. "The wife, Mrs. Taggett, brought her son to the hospital multiple times. This was years ago, when her son was a toddler and a preschooler. One of the doctors mentioned the possibility of child abuse. Then the son's hospital visits stopped."

"Can I read some of the notes?"

"No problem. Pull a chair around."

Aaron sat at the computer beside Rachel and scanned medical reports on the computer screen for several minutes.

"Look at this," he said. "One of the consultant reports mentions Munchausen by Proxy. They thought she might've been hurting her son on purpose to gain sympathy and attention from her friends and doctors."

"I've heard of that."

"It's a rare psychiatric disease. As I recall from medical school, it can be hard to treat, and the children can develop psych problems of their own."

"How do they treat it?"

"Mainly psychotherapy and counseling, I think. I'm pretty sure there's no specific medication for treating it."

"I thought by now we had medicines for everything," Rachel said.

"Unfortunately not. To make matters worse, some patients with these types of illnesses don't even believe they're sick and don't follow through with any kind of therapy."

"I hate to ask. Does it say how she hurt the poor child?"

Aaron studied the reports. "They weren't absolutely sure that she was abusing her child, but they suspected she overmedicated or poisoned him once. Another time, he had suspicious cuts on him, like from a knife. Her story was that he'd fallen and cut himself on broken glass in the carpet. I guess the doctors believed her."

"Do you know her son, Dr. Rovsing?"

"She has a son who lives in her house. I assume that's the child we're talking about. I don't know this family very well yet."

"She may be one sick lady."

"I have a feeling that's true." Aaron stood and shook her hand. "Thanks for your time."

He noticed deep dimples at the corners of her smile.

Aaron fired up the Volvo. *This is getting very interesting.*

He stopped at a roadside cafe for lunch and ordered a large lettuce salad with walnuts and cranberries. As he drove back to his town, he hatched a plan. He pulled into a parking place in front of the diner where Wanda worked and walked up to the front entrance. Wanda was there, waiting on a customer.

Aaron hurried back to his car, dropped by his house to pick up his medical bag and drove to Wanda's house. He climbed the steps to the front door and punched the doorbell. After a minute, he knocked but still heard no response, and since the front door was locked, he walked around the side of the house and peered into several windows. Curtains were pulled closed, and he gained no visual perspective until he reached a window at the rear of the house. He could see through a slit at one side of the curtain, and with multiple viewing angles, he was able to make out a bed in the middle of a room. A portable toilet was nearby, and a person lay in the bed, covered up to the head with a sheet.

Aaron tapped on the window, but the person didn't stir. He tapped louder, and then he saw movement. A man pulled himself up in bed, turned his head, and looked toward the window.

"Open the back door," Aaron shouted, then he trotted over to the door.

He heard movement and then the release of latches, and the door creaked open a crack.

Sid Taggett was on his knees, his shoulder propped against the doorjamb.

"I'm Dr. Aaron Rovsing. Can I talk with you?"

Sid swung the door open wide, and Aaron stepped into the house. He winced at the smell of urine as he helped Sid to his feet.

Aaron looked up at a frail man, about six feet tall, with sunken eyes and skin hanging from his cheekbones like beige crepe on a skeleton.

Sid collapsed into Aaron's arms. "You're just skin and bones," Aaron said.

"I used to be strong."

Aaron helped him back to the edge of his bed.

"Does Wanda know you're here?" Sid said.

"No."

"You've got to help me, Doc."

"What's happening to you? Why are you sick?"

"I don't know. I'm real weak." Sid struggled to speak. "I fall asleep all the time . . . and I'm getting these horrible headaches when I'm awake." He took several breaths and lowered his head. "Look. In the last few weeks, my hair has been falling out."

Aaron noticed his scalp with random swatches of white hair among patches of baldness.

As he raised his balding head, Aaron's eyes widened. Sid had no eyelashes.

"How long have you been feeling bad?" Aaron said.

"I can't remember exactly. I have trouble remembering things . . . It's got to be months and months." He put his hand on Aaron's shoulder and took several deep breaths. "I feel like I'm dying. I can't go on like this."

"What did the hospital doctors tell you?"

"That I have some kind of nerve disease . . . Wanda says they don't know which one."

"Are you on any medications?"

"I think I was, once . . . Now, Wanda gives me a liquid medicine."

"What kind of medicine?"

"She says it's strong vitamins, to build my strength."

"Where does she keep it?"

"She locks it in a cabinet . . . in the kitchen, I think."

Aaron walked to the kitchen area and spotted a cabinet with a lock. He pulled on the cabinet knobs, but the doors wouldn't open. "Do you know where she keeps the key?"

"I'm sure she keeps it with her."

Aaron looked around the area and opened a few drawers but didn't find any keys.

"Doc, I need to lie down."

Aaron returned to Sid's bed and helped him recline.

"Wanda checks on me every few hours . . . Sometimes she calls, but sometimes she comes home." He took several breaths. "I don't think she'd be happy to find you here."

"Can I do a quick physical exam on you?"

"Sure. Let me know if you find anything."

Aaron opened his medical bag, pulled out his stethoscope, and applied it to Sid's bony chest. He then palpated the abdomen and extremities. "You've definitely got some unusual, wasting illness."

"That's how I feel, like I'm wasting away."

Aaron saw something under the edge of Sid's pillow. "What's this?" He held up a black cloth pouch, tied at the top with cord.

"I don't know. Wanda puts it under my pillow. She says it'll help me get better."

Aaron felt hard round objects in the pouch. He loosened the cord and looked inside. Mixed in with dust were several stones of various bright colors, long strands of white hair, small bones, and a dried lizard.

Some kind of witchcraft? Aaron thought. His palm began to feel heat from the pouch. "Geez." He retied the pouch and thrust it under Sid's pillow. *I'll leave that thing alone for now.*

"I'm leaving," Aaron said. "I'll research this to see if any tests are indicated that I can do. I'd like to find out what's really wrong with you."

If Wanda's his legal caretaker, I'll probably have to get her consent to test him.

Aaron repacked his medical bag and looked at Sid. "Do you need to lock up behind me?"

"No, she'll just think Race came in."

"Race is your son?"

"He's my stepson, Wanda's son. I adopted him when he was a child."

"Where is he?"

"Probably at work at the cemetery . . . I don't talk to him much anymore."

"What does he do at the cemetery?"

"Odd jobs whenever they need him . . . He digs graves." Sid took a deep breath. "Most people steer clear of him. You probably should, too."

Aaron walked toward the back door and stopped. He looked back at Sid. "I'll do my best to help you."

He saw a flicker of a smile on Sid's face.

As Aaron stepped out the back door, he heard soft snoring from Sid's bed. He stopped at his car and stared back at the Taggett's house.

Something's not right in there. Why would she lock up vitamins, and what is that pouch under the pillow?

He glanced in his rearview mirror as he drove away. *Why would Sid say that I should avoid his stepson, Race Taggett?*

Aaron remembered what the car dealer Dale McCorkindale had recommended, so for dinner he savored spicy Tex-Mex chicken enchiladas and a fruity margarita at a restaurant about twenty minutes from his house.

After the meal, he explored country roads that bordered his town and the Big Thicket nearby. At one point, he stopped his car at the side of the road and stepped out. He was alone on the road, and the wind ruffled his hair as he looked up at towering trees swaying in tight rows just a few feet from the road shoulder. At times, he heard the breeze moan from deep within the forest. A chill passed over him.

He lifted a hand up to the trees. "Why am I even here? I'm a New Englander. What the hell am I doing in this strange place?"

A gust of stale wind blasted his face and knocked him back.

Aaron jumped back into his car and sped off to town with his windows down, eventually turning onto the road to his house. His car headlights were on low beam, and the moon over him was almost full. He hummed along with a country song on the radio. "Wow, that is one vengeful lover." He glanced at the radio song information: 'Tornado,' by Little Big Town. "That poor sap sure picked the wrong woman to cheat on."

As he approached the intersection near his home, he saw Marley and Cristal Brighton walking up their driveway. Pulling his car to the side of the road in front of their house, he waved and walked over to them.

"I saw you two out here and thought I'd stop and say hello."

"How are you? We had a good day, didn't we Cristal?" Marley said.

"We played in the park," Cristal said.

"I wonder if I could have a neighborly chat with you," Aaron said to Marley.

"Sure, come on inside." She unlocked the front door, and a large Golden Retriever barked greetings at them. "This is Princess."

Princess jumped up and put her front paws on Aaron. "I'll bet I know who named her," Aaron said.

"I did." Cristal hugged her dog. "Genie told me to."

"Down, Princess. Calm down," Marley said.

"That's okay. I like dogs," Aaron said.

Marley smiled. "She can tell."

Aaron followed Marley into the living room.

Marley stroked Cristal's hair. "Go check on Genie and get ready for bed." Cristal and Princess ran to her bedroom.

Marley motioned toward a chair. "Please sit down. Do you want some water or a soda?"

"No, thanks," Aaron said.

They settled into soft living room chairs next to each other.

"How has your first week been?" Marley said.

Aaron sighed. "It's an adjustment. The country life is all new to me."

"I like it."

"It seems more relaxed. Some songs talk about the low-key country lifestyle."

Marley stood up. "What kind of music do you like?"

"I've been listening to country music."

"Good. I'll put some on." She walked over to a stereo.

"I just heard a sad song on the radio," Aaron said. "It talked about falling in love with an illusion. The real person turned out to be quite different from the illusion."

Marley sat down in the chair, one leg bent under her. "Shades of 'The Great Gatsby.'"

Aaron sat forward and touched her hand. "You've read 'The Great Gatsby'?"

Marley chuckled. "I know you think we're all hicks—"

"No. I didn't mean to imply—"

"That's all right. We get that a lot from strangers. We're used to it."

She looked at Aaron and smiled. "Your face is bright red. Don't be embarrassed."

Aaron nodded. "It gives me away. Everyone knows when I'm embarrassed."

"Well, I think that's cute."

He took a few deep breaths and turned to face her. "Do I look okay now?"

"You look fine."

"Good. You made an interesting point about the book. Some songs talk about falling in love with someone you put on a pedestal, like the book does. People are far from perfect."

"How well do I know that."

They talked more about country music and good books.

"I hear songs about beer and whiskey and tequila and Southern Comfort. Do cowboys drink a lot?" Aaron said.

Marley laughed. "No more than anybody else."

"And I'll think twice about cheating on a cowgirl. At least in the songs, those guys have bad ends."

Marley frowned and looked down.

Oops, I hit a raw nerve, Aaron thought.

He took a deep breath. "Would you like to have dinner some evening?"

Marley stood. "I'll have to think about that."

Okay, I'm not doing very well here. Aaron followed her to the front door. *Try something else, Aaron.*

He took another deep breath. "Well, at least you could show me around these parts. Let's take a drive tomorrow. It's the neighborly thing to do."

Marley smiled. "Okay."

Aaron exhaled. *Good move.*

"I'll pick you up around one o'clock?" he said.

"We'll be ready."

Aaron's heart raced as he started his car and pulled out into the road. He pumped his fist in the air. "Yes. I think she likes me." He drove down the road toward his house.

"Yikes." He jerked the steering wheel to the left and slammed his brakes as something darted in front of his car. He screeched to a stop at an angle in the road. Looking over his shoulder, he saw a figure disappear around the side of a house.

Another near miss. I'm going to have a heart attack driving on these roads.

He steered the car over to the side of the road and jumped out. Sprinting in the direction of the running figure, he rounded the corner of the house and spotted a man vaulting over the fence that bordered Grant Belkin's ranch.

He cleared that fence by several feet.

Aaron stopped to catch his breath as the man bounded away, his hair flaring up in the air. *Who the heck was that?*

Chapter 8

Aaron awoke with a start early Sunday morning.

He lay in bed for a minute but didn't hear any unusual sounds. It was before dawn.

After pulling on shorts and a T-shirt, he searched the house. Finding no cause for alarm, his jitters subsided. In the kitchen, he punched on the coffee brewer, walked to a rear window, and pulled back one side of the window blinds.

Just outside the glass, two wide-open eyes stared at him.

"Whoa." Aaron lurched back and fell into a small dining table. He righted himself and stumbled back to the window, flipping the blinds open.

The eyes aren't there. Was it an illusion?

His heart pounded as he slid into running shoes and peered out into the back yard. He strained his ears but heard only the hooting of an owl, so he ventured out into the dim moonlight. Standing still next to his fence, he sensed no movement in the yard or the pasture.

A voice rang out, "Stay away from the Taggetts."

Aaron jumped and fell against a fence pole. He looked toward the source of the voice and saw glinting eyes, the same eyes that were at his window, and the silhouette of a figure.

Aaron took a deep breath. "Why?"

"You can't help. No doctors can help us. Stay away or you'll be sorry."

Then the eyes were gone.

Aaron looked around the yard and walked back through the house to the front door. Noticing nothing unusual in the front yard or street, he glanced at the nearby tree grove and listened. The owl was quiet.

He locked all the doors and windows of the house and sat in the living room until he spotted the faint glow of sunrise.

After two cups of coffee, he ventured outside again and wandered around the house. Familiar objects emerged into view in the early dawn.

Aaron dwelled on those strange eyes.

That had to be Race Taggett, and he's hurting.

A shiver passed over him.

He's also one hell of a scary dude.

Aaron spent the rest of the morning unpacking boxes and arranging his home. Despite the soreness in his leg muscles, a pleasant reminder of his jog the day before, he danced from box to box to the sound of country music from a small radio.

Maybe I'll take country-dance lessons with Marley.

He nourished himself with a breakfast of juice and cereal with soy milk, then he decked out in blue jeans, a dark blue-and-gold cowboy shirt, and his new boots.

He pulled into Marley's driveway right at 1:00 p.m. She and Cristal walked out to his car, and Marley slid a picnic basket into the back seat.

"A picnic. Great idea," Aaron said.

"We love picnics, don't we Cristal?"

In the back seat, Cristal raised her arms. "Picnics are fun."

Aaron turned to Marley. "I'll drive, but you can be the tour guide, okay?"

Marley smiled. "Sure, I've got a route in mind. Get ready for some interesting sights in the Big Thicket."

Aaron backed out of the driveway and headed out of town on a county road as Marley pointed the way.

They cruised north and south and sometimes east and west on two-lane roads bordered by pastures and marshes and piney woods, crossing several creeks on their journey. Marley pointed out various birds and four-legged creatures along the side of the road.

"You're a careful driver," Marley said.

"Well, since I moved here, I've become much more alert for surprises in the road."

Aaron slowed and stopped near a sign. "What's this?"

"The entrance to Bragg Road. A lot of folks call it Ghost Road." Marley turned to him. "Don't come here at night." She pushed the car AC to the max setting.

Aaron moaned like a ghost. "Is it scary?"

She turned up the radio volume so Cristal couldn't hear her speak. "At times, along the road, a strange light appears at night out of nowhere. People think it's a lantern carried by a ghost looking around for his head, the ghost of a railroad worker who was decapitated."

Aaron turned onto the dirt road and crept along in the car, studying the forest and the ruins of an old railroad track. After several miles, a shiver gripped him. "It does feel creepy out here, alone in the trees."

"Mommy, let's go back," Cristal said.

Marley nodded and touched Aaron's shoulder. "We should turn around."

"You got it," Aaron said. "The air is heavy in here. It's hard to breathe." As soon as Aaron returned to the paved roads, he stopped the car and jumped out.

"What's wrong?" Marley said.

Aaron gasped for air with his hands on his hips. "Whew. I couldn't breathe back there." He calmed down, stepped back into the car, and turned to Marley, pointing to Ghost Road. "I'm adding that to my bucket list."

Marley laughed. "Join the club."

After another hour of cruising around East Texas, he turned onto a road that led into a state park. "We can picnic here," Marley said.

"Looks good. I think we're far enough away from Ghost Road."

Marley smiled. "I think you got spooked."

"Well, thanks for the history lesson about it. At least, now I know what to expect." Aaron stopped near a few unoccupied picnic tables.

Moisture from a short rain earlier in the day glistened on the grass and trees. "Look all around us," Aaron said. "Everything is bright green."

Marley nodded. "It's amazing the way the rain can bring out that intense green. It's a chance for all the plants to show off."

Marley and Aaron spread a red and green tablecloth over a nearby table. She opened the picnic basket and arranged peanut butter and jelly sandwiches, water, and vegetables with dip on the table.

Aaron stood and turned in a circle with his arms wide. A breeze carried the scent of the pines across his face. *A little slice of heaven on earth.*

Marley and Cristal sat at the picnic table and sampled their sandwiches. "C'mon, join us," Marley said to Aaron. "I brought fresh strawberries, too, from a local strawberry field."

"Yummy, an honest-to-goodness alfresco lunch," Aaron said.

After several bites into his sandwich, Aaron looked at Marley. "The guy with the ranch behind us: Grant Belkin . . . He's an interesting person."

"He's different," Marley said.

"Did you know his wife?"

Marley put her sandwich down. "Not very well."

"He told me she died two years ago."

Marley was quiet.

"I thought hairdressers knew everything."

Marley chuckled. "Usually you'd be right. I guess some things fly right past me."

Aaron and Marley polished off their meals, and even Cristal ate most of her sandwich.

"Everything's delicious," Aaron said.

"Go ahead, enjoy that last strawberry," Marley said.

"You don't have to twist my arm."

"You've got a few red stains on your shirt," Marley said. She stood and wiped his shirt with a moist napkin.

"Thanks," Aaron said. "As a memento of my first picnic, I'll cherish those stains forever."

Marley laughed. "You had a deprived childhood. Everyone should picnic now and then."

Aaron looked down and shook his head. "I've been deprived of many things."

Marley played a pretend violin and hummed a song.

Aaron laughed. "What song are you playing?"

" 'I'm So Lonesome I Could Cry,' by Hank Williams, Jr."

Aaron began to dance with Cristal. They moved in circles and he twirled Cristal under his arm.

Marley looked up. "I can hear the birds warbling louder now. They're watching you."

Aaron stopped and listened. "The birds must like it when folks picnic around here. They can all fly in and join the party."

He bowed to Cristal. "Thanks for the dance."

Cristal continued to dance solo as Aaron broke into the moonwalk dance.

"Mommy, look at him." Cristal pointed at Aaron sliding backward across the grass, his hands on his hips and a big smile for Marley on his face.

Marley giggled. "You've got some great moves."

"I'm glad you think so."

After the dancing, it was time to clean up the picnic table.

Aaron took a deep breath. "I want to learn how to line dance in a real cowboy dance hall. Can we go some evening, and you can show me how?"

Marley nodded. "Sure."

"How about this Wednesday?" He held his breath.

Marley sighed. "Okay."

Aaron clapped his hands together. "Awesome. I can't wait. Dinner's on me, too."

Marley walked away and tossed trash in a nearby bin.

"Since there's a day for just about everything, I'll bet we have a National Picnic Day," Aaron said.

"That would be a safe bet. There is one, in April."

"Yeah, I would've guessed sometime in the spring. Let's picnic again on the next official day, and maybe before then, too? This is a great way to spend an afternoon."

Marley turned and carried the picnic basket to the car.

Maybe I'm coming on too strong. Slow down, Aaron.

Cristal ran over to a nearby trail. "Come with me," she said, waving her arms.

Aaron motioned to Marley. "Let's go. You'll have to tell me about any critters we come across."

"Okay, follow me," Marley said. "Now for another lesson. Over 300 species of birds live in the Big Thicket, and many are on the endangered list. Look for orchids. Twenty types of orchids grow in here, along with, get this, more than one thousand species of plants and ferns."

Aaron whistled. "I can't get my head around all that."

They walked and skipped along the narrow trail for a while, accompanied by chirping birds and scurrying squirrels. Marley pointed at a bluebird as it flew over them. At one point, Aaron heard rustling in the bushes at the side of the trail. Marley parted branches and peered in. "Look, our nine-banded armadillo." Aaron bent forward to see and jumped back as the armadillo scurried away.

Marley laughed. "It won't hurt you."

Cristal ran up to Marley. "Look, Mommy." She held out her hands cradling a large green frog. "Can I have him? Please?"

"No, his home is here. Let him down gently."

As Marley stood up from crouching, her hair glistened in a breeze. Aaron marveled at the intense colors of fluttering birds and swaying foliage behind her.

"Why are you smiling?" Marley said.

Aaron blushed and put his hand to his forehead. "I had this vision of the Garden of Eden. What it might've looked like." He shook his head. "Sorry. I know that's crazy."

"No, it's not. I get that feeling in here sometimes, too."

After about an hour's time, they returned to their picnic area.

Aaron wiped his sweaty forehead with his handkerchief. "Okay, nature girl, you've convinced me. There's a huge variety of plants and critters in the Big Thicket."

Marley smiled. "We've only scratched the surface."

During the drive back to town, they sang along to country music and Marley knew the lyrics to most of the songs. Aaron drove with the windows down and the music loud.

He hadn't thought about those strange eyes outside his window.

Aaron drove farther away from his home that evening for dinner and strolled into a dimly lit Italian restaurant. After wolfing down grilled salmon with pasta and vegetables, he complimented the server and left a generous tip. "Now I know where I can get a decent salmon dish."

As he walked out, he caught a glimpse of the side profile of a man at a table in one corner of the restaurant. *That looks like Dale McCorkindale, the car dealer.*

Aaron watched as the man's hands flew back and forth in front of him, directed at another man sitting opposite with crossed arms and a grim look on his face.

Probably just an animated discussion between friends, Aaron thought.

Back home, Aaron checked computer emails and messages at his desk, and then he sat back, his hands behind his head.

So, Race Taggett wants me to stay away, and maybe I damn well should.

He sighed. *But Marley and Grant asked me to check on them.*

Aaron shook his head. *Race's eyes . . . the way they glinted at me.* A shudder shot down his back. *Kind of reminds me of the chief of staff back at my old hospital.*

****

Not far away, Grant Belkin sat at a table in his kitchen. His words echoed throughout the house.

"Your hair looks whiter today." He directed the words across the table to an empty chair. "It's gettin' longer, too. I like it."

He smiled at the chair, and then nodded. "Yeah, I'm sure it does take quite a while for you to brush all that hair."

Grant sipped from a glass of water. "We have a new doctor in town," he said. "I need to look after him."

He listened for a few seconds.

"Now, don't you worry your pretty head. I'll keep my distance. He won't know I'm watchin'."

Chapter 9

Aaron had the impression that his neighbor—the owl—hooted during the night.

I wonder what challenges are in store for me this week, he thought as he opened the clinic door.

A short while later, he watched from the waiting room as Rocky Donnigan, his alcoholic patient, pedaled a shiny red bicycle into the parking area. Rocky was registered and escorted to a room.

Aaron winced at the smell of cigarettes as he entered Rocky's room. *I'll ask Stella to deodorize in here.*

"How's the infection?" Aaron said.

"Fine, Doc." Rocky held up his forearm. "It's doing real good."

Aaron examined the infected area. "Great. Go ahead and finish the antibiotics."

"I will."

"That's a nice bike you have."

"It's how I get around, so I take good care of it."

Aaron stepped back. "Any more weirdness going on lately?"

Rocky looked down and squinted his eyes. "Come to think of it, I saw something strange a couple of days ago."

"What was that?"

"There's a woman that lives down this road. It dead ends at her house."

"Wanda Taggett?"

"That's her. I saw her buying something, drugs probably, in an alley in town."

Aaron's eyes flew open. "Buying drugs?"

"Yeah. I know the guy she met up with. He's a drug dealer, and I'm pretty sure she handed him money."

On his way out, Rocky stopped at the door of the room and turned to Aaron. "When your car needs maintenance or has a problem, shoot it over to my shop. I'll take care of it."

"It's a deal. So you're good with bikes and cars."

"Yes, sir, I am."

Just after lunch, Stella motioned to Aaron in the hallway. "This next patient is Buck Bogarty. He's a troublemaker and he's always getting into fights. I removed his bandage so you could see his hand wound."

Aaron walked into the room and greeted a young man with short black hair and several small scars on his face. He held up a bloody left hand.

"I got cut," he said.

Aaron examined the wound. "How did it happen?"

"A fight, last night."

"So you hit someone in the mouth? Are these teeth cuts?"

"I guess."

"We'll tend to those wounds and put you on antibiotics to try to prevent infection. Did you report anything to the police?"

Buck laughed. "Hell, no. Don't want no cops."

"Keep the hand elevated as much as you can, and let me know if you have any problems. My nurse will show you how to take care of your hand at home."

Stella cleaned and dressed the wounds, and Buck strutted out of the clinic with his prescription.

"You said he's a troublemaker. I guess he grew up around here?" Aaron said to Stella.

"He did. He had a rough family life, but he did manage to graduate from high school."

"A rough family life?"

"Problems in the marriage. His father left them. Buck still lives with his mother."

"He has a wild look about him, like a hungry tiger."

"Oh, yeah. Everyone knows Buck Bogarty. If you see a fancy hot rod around town, it's probably Buck showing off."

Aaron closed his clinic an hour early and drove over to Constable Greevy's office. He could have asked his questions over the phone when he'd called earlier in the day, but he figured he might be more convincing in person.

As Aaron walked into the office, he detected a faint scent of coffee. In the middle of the room, Keller Greevy sat behind a desk strewn with papers.

"Have a seat, Doc. What's on your mind?" Keller said.

"It's the Taggetts. I'm worried about those folks."

"Well, I know Sid is sickly, and Race is a bit strange. They've been that way for a long time."

"I looked up some medical records at the hospital. It seems that Wanda was suspected of possible child abuse when Race was young. Recently, she took Sid to the hospital several times and they couldn't find out what was wrong with him."

"Okay, plenty of doctors have tried to help them. Maybe that's the way it is. Some things can't be helped, right?"

"That's true, but Wanda has been giving Sid some kind of liquid medicine, and yet he's begging for help."

"Begging for help. Now, how would you know that?"

"Sid told me."

"You were in the house?"

"Yes. And Rocky told me he saw Wanda buying drugs in an alley downtown."

"Rocky Donnigan?"

Aaron nodded.

Keller threw his hands up. "He's a drunk. He's liable to say anything."

Keller stood up and took several steps away from his chair.

He turned to Aaron. "What do you want from me?"

"Get a search warrant and let's find out what Wanda is giving him to drink."

Keller pointed his finger at Aaron. "You're way out of line. The state has already looked into their situation. That family has been that way for a long time, and Sid has been checked by doctors. He's a sick man, and Wanda takes care of him. Let them be."

"But—"

"This meeting's over," Keller said.

Aaron shook his head and stood up.

Just like Marley said, there's something very wrong with Sid, and we don't even have a diagnosis, he thought as he walked out. *I'll have to pursue this in my own way.*

Aaron drove away from Constable Greevy's office, and after several miles, he pulled into a long curving driveway that led up the hill to the home of Brad Benningham, the oilman. He'd called earlier from his office to ask if he could drop by and discuss Preston's struggle with addiction.

Aaron stopped in a porte cochere at the front of the house and stepped out as the front door swung open. V. Brad Benningham stood at the threshold, filling most of the open doorway space, the crown of his head almost touching the top of the door.

Brad motioned to Aaron. "Come on in."

Aaron followed him into the mansion and to a spacious living room with earth-toned furniture. A sparkling crystal chandelier hovered over the room. Brad gestured toward a collection of chairs and couches. "Have a seat. Can I get you a drink?"

"No, thanks." Aaron sat in a plush chair. He noticed a faint sweet scent in the room. *Apples?*

Brad wore boots, a plaid shirt, and jeans secured by a large silver belt buckle. He stopped near Aaron's chair. "I'm sorry about the incident in your office. As you can tell, my son has a problem."

"How's he doing?"

"He's in rehab, in a hospital a few hours from here. We want to avoid recognition."

"He's had a drug problem before?"

Brad sighed and put his hands in his pockets. "He's been in rehab twice over the last five years, for alcohol or drugs."

Brad turned as a tall redheaded woman walked into the living room. "Myra, this is Dr. Rovsing."

She put her hands to her temples. "Oh, my gosh. I'm so sorry you had to see our son that way."

"At least he's in a good place now," Aaron said.

Myra sat in a chair near Aaron. She shook her head. "I don't know if anything will work with Preston. We've been down this road before." She looked at Aaron. "Maybe it's bad genes?"

Aaron nodded. "Genetics could be involved."

"Or maybe we weren't good parents."

"Now, don't start with that," Brad said as he glared at Myra. "When he gets back, he'd better get a job or I'm kicking him out of here, and I'm not keeping him out of jail anymore."

"But he says there aren't any jobs," Myra said.

"He doesn't try to find one. He doesn't want to work."

She put her face in her hands. "Will this nightmare ever end?"

Brad left the room. Aaron stood and put his hand on her shoulder. "I'll help in any way I can. This has got to be tough for you."

Myra groaned, her head down. "You can't imagine."

Aaron walked toward the front door and stopped when he heard the clunking of boots behind him.

"Doc, let me buy you a drink," Brad said. He put his hand on Aaron's back. "I'll take you to my favorite bar. How about it?"

"Sure."

Brad led Aaron outside to his truck. "They have great appetizers there, too. We can make a meal of it."

In the still night air, an owl hooted in the distance as they shut the truck doors.

"Sometimes I just need to get away for a drink. Know what I mean?" Brad said.

Aaron nodded. "Yes, I do."

Brad drove away from his home. "Our son is a real problem."

"Drug addiction is a problem everywhere. A lot of families suffer."

Brad turned up the volume on his truck radio. Along the way, he pointed out businesses and homes of people he knew. He drove for almost twenty minutes to a lounge with a packed parking lot in front.

As they entered the lounge, two men walked away from a small table in a corner. Brad and Aaron sat down at the table and ordered drinks and sausage-and-tomato flatbread.

"This drug addiction is tearing Myra and me apart. She thinks I was an absent father and should have been more involved with Preston when he was young."

"It's not that easy."

"I've protected Preston," Brad said. "I've kept him out of jail, so far."

"Out of jail, for what?"

"He robbed some houses, to pay for his drugs."

Aaron's stomach tightened. An image of a drugged robber and the bloody bodies of his parents floated into his mind. His head began to swirl.

"What's wrong?" Brad said.

Aaron took several deep breaths and a few sips of water. "It'll pass." After a few seconds, he nodded. "I'm all right."

A tall mug of foamy beer appeared for Brad and a glass of red wine for Aaron.

"By the way, how do you keep someone out of jail?" Aaron said.

Brad snorted. "Let me put it this way. I have an understanding with the law around here."

Aaron studied Brad's face. *Does that mean he bribes them?*

Brad had four beers over the next hour, while Aaron nursed his glass of cabernet. Brad talked about his son growing up with such potential and his excelling in high school academics.

"College was not good for Preston. That's when the trouble started." Brad gulped the last of his beer and wiped his mouth with the back of his wrist. "Maybe he'd be better off if he did some time. What do you think?"

"Don't give up on him."

"I once hoped he'd become an engineer like me, like my father and grandfather."

"All in the oil business?"

"Yep. My father was vice-president of an oil company, back when things were better."

"Business is slow now?"

"It's harder. A lot more regulations to deal with, and more folks talking trash about oil."

"Your oil family goes way back. I'll bet you've heard some great stories."

"I have." Brad drained his water glass. "My father knew T. Cullen Davis and followed his trials. That was a crazy time."

"I remember that. He was acquitted of murder, right?"

"Yeah, but my father had his doubts. I wonder if Davis got away with murder." He shook his head. "I guess some people do."

Brad paid the bill and they walked out.

"Thanks for the food and drinks," Aaron said.

They climbed into Brad's truck and drove away. Brad cranked up the country music on the way back, and he sang along at times. Aaron heard several songs about angel eyes and cold beer.

Brad pulled into his driveway and stopped the truck beside Aaron's car. Aaron jumped as Brad slammed his palm against the dashboard. His words were slurred. "I'll tell you. I'm worried about Preston."

"I would be, too."

He cleared his eyes with the back of his wrist and looked at Aaron. "He's all I got."

As Aaron turned to open his door, he flinched as a large hand squeezed his arm. Brad's eyes were wide and his lips contorted.

"What's with you medical doctors anyway? We pay you all this money to fix things. Why can't Preston get well? Why can't he?"

Aaron looked at Brad and sighed.

Brad released his grip. "I'm sorry. This is hard on me."

"I know it is, but there's always hope. People can get better, especially if someone is there for them."

Brad nodded. They stepped out of the truck, and Brad lumbered away to his front door.

Aaron mumbled under his breath, "Unfortunately, we can't fix every problem."

Later that evening, Aaron collapsed into his bed and pulled the sheet up to his neck. He yawned, closed his eyes, and drifted off to sleep.

A line of tall trees appeared, swaying in the breeze. He walked toward the trees and turned as he heard a voice behind him. "Don't go in there." A woman with short blond hair held her arms out toward him, and then she faded away into mist. Aaron ran after her, but he couldn't find his way in the thick mist, and he tripped and fell.

His body jerked and his eyes flew open. Stumbling to the bathroom to towel off his sweaty skin, he couldn't recall the woman's face.

Chapter 10

Buck Bogarty, the hot rodder, leaned against the bar counter inside a lounge. Some of the late evening drinkers sang along to country music blaring overhead. Buck sipped from a beer mug as two women leaned on him, one on each shoulder.

One woman lifted Buck's cowboy hat off his head and slipped it onto her heap of brunette hair. She stroked his hand. "Did my sweetie get into another fight?"

Buck nodded. "Yep."

"It wasn't over another girl, was it?"

"I'm sure it was," the other girl said. "Tell us the truth. You have other girlfriends, don't you?"

Buck smiled and looked at each girl. "There's only you two." They laughed and hugged him.

A group of guys swaggered close to Buck. One of them stopped and clapped Buck on the shoulder. "Who did you whup this time?"

Buck belched. "He sat on my car."

"Yeah, I figured something like that," the man said, then he shook his head at the group standing by Buck. "Don't ever sit on his car."

Buck unlocked the front door of his house, scraped the bottom of his boots on the welcome mat and walked in.

"Is that you, Buck?" a voice said from down the hall.

"Yeah, Mom."

She walked into the living room, a robe wrapped around her nightgown. "You're awful late."

"I met friends."

She touched his hand. "What happened?"

Buck sat down on a couch to pull off his boots.

"Let me help you." She kneeled in front of the couch and tugged on his boots. "You hurt your hand when you beat up someone, didn't you? His father called me about it."

"He had it comin'."

"I'm worried about all these fights. One of these days, you're going to get hurt bad." She sat down by him. "I don't want that. You're my only child. You're all that's left to carry on the family name."

Buck sat back on the couch. "Why do you keep tellin' me that?"

"Because I know you can make something of yourself, if you try. You take after—"

"I know, I know. I remind you of Grandpa."

"Well, you do. That's a good thing." She touched his knee. "There is good in my side of the family."

He sat up and his eyes went to the long irregular scar on her deformed ear.

She held up her hand. "I know what you're thinking. Don't bring your father into this. He's rotten to the core. You're much better than that."

Buck shook his head, stood up, and walked away down the hall.

Chapter 11

Constable Keller Greevy cruised around town on his morning patrol. He peered down several alleys where he suspected that drugs were sold from time to time. So far, this Tuesday morning was quiet, and last night had been uneventful.

His two-way radio crackled, "Disturbance on Pine Street." The voice went on to say that Keller's office had received several calls about a man acting strangely in the street.

Keller eased his car along Pine Street, behind a long line of traffic, until he saw a man in the road ahead. After parking at the curb, he rested a hand on his holstered weapon as he approached a short man in a bright orange shirt and purple pants. Wide-eyed drivers stopped their cars as the man tapped on the side windows and yelled at them. The man handed papers to any occupants who lowered their windows.

Keller walked up to the man. "Tucker Boudreaux?"

Tucker turned and reached out to Keller. "Great, I'm glad you're here. Help me hand out these flyers."

"You can't do this. Get out of the road. You're obstructing traffic."

"I'm running for governor. Texas needs a Cajun governor. I have to let everybody know, so they'll vote for me," Tucker said as Keller guided him to the sidewalk.

He's out of his head again, Keller thought.

"I've got letters of support from the governor and the president. I've got great plans for this state. Just think, I'll build the perfect society, unemployment at zero, no child goes hungry, one hundred percent high school graduation rate, immigrants put to work so everyone will contribute, people will come here from all over the world—"

Keller held his hand up. "Slow down."

"Tucker," a woman yelled.

Keller turned toward the woman. "Good, your mother's here."

"I wondered where you'd gone to," she said as she trotted up to them out of breath. "What's happening?"

"He was out in the street stopping traffic. Thank goodness, no wrecks have been reported."

"I'm sorry, I didn't know he'd left the house." She scanned one of the flyers in Tucker's hand. "He's been writing hundreds of letters over the last few days, to politicians and all the people he knows."

Tucker held up a flyer. "I need to get the word out about voting for me for governor." He nodded at Keller. "Just you wait and see. I'll be president someday."

Keller pointed at Tucker's mother. "Get him some help, before somebody gets hurt."

Tucker stared at Keller, held up his hand and babbled. "How's yo' mama and all dem doin'? *Arrete, arrete,* stop, stop, stop, woman, wanting, wanting woman."

"What the hell?"

"I'm so sorry, Officer," Tucker's mother grabbed her son's arm. "Let's go home."

She led Tucker away. "Have you been taking your medicine? I need to call your psychiatrist."

Chapter 12

Aaron worked out a plan of attack. At lunchtime on Tuesday, he hopped into his car, drove to Wanda's diner, and walked up to the entrance doors. Spotting Wanda inside, he jogged back to his car and sped away to the Taggett's house.

After shouting and pounding on the back door for several minutes, Aaron stood at a side window and saw Sid wake up and roll out of bed. Sid lay on the floor for a minute or so and then crawled over to the back door. Aaron ran to the door as he heard the locks release.

Aaron opened the door and stepped into the house. Sid was back down on the floor.

"Sid, are you okay?"

"Hey, Doc." His words were slurred. He struggled to raise his eyelids, looked at Aaron, and then closed his eyes again.

Aaron gathered Sid up in his arms and carried him back to his bed. He soon heard Sid's rhythmic breathing of sleep.

Aaron checked the kitchen cabinet, which was locked, and then he walked into a laundry room near the kitchen. Across from the washer and dryer was a sink with a counter and cabinets. He opened the cabinets above the sink and sifted through common household wares, towels and old magazines.

In a lower cabinet, he spotted a crumpled brown box with a product name he didn't recognize and the word "rodenticide" written on it. He shook the box; it felt empty. He opened the top of the box, pulled out a small jar from his pocket and tapped the box over the jar. A few flakes of off-white powder fell to the bottom of his jar. Tightening the jar lid, he replaced the brown box in the cabinet and washed his hands in the sink, then he found a paper towel nearby and dried his hands and the sink. He put the towel and the jar in his pocket and walked back to Sid's bed. Sid was in a deep sleep.

Back at his clinic, Aaron printed a lab request for analysis of the few grains of powder he'd found at the Taggett's house.

"What is that?" Stella said.

"Something I found in Wanda's house."

"Wanda was there?"

"No, she was at work. Sid let me in."

Stella looked at the flakes of powder in the jar. "What do you think it is?"

"I don't know, but I'm worried about Sid. I might as well check this out."

Stella had the powder picked up that afternoon for delivery to a laboratory testing facility located in a nearby county.

Later in the afternoon, Juliana walked up to Aaron. "While you were at lunch, a man stopped by and asked for you."

"A man? What was his name?"

Juliana shrugged her shoulders. "He didn't give me his name, and he wouldn't leave a message. He said you'd know who he was, and that he'd come back some other time."

"What did he look like?"

"Tall. Stocky. He was bald."

"Did he have bushy eyebrows?"

"Yes, he did."

Aaron sighed and looked out the front window. *So, the machete guy has found me.*

"Do you know who he is?" Juliana said.

"Yes. Let me know if you see him again." Aaron turned and walked away.

Aaron motioned to Stella in the hallway. "I've noticed we get really warm in here in the afternoons. Do you feel it?"

"Oh, yeah. I think every time the front door opens, cool air rushes out. I'll pay more attention to the AC settings."

After glancing at the registration information, Aaron walked into a patient room. A young man with a prominent jaw sat on the examination table. He stared over Aaron's shoulder with a faraway look in his eyes.

"Daniel, how can I help you today?" Aaron said.

Daniel brought his eyes into focus on Aaron and took a deep breath. "I'm having trouble getting my life together, sir."

"You're having emotional problems?"

Daniel was quiet for several seconds. "I'm in the Army. I got back from a tour of duty six months ago." He struggled to speak. "I can't seem to straighten myself out."

"Has this ever happened before?"

Daniel's eyes filled with tears. "A friend of mine was shot dead by a sniper." He put his hand to his eyes. "He was right next to me. I carried him to shelter and tried to help him."

"I'm sorry. I'm sure you did what you could." Aaron handed a tissue to Daniel.

"I can't sleep." Daniel blotted his eyes with the tissue. "I keep reliving that scene, with his blood splattering all over me, and the way his eyes looked at me before he died." Daniel had that faraway look in his eyes again.

"Have you seen a counselor or psychiatrist?"

Daniel focused his eyes on Aaron again. "Sure. They told me I had PTSD."

"We have ways of treating that."

"I know, sir, but my problem today is, I think I'm really short of sleep. Can you give me something to help me sleep?"

"No problem." Aaron examined his heart, lungs and pupils, and printed him a prescription. "Keep up your counseling sessions."

Daniel nodded.

Aaron touched his shoulder. "I appreciate you. We all appreciate your service."

Daniel sighed and walked out.

Aaron studied his surroundings after he walked out of the clinic after work. He watched his rearview mirror as he drove to a cafe for dinner, and he looked over the diners inside the cafe before he checked in to be seated. At his table, he sat with his back to the wall. He forced himself to eat his appetizer crab cakes as he surveyed the dining room every few minutes, and between bites, he scrutinized all newcomers at the check-in area.

Back at his home, he checked the yard, all the doors and windows, the closets and even under the bed, and then he armed his house alarm system.

I probably won't sleep well tonight. He sighed. *But that's nothing unusual lately.*

Chapter 13

Late that evening, Race Taggett stood in the trees outside a crowded lounge. His body was still as he watched, except his long hair, which swayed at times in the breeze. At one point, he slid over to another tree, and a crow screeched as it flapped away.

Race was close to a particular car in the parking lot, which was about half-full with trucks and cars. People came and went through the entrance door of the lounge, and some folks wobbled or needed support to make it to their vehicles.

After an hour or so, two young women walked out to the parking area. They stopped and talked with each other for several minutes and then separated to their respective cars. As the shorter woman approached her car at the rear of the lot, she reached into her purse, looking for her keys.

Race held up a long, round bat-shaped object and swung it against the woman's temple, the impact causing a hollow thud, as if her head was a coconut. Catching her as she groaned and collapsed, he lifted her limp body and draped it across his shoulder, and then he trotted into the trees. In the inky shadows of the Big Thicket, he alternated walking fast and jogging for several miles along a narrow, zigzag path through the thick trees and underbrush, beneath faint moonlight that filtered at intervals through the tree canopy. He exploded into a small clearing and laid the bat and the unconscious woman on the ground near a tree. Although his shirt was splotched with sweat, he was not out of breath.

Race covered the woman's mouth with duct tape, pulled her arms behind her, and wrapped her wrists and lower legs with tape. A heavy chain was secured around a tree near the woman. He encircled her waist with one end of the chain and joined chain links behind her back with a metal clasp. He tested the chain; it was snug around her waist.

Race tossed dry wood into a campfire pit in the center of the clearing. After a few minutes, a blazing fire lit the clearing. He turned as the woman opened her eyes and moaned, his body and face reflecting the flickering yellows and reds from the flames.

He pulled a long knife out of a nearby backpack and swaggered over to her, smirking as he held the gleaming knife in front of him. He leaned down, his contorted face inches away from her wide-open eyes.

"Remember me? You were mean to me in school." He spat on her. "You're not mean to me now, are you?"

Chapter 14

The big day has arrived, Aaron thought as he walked into his clinic. He pumped his fist in the air. *My date with Marley is tonight.*

Midafternoon, Stella approached Aaron in the hallway. "Dale McCorkindale is here. He wants to ask you something."

"That's Boots, the car dealer, right?"

"One and the same. He likes to be called Dale."

Aaron walked to the waiting room and spotted Dale sitting in a chair.

Dale stood and they shook hands. "What can I do for you today?" Aaron said.

"You ever been fishing?"

"No." Aaron raised his hand. "Well, I take that back. I went once as a Boy Scout. I don't remember much about it."

"I like to take new folks fishing. Why don't you and I go one weekend morning?"

"Okay. Let's do it."

"Good. You'll find it relaxing."

Dale stopped at the front door. "Don't forget about my offer on the pickup truck."

Aaron snorted. "I won't. Maybe someday."

Aaron was about to enter a patient room when Stella stopped him.

"This guy is an odd one," she whispered. "Be ready for a wacky story."

"What was his name? I saw it on the computer."

"Cam Fillmore."

Aaron nodded and walked into the room. A lanky man with long dirty blond hair sat on the examination table, a guitar hanging from his neck.

"How can I help you, Mr. Fillmore?" Aaron said.

Cam strummed a few chords. "I'm out of my medicine. I haven't taken it for a while. My doctor says I need it."

That's easy enough, Aaron thought. He'd read in the patient record that the man was on an antipsychotic medication.

"I can help you with that, and I'm glad you're following your doctor's wishes."

He strummed a few more chords. "Sometimes I don't think I really need the medicine."

"Just remember, it helps you think straight."

"I guess so."

"Where is your doctor?"

"Montana."

"You're a long way from home."

"I moved here not too long ago."

"Montana must be a nice place. Why did you move away?"

Cam strummed more chords, louder this time. "I had to get away."

"So it was time for a change."

"I had to get away from them."

Aaron raised his eyebrows. "I see. Anyone in particular?"

"The police."

A fugitive from justice?

"They follow me everywhere. They try to zap me with beams."

"What beams?"

"Beams of radiation. They're trying to boil my blood with their beams. Here, feel my arm. Feel the heat from my hot blood." He looked at Aaron with wide eyes.

Aaron touched the man's forearm. "They followed you here?"

"Yep. They were outside my house a few days ago. They didn't know I was home."

"Where are they now?"

"Gone. As long as I'm behind my beam blockers, I'm okay."

"Beam blockers?"

"Sure. Drive by my house and I'll show them to you."

"I might do that. Thanks."

A few minutes later, Aaron handed him a prescription. "Be sure and take your medicine."

"That's what everyone tells me." He jammed the prescription into his pocket.

"By the way, is Cam short for something?"

Cam strummed one last chord. "No."

After work, Aaron drove to Rocky Donnigan's auto shop on the outskirts of town. He checked his rearview mirror more than usual but saw nothing suspicious.

Aaron parked near the door to the small lobby of the shop and walked inside. Rocky stood by the counter. "Hi, Doc."

"Can I get maintenance on my car?"

"No problem. I'll take care of it," Rocky said.

"My Volvo is a good car, but I'll bet you miss the old days. It must have been easier to work on cars back in the day."

Rocky looked out the window. "I do miss the old classics. They were fun to fiddle with."

"What's your favorite classic car?"

Rocky scratched his chin. "Can't go wrong with a '57 Chevy. That was a beauty. But if I could have only one, I'd make it a red '64 Pontiac GTO two-door convertible with a four-speed transmission. Those were fun cars to work on and drive."

"You have fond memories of that car?"

"One of my good buddies back then had one, and we used to drive around town showing off." Rocky sighed. "Well, back to work. I'll get to your car soon."

"No problem. Take your time."

Rocky finished work on a Toyota Camry, and then he drove Aaron's car into the garage and power-lifted it off the ground.

He motioned Aaron to walk to the edge of the car bay. "Volvo is a real sturdy car," Rocky said. "They're like tanks." He walked around and underneath the car, checking various parts. "You're going to need new tires soon."

Aaron nodded. "I'm not surprised."

"Folks go through lots of tires around here."

Aaron watched as Rocky maneuvered around the car and through the engine, every step and hand action choreographed with no wasted motion.

After a short while, Rocky straightened and stood tall, wiping his hands on a towel. "I'll clean it up, and you're good to go."

On his way home, Aaron slowed his car in front of a house set back from the road.

What in the world is that?

Several shiny silver rectangular partitions stood upright in the front yard. Aaron stopped at the side of the road, and a gangly man walked between the partitions and waved, a guitar hanging from his neck.

It's Cam Fillmore, my schizophrenic patient.

Aaron pulled into the driveway, and Cam leaned down to Aaron's window.

"Hi, Doc. How do you like my beam blockers?"

"Do they work?"

"They sure do. I covered some wooden planks with aluminum foil, and they do the job real good. My skin doesn't heat up when I'm behind them."

Aaron studied the foil-covered partitions. "They look sturdy, put together well."

"It was a snap. I'm a carpenter."

"Are you taking your medicine?"

"Sometimes I forget."

"You should remember. The medicine helps you think clearly."

"That's what they tell me."

"Did you recognize my car just now?"

"Yep. I know your car, and I watch the cars on this road, for my own protection."

"But you can't possibly spot every car that passes by."

"I don't have to. When bad guys get close, my beam blockers signal me. They start to jiggle."

"I see."

Aaron shook hands with Cam. "I've got to move along. Stay healthy." As he backed into the road, pleasant chords from Cam's guitar floated on the air through his window. He felt Cam's eyes on him as he drove away.

Aaron pulled into Marley's driveway that evening, singing words from a song he'd just heard on the radio: 'Begin Again,' by Taylor Swift.

He rang Marley's front doorbell, and his heart pounded as the door opened.

Marley stood in the threshold in a flowery sundress, a black cowgirl hat, and red boots.

Aaron caught his breath. "You look great."

Marley smiled. "I'm glad you think so."

Thank goodness I wore my boots, he thought.

Aaron drove to a popular steakhouse restaurant about twenty minutes away. He held the entrance door for Marley and glanced around inside the dining room. He didn't spot any suspicious bald men.

They were escorted to a table and Aaron pulled out her chair.

"I read 'The Great Gatsby' again," Aaron said as their Caesar salads were served.

Marley shook her head. "Daisy had problems. She didn't seem to care much for her child."

"You wonder how that child would've turned out later in life."

"I'll bet an unhappy person, because Daisy was probably not a good mother." Marley put down her fork. "I don't want to be like her."

Aaron nodded. "And Daisy got away with murder, or at least manslaughter."

"She let someone else take the blame. I wonder if I'd be weak like that."

Aaron shook his head. "Somehow I don't think so."

Marley's face beamed.

She sipped her iced tea and then leaned toward him. "Race Taggett had a difficult childhood. Have you been able to check on that family?"

Aaron coughed into his hand. "Race is one disturbed man."

Her eyes narrowed. "Don't let that stop you. You might make a real difference with them."

Aaron's chest swelled. "Thanks for the vote of confidence. I am checking on some things about Sid Taggett." He didn't remember later how his entree tasted.

"Are you ready for some line dancing?" Marley said as they left the restaurant.

"Let's do it."

Marley directed him south of their town to a dance hall and saloon in Beaumont. As they walked to the entrance, Aaron heard music and laughter from the festive dancers inside.

"Let's watch first, so you can get the hang of it," Marley said.

They sat at a small table and ordered drinks. Aaron studied the dancers as they stepped and turned to the music. "They don't touch each other while they dance," Aaron said.

"Usually not."

They watched the dancers through several songs, then Marley grabbed Aaron's arm. "We've seen enough. Let's join in. This song is a dance classic: 'Boot Scootin' Boogie,' by Brooks & Dunn."

Aaron got into the flow of the synchronous leg and body motion.

"You catch on quick," Marley said.

Aaron pointed at her. "I've got a good teacher."

After several songs, Aaron was a bit out of breath. "This is fun, and it's good exercise, too."

"I figured you'd enjoy it."

"I'm glad the AC works good in here. I haven't even broken a sweat."

They walked back to their table.

Aaron clapped his hands. "I'm getting into this. Let's close this place down."

Marley laughed. "That would be fun, but it's time for me to get back home."

Aaron smiled. "I was afraid you'd say that."

As Aaron walked Marley out of the dance hall, he didn't notice Constable Keller Greevy following them out into the parking lot.

Aaron drove back to Marley's house. "How much time do we have?" he said as they walked in the front door.

"I have to pick up Cristal in thirty minutes." Marley turned on her stereo with country music.

Aaron embraced her, and she responded with a tight hug. He sensed a faint pleasant perfume. *Some kind of flower. Maybe honeysuckle?*

She laid her head on his shoulder as they slow-danced. He felt wetness through his shirt.

"What's wrong?" Aaron said.

She lifted her head. "I don't know. I need more time."

"I don't want to let you go."

"I don't know what's happening."

"Are you really expecting him to come back?"

"I think I want him to. I know Cristal wants him to."

They danced to the music of several songs.

Marley sighed. "He was always attractive to women, since high school. He can't say no. But I think he still loves me."

"Has he called you since he left?"

"No, but he's done this before."

Aaron stopped dancing. He held her hands. "How can you put up with him?"

"I know him better than anyone else does. He always comes back. Other women get tired of him."

"I'm not sorry to say this. I think he's an idiot."

Marley led Aaron to the living room chairs. Aaron noticed that she sat in her characteristic position with her leg bent beneath her. "He was our high school quarterback, and he got a bad concussion and had to quit football. He was in a coma for several days."

"Wow, that was a serious injury."

"It changed him. It affected his thinking. He was embarrassed in school, his grades got worse, and he didn't even try for college. The high school just let him graduate."

"What kind of future can you have with him?"

"Deep down, he's a good man and only I know how to take care of him." She looked down. "I know he'll settle down someday."

"I . . . I want to ask you something." Aaron held up his hand. "Don't worry, you won't hurt my feelings."

"What?"

"Is it my face?"

Marley's jaw dropped. "Of course not. You're a good-looking man, in a rugged way."

"Okay. Rugged is good."

From his parked car, Constable Keller Greevy watched Aaron drive off down the road. He stepped out but didn't close the door, and he stood and watched Marley's house. After several minutes, he shook his head.

What in the world was crazy Cajun Tucker Boudreaux babbling about in the street yesterday?

He stepped back into his car and drove away.

It was probably just Tucker's idiot nonsense.

****

Marley sat on the edge of her bed, alone in the darkness. Cristal was asleep in her own bedroom down the hallway.

Marley put her hand over her eyes and bowed her head, sobbing into a tissue. Some tears escaped and dripped onto her thighs.

"God, what should I do?"

She shouted and stiffened as something touched her leg.

"Cristal, angel. You should be asleep."

Cristal gazed up at Marley and hugged her thigh. She climbed up into Marley's lap and rested her head against Marley's chest.

Marley dried her eyes with tissue and stroked Cristal's hair. After several minutes, she heard Cristal's soft snores.

As Marley stared ahead, her vision cleared, and she gave a faint nod.

She lifted Cristal across her arms, kissed her forehead, and carried her to her bedroom.

"Everything will be fine," Marley whispered as she pulled the sheet over Cristal's chest.

****

Aaron lay on top of his sheets. His eyes were open, but his mind was elsewhere.

That's it. I'll book a cruise. Maybe a Caribbean cruise, or one to Alaska. I'll bet Cristal would like Alaska.

Chapter 15

With vacant eyes, V. Brad Benningham sat on his living room couch and stared out the window. Orange and caramel colors washed over the evening horizon.

He leaned forward to a table and opened an album of photos. Leafing through the pages, he studied family images from the past, pausing at times to stare at certain photos of his son, Preston, before the days of the addiction.

Myra walked into the living room. "Dinner is ready."

Brad didn't look up. Myra sat down beside him on the couch.

Brad continued to gaze at the photos, page after page.

Myra smiled and pointed to a photo of Preston with her. "There's Preston in his Tiger Cub shirt. Remember that?"

Brad closed the album and walked to the window. "I wasn't there for him."

Myra joined him and put her hands around his arm. "You're there for him now, and he needs you."

"I hope it's not too late."

"He's coming home tomorrow. Maybe this time, he'll be okay."

They looked out of the window until the colors of the sunset faded.

It was a hot, muggy day when Preston Benningham came home from rehab.

Brad pulled into the driveway of their house. He and Preston had spoken only a few words on the trip back from the rehab center.

Myra greeted them at the door, and Preston carried his suitcase to his bedroom.

"How is he?" Myra said.

"It's too soon to tell."

After a few minutes, Preston walked into the living room.

Brad turned to Myra. "We're going to see the doc. Preston wants to apologize."

Chapter 16

Stella fanned her face with a clipboard as she escorted Brad and Preston into a patient room. "I'll get Dr. Rovsing."

Aaron entered the room. "Hello, Preston. You're looking better."

"Thanks. I'm doing okay."

"I can tell. You're headed in the right direction."

Brad cleared his throat. "Preston has something to say."

A pasty-faced Preston looked at the floor. "I was out of my head that day. I'm sorry I pointed a gun at you."

"You've got an illness that has to be managed. There's a lot of help around for you," Aaron said.

Brad put his hand on Preston's shoulder. "We're going to make it."

Preston sighed and looked up at Aaron. "Addiction is rough, isn't it?"

"It can take complete control of you. It can ruin your life."

"You must see other patients like me."

"Yes, I do."

"Some of them recover, don't they?"

"They can recover, with the right kind of help."

"Isn't everyone addicted to something?" Preston said.

"Everybody has the potential to fall into some kind of addiction."

Brad looked up. "Heck, some people are sugar addicts. Right, Doc?"

"I agree."

"Does it ever go away?" Preston said.

Aaron shook his head. "The trap will always be there."

"For the rest of my life?"

"It's best to assume that."

"That's what they told me in rehab. I guess every day is going to be a battle."

"Yes, it can be, but it's a battle you can win, one day at a time."

Brad patted Preston's shoulder and nodded. "That's why we need doctors and counselors."

Aaron stepped closer to Preston. "Can I ask some personal questions?"

"Fire away."

"Did you grow up around here?"

"I was born here," Preston said.

"You must be about the same age as Race Taggett. Did you go to school with him?"

Preston chuckled. "Now, there's a guy with real problems. He was a year ahead of me. I don't think he finished high school."

"What was he like?"

"A loner. He didn't have any friends that I knew of. He skipped class a lot."

"Did he talk to people?"

"I guess so. I talked with him a couple of times. He didn't have much to say, and he acted weird sometimes. Word went around that he used to cut himself."

Aaron's eyes widened. "You mean, like with a knife?"

"Yeah. I remember seeing bandages on his arms."

"I'm sure the school tried to work with him."

"Maybe so. He was really good in sports. He was strong and fast. He could've been a star athlete."

"I believe that."

"He never had a girlfriend, either, at least that I knew of. Some of the girls used to make fun of him, all the time. They were worse to him than the guys. Once he tried to hug a girl, but she screamed and called him an icky freak."

"Why all the questions about Race?" Brad said.

"I just want to get to know folks in the community. I might see him someday as a patient."

"Good luck with that," Preston said. He held up his hand. "I just remembered something. After Race left school, two of the teachers disappeared."

"That's right," Brad said. "They were never found, and there was a rumor that Race might've been involved somehow. Looking back on it, I wonder if that rumor got started just because Race was such a weird guy. They probably just moved somewhere else without telling anyone."

As they walked out of the room, Brad turned to Aaron. "Do you hunt?"

"I've never been," Aaron said.

"I go deer hunting every year. Why don't you come along next time?"

"Thanks. I'll think about it."

"Believe me, it's good for you. You can reconnect with your manhood, with that hunter instinct in you that's deep in your DNA."

Aaron puffed out his chest. "Manhood DNA. Sounds good. Can you teach me how to shoot?"

"We'll go to the shooting range, and you'll be good to go."

Then I'll be a real Texan, Aaron thought.

Stella frowned and fanned her face as she watched Preston and Brad walk out of the clinic.

Aaron approached her. "You weren't happy to see them, were you?"

"I wish I never had to deal with a drug addict again."

After lunch, Aaron spotted the drug rep in the hallway. Aaron didn't offer to shake his hand.

"Hi, Doc. Were you able to prescribe my antibiotic?"

"Yes, I'm using it in my patients. I think it works well."

"Great. Say, I was wondering, a lot of doctors invest. Do you? I can steer you to some great investments." He held his hands behind his back as he rocked on his heels.

129

"Are you talking about the stock market?"

"Actually, there are some promising new medical devices. I've studied these products, and I think one of them in particular will be a gold mine for investors. A gold mine."

Aaron hesitated.

"Don't miss out on this. It could make us both very rich."

Aaron sighed. *Oh, boy. I've heard that line before.* "Thanks, but I'll pass on that for now."

"Maybe later then. Here's some info about that 5K I told you about." He handed Aaron a flyer. "It's a popular race every year."

"Good. I've already started jogging again."

The rep pulled out his hand wipes and turned to leave.

Aaron held up his hand. "Wait, you mentioned last week that you knew Forrester Brighton, Marley's husband."

"I was a few years behind him in high school."

"What was he like?"

"He was a good football player, until he had that brain injury. He never was right in the head after that. He began to act like a mean little kid."

"He acted immature?"

"He sure did. He wanted his way all the time and picked fights if you didn't go along with him. He bragged about all the girls he scored with."

"Was he always a womanizer?"

"Not before, I don't think so. He was a different person after the injury. It turned everybody off." He stopped rocking on his heels and leaned toward Aaron. "And the girls said he couldn't even do it. He wasn't scoring at all."

Aaron's eyes flew open. "You mean, he's impotent?"

"That's what I mean."

"But he and Marley have a child," Aaron said.

"She's adopted."

Aaron shook his head. "I'm amazed Marley stuck with him. She must be an angel."

****

Preston walked outside under the porte cochere of the Benningham mansion and gazed at the orange and red colors oozing over the evening horizon. He spotted Rocky Donnigan on the street and watched as Rocky pedaled his bicycle up the driveway toward him.

"How're you doing?" Rocky said, braking his bicycle near Preston.

"Better, thanks."

"I'm glad. You're still young. You have your whole life in front of you."

Preston put his hands in his pockets. "I've heard all that."

"I blew it when I was your age, and look at me now."

Preston glanced up at Rocky.

"I was addicted to cocaine for a while," Rocky said. "I got off it and on to booze. My father kicked me out when I was twenty."

"Everyone can get addicted to something," Preston said.

"Sure, but you're a good man, and you have a future. You still have your father."

"Where is your father now?"

"He's dead." Rocky looked at the ground. "After I left, I never saw him again." He pedaled off on his bicycle, made a U-turn and rode by Preston. "You can lick this. You can end up better than me."

Chapter 17

On his way home that evening, Aaron passed Rocky Donnigan's trailer home and spotted Rocky's bicycle lying in a heap in the front yard.

"That's not like Rocky. He takes good care of that bike."

Aaron stopped his car on the right shoulder of the road and stepped out. He heard a faint humming, which seemed to come from behind the trailer. Aaron hurried to the back yard and saw Rocky sitting with his back against the trailer, drinking from a wine bottle.

"Rocky, it's me. Are you okay?"

Rocky turned to Aaron. "Hey, Doc." He sat forward and showed Aaron his bottle. "I wish I had some . . . to share . . . but it's almost gone." His words were slurred.

"Why are you out here?"

Rocky let out a loud belch. "Drinking my cares away."

Aaron sat down beside him. Rocky drained the bottle, took a deep breath, and stumbled over a few words from a country song.

I know that song, Aaron thought. *It's 'You and Tequila,' by Kenny Chesney.*

Rocky sang a few more verses and stopped. "Doc, I'm no good."

"You're a decent man, a good mechanic. People in town like you. I like you."

"Thanks . . . but I'm really no good. He dropped his head. "I've made a stinking mess of my life."

"Come on, let me help you to your bed. You need a good night's sleep."

Rocky pulled up his knees, hunched over, and began to sob. "My life ain't worth a plug nickel." He rocked back and forth a few times, then he grabbed the empty wine bottle and hurled it into the trees.

He put his head in his hands. "I killed ... I killed my own son," he said between sobs.

"What?"

Rocky moaned and resumed the rocking motion. "I was drunk one night. I came home . . . My baby boy was crying in his crib . . . I picked him up and hugged him . . . and put him in bed beside me . . . I woke up in the morning . . . and I was on top of him. He wasn't breathing." Rocky sobbed in his hands.

"I'm sorry."

"My wife couldn't take it. She left me."

Aaron put his hand on Rocky's shoulder as he moaned and sobbed and rocked.

"Sometimes I wish I was dead . . . Then maybe I could see my son in heaven . . . and maybe he could forgive me."

Aaron's eyes welled with tears. *We all have our demons, my friend.*

He sat with Rocky for a while, until the rocking stopped.

Rocky mumbled something. His eyes were closed. Aaron leaned closer and he heard Rocky whisper, "I've got to help Preston."

A minute later, Aaron heard soft snoring. He lifted Rocky in his arms and carried him inside the trailer to his bed. Rocky didn't stir as Aaron arranged him in a comfortable position, pulled off his boots, and slipped a pillow under his head.

He switched on a lamp and looked around the trailer. Automobile books and magazines were strewn about on chairs and tables. He walked over to a small model car on a nearby table and studied the shiny body.

I wonder if that's a '64 Pontiac GTO.

Several minutes passed, and Aaron heard no sound except Rocky's regular breathing. He covered Rocky with a sheet up to his chest.

As he stood by the bed, he felt a gnawing tightness in his stomach. He reached out and touched Rocky's forehead. *Sleep well, my friend.*

Aaron turned off the lamp and walked out into the night air behind Rocky's trailer. He heard branches of the tall pines in the Big Thicket whisper in the breeze.

Chapter 18

Aaron was in and out of sleep all night. He woke up shouting, his hands above him, as he saw the machete swinging toward his face. He sat on the side of the bed in a cold sweat. It was several minutes before the alarm was set to ring.

The machete guy is in town. Juliana saw him in the clinic a few days ago. I've got to stay alert.

He stumbled to the bathroom to wash his face and then looked around inside the house. *Should I even go outside?*

Aaron eased the back door open, stepped out, and tiptoed around the perimeter of his house in the dawn light, searching for anything unusual. He heard noises from inside a tree grove that bordered the western side of his property.

Aaron turned to sprint back to his door.

"Hey, you." A figure emerged from the shadows, a man with long, flowing hair and a mustache and beard.

Aaron stopped in midstride. He recognized the silhouette. "Race Taggett?"

"Yeah."

Aaron hesitated and then, despite shakiness in his legs, hobbled across the yard toward the trees.

Race's eyes bore into him. "You've been to my house. Like I told you before, you'd best stay away from there. We don't like visitors."

Aaron's voice trembled. "I'm just trying to help."

"There was a doc before you," Race hissed, baring his teeth. "He reminded me of a doc when I was a kid, when they all looked at me like I was a freak." Race nodded. "I scared him off all right."

"Your father is very sick."

Race looked down. "Mom's taking care of that."

Aaron took a deep breath. *Maybe he's right. I should just forget about this screwed-up family.*

Race stepped forward and pointed. "Don't come around my house."

Aaron turned and hurried away. He reached the door and looked back. He could make out the figure of Race in the trees.

His hair. He's the guy that ran in front of my car and jumped the fence a few days ago.

"Are you all right? You look like you didn't sleep a wink," Stella said as Aaron walked into the clinic.

"I'm worried about Rocky Donnigan," Aaron said. *Among other things,* he thought.

"Did anything happen to him?"

"He was really down last night. I'm afraid he might get suicidal."

"Usually he's okay when he sobers up."

"I hope you're right."

"I'll phone him this morning and talk with him."

"Good idea."

Later in the morning, Marley carried Cristal into the clinic. "She's not acting right," she said to Stella.

"What's wrong, Cristal?" Stella said.

Cristal opened her eyes. She stared up toward the ceiling.

Stella's brow furrowed. "Follow me." She led them to the first empty patient room. "Lay her down on the table. I'll get the doctor."

Aaron walked into the room. Marley stood beside Cristal, who lay motionless on the table, her hand resting on the plush Genie at her side.

"She looks sick," Aaron said to Marley. "When did the symptoms begin?"

"She said she felt bad yesterday afternoon. She normally doesn't complain much." Marley stroked Cristal's hair. "She had 102-degree fever last night, and she didn't sleep well."

"She's got a rash. Was it there yesterday?"

"I noticed it on her forearms this morning. I think it's spreading."

Aaron examined Cristal, who stared off into space.

"Cristal, do you feel bad?"

She looked at him with glassy eyes. Her voice was weak. "I've got Genie."

"Yes. I'm glad." He turned to Marley. "Has she been around any sick kids recently?"

"No, I don't think so."

"How about mosquito or insect bites?"

"I don't know of any insect . . ." Marley touched her cheek. "Well, wait a minute. I did pull a tick off her stomach."

"When was that?"

"I believe it was a little more than a week ago."

"We've got to get her admitted to the hospital. She may have an infection that requires IV medication."

Marley put her hands to her temples. "Is it that bad?"

"It can be. But I think we've caught it in time."

"What kind of infection is it?"

"It might be a tick-borne infection, possibly Rocky Mountain Spotted Fever."

Marley covered her mouth. She had tears in her eyes.

Aaron put his hand on Marley's shoulder. "We've got treatment for this. I think she'll be all right."

Aaron stepped out of the room and jogged over to Stella. "Call for an ambulance. I'll finish up here and meet her at the hospital. Please tell any patients waiting that I had to leave for an emergency."

Fifteen minutes later, an ambulance pulled up to the front of the clinic. Aaron briefed the two medics about Cristal's illness, and they loaded her on a gurney and into the ambulance.

As Aaron walked out of the clinic toward his car, the air felt hot against his skin. He turned up the air conditioning but left the radio silent as he sped to the hospital. Along the way, he stayed alert for police cars and any other suspicious cars following him.

He pulled into the emergency department parking area and saw the ambulance near the ER entrance doors. He hurried into the ER registration area and found the triage nurse.

"A little girl named Cristal just came by ambulance. I'm her family doctor."

She checked the patient log. "Yes. Cristal Brighton?"

"That's her. Can I see her?"

"I'll take you back to her."

They walked through the main ER, passing by patients on stretchers in rooms and behind curtains. Aaron was led to a room with several hospital personnel clustered around Cristal's stretcher, one nurse placing nasal oxygen and another preparing an intravenous line. Marley sat in a chair in the room with Genie in her lap. An ER doctor at the side of the stretcher looked up as Aaron and the triage nurse entered the room.

"This is Dr. Rovsing, Cristal's family doctor," the nurse said.

"She's incoherent at times," the ER doctor said to Aaron. "She has a febrile illness with a rash."

Aaron walked up beside the ER doctor. "Her mother pulled a tick off of her recently. I wonder about Rocky Mountain Spotted Fever."

"Yes, that crossed my mind," the ER doctor said as he bent over and examined Cristal's skin. "The rash is consistent with that. I'll order the appropriate antibiotic IV." He rushed out of the room.

Aaron walked to the head of the bed. Cristal's eyes were closed. She opened and closed her eyes when the nurse inserted the IV needle into a vein in her forearm.

Marley walked up beside Aaron. Her eyes were reddened. "In the ambulance, she was out of her head, talking crazy," she said.

Aaron put his arm around Marley's shoulders. "She's where she needs to be." *I hope we're in time,* he thought. Queasiness gnawed at his stomach.

After a short while in the ER, Cristal was admitted to a bed in the ICU.

Aaron and Marley sat at her bedside. Several minutes after the ICU nurse left the room, Aaron nodded off. He woke to see Marley standing over him, her hand on his shoulder.

"You should go home and get some sleep," she said.

Aaron stretched, and then stood and looked at Cristal. "Her vital signs are stable, and she's getting the treatment she needs."

Marley blotted her eyes with tissue.

"I know how worried you must be," Aaron said. "But we should stay hopeful about this."

"I will." She looked up at Aaron. "There's something else. I'm concerned about Forrester. I think he's in trouble, and I don't know where he is."

"Forrester? What kind of trouble?"

"He called me yesterday, and he'd had another memory lapse. When this happens, he doesn't remember what he's been doing or how he got to where he is."

"Did you call the police?"

"Not yet."

Aaron shook his head. "You have a lot on your mind."

"I'm sorry to burden you with all of it."

"It's not a burden. That's what I'm here for." He touched her arm. "Can I do anything for you?"

"No, but thanks." She sighed. "This has happened before with Forrester, and it's worked out. I'll be fine."

Aaron frowned as he studied Marley's face. *Forrester is dragging her down, and she's really stressed. I don't know if I'd be able to handle it.*

Aaron yawned several times but managed to stay awake during his drive back to the clinic. His car wasn't followed.

"Everything's good here," Stella said. "How is Cristal doing?"

"She's got a bad case. I hope we're in time."

"Well, you did what you could. I'll pray for the little angel."

Aaron nodded and turned to walk away.

"I called Rocky Donnigan's auto shop and he's at work today, so I guess he's okay," Stella said.

Aaron took a deep breath. "I'm glad to hear that."

After work, Aaron drove to the happy hour bar he'd visited the week before. He smiled as he saw Red Relford in his usual place and the chair next to him leaning against the bar.

As Aaron walked toward him, Red straightened the chair. "I saved the seat for you."

"Thanks." Aaron ordered his cabernet and sat down.

Red swirled his brandy. "Do you like any particular cabernet sauvignon?"

"I'm learning as I go. You can't go wrong with California wines, but I've found some good prices for South African cabernets, and they taste good, too."

"I'll remember that."

Aaron sipped his wine. "What kind of dog do you have?"

"A black Labrador retriever. I just got him a few years ago. He's three years old."

Aaron had bread and a bowl of chicken noodle soup with his wine. Red was quiet for several minutes.

Aaron turned to him. "Is everything okay?"

"I got a letter from the widow of a friend of mine. He died a few weeks ago. We served together in the war."

"I'm sorry."

Red nursed his snifter of brandy. "I haven't thought about the war in a while."

"Which war?"

"The Second World War."

"Which branch were you in?"

"Navy, Pacific Theater."

"That must have been an interesting experience."

"Well, I'm glad I did it. I learned a lot about battleships, and war."

Aaron stared at his wine glass. "World War Two sure turned this country around."

"We had a lot of pride. You could feel it. The day after Pearl Harbor, lines at recruiting stations went on for blocks."

"Did you see combat?"

"I sure did. My ship got hit by a kamikaze once, starboard side. Killed a lot of good men." He sighed and looked down. "We shoveled bodies and arms and legs overboard. There was blood everywhere on deck."

Aaron sat in silence, but Red said no more. After a few minutes, Red swallowed the last of his brandy and looked at his pocket watch. He turned to Aaron. "It was nice talking with you."

Aaron stayed alone at the bar for a short while and finished his wine. As he walked out of the bar, he didn't notice the man who stood up from a nearby booth to follow him.

On his way home, Aaron thought about his discussion with Red and paid little attention to the rearview mirror. As he drove into his garage, the street behind him lit up. *That must be the car headlights of one of my neighbors.*

At his office desk, Aaron turned on the laptop computer and began to scan email titles. He opened the first message, which was a medical information update from his Family Practice Society.

He read from the top story: "Is there evidence-based research to support the medical use of marijuana? If so, what are the indications and what dose—"?

"Yikes." He lurched back as someone pounded on the front door.

Aaron's heart raced as he ran to the door, switched on the porch light, and peered through the peephole. No one was outside. He pushed the door open and walked out, scanning the yard and street and nearby trees. He spotted nothing out of the ordinary—no movement—and the only sound he heard was his own rapid breathing.

He turned around and then froze with his hand on the front doorknob. A piece of paper was taped to the door. Aaron peeled it off and read the message: "You won't know when or where, but I will get my revenge."

Aaron slammed and locked the front door and checked all doors and windows in the house, then punched buttons to arm the alarm system.

He stared at the message again and shook his head. "This time, asshole, I'm not going down without a fight, even if it kills me."

He called Constable Greevy and recounted the whole machete story. Keller said he'd put out an APB.

Aaron sat up in bed for several hours listening for any unusual noises, until he faded off to sleep.

Chapter 19

Later that evening at the Benningham mansion, a peal from the front doorbell surprised Brad. Myra hurried to the door, switched on the outside light, and looked through the peephole.

"It's Rocky Donnigan," she said to Brad. "I wonder what he wants." She opened the door.

"Is Mr. Benningham home?" Rocky said.

Brad walked to the door. "Is anything wrong?" he said.

"I need you to come. Preston is out cold."

"I thought he was out with friends," Myra said to Brad, who wheeled around and ran to the garage.

Rocky climbed into Brad's truck and directed him for several miles to a downtown alley.

Brad parked at the curb, and Rocky hopped out of the truck. "He's right over here."

Brad spotted a person on the ground. He kneeled down by the body and heard slow deep breathing. "It's Preston." He shook his shoulders. "Preston," he said into his ear. Preston moaned.

Brad picked up his son and carried him to the truck. Rocky brushed the dirt off Preston's clothes and then climbed into the front seat. Brad laid Preston in the seat, propped against Rocky. Preston dozed as Brad drove back to his house and stopped near the front door.

"Thanks, Rocky," Brad said as he gathered Preston in his arms.

"I hope he's okay," Rocky said.

"Have you been watching him?"

Rocky sighed. "Yeah. I guess I just want to help him any way I can. My son would've been about his age."

Brad watched Rocky ride away on his bicycle, then he closed his eyes and shook his head. "Damn drugs. I don't know if anything will work."

He carried Preston into the house and laid him on the living room couch. "Is he all right?" Myra said.

"I think so, for now. We'll see. He's not hurt as far as I can tell."

Myra put her hand on Brad's shoulder.

Brad slammed his fist against the palm of his hand. "We're running out of options."

Myra kneeled down in front of the couch and stroked Preston's forehead. "At least he's still with us."

Brad sighed and sat down by Preston. "Rocky tries to help him."

"We're lucky Rocky was there."

Brad looked at Myra. "Didn't something happen to Rocky's son? I seem to remember a story about that."

"I heard Rocky was involved with his death somehow," Myra said.

Three hours later, Preston stirred on the couch.

"Are you awake?" Brad said.

Preston opened his eyes, yawned, and sat up. He looked around the room and then at Brad.

"You came for me?"

Brad nodded.

Preston looked down, and his voice broke. "I'm sorry."

Myra hugged him. Preston couldn't stifle several sobs.

Chapter 20

Deep in the forest several miles away, a bonfire raged in a clearing in the trees. A large crowd of girls and guys milled about near the fire, helping themselves to free and plentiful beer from kegs scattered about on pickup truck beds. A speaker in one of the trucks blared country music, and dancing broke out at times in the crowd.

"There's Buck," someone yelled.

A sleek hot rod with a flame paint job motored through the parting crowd and past the area where the pickup trucks were parked. A pair of cattle longhorns was perched on the front of the hood, and the car seats were lined with brown fur. Buck Bogarty stopped the car just short of the trees, swung the door open, and stepped out. A crowd of people collected around him. Flickering light from the bonfire reflected in his face as his eyes panned over the crowd.

"Don't touch the car," a man said to a girl.

"When are you gonna race this hot rod again?" someone said.

"Yeah. I'd like to see you race again," another man said.

A girl brought Buck a cup of beer, and he nodded at her as he took it. Several bandages were stuck to his left hand.

"I remember the days when you were riding broncs in the rodeo," a man said from the back of the crowd. "When are you riding again? You were one of the best around here."

"One of the best?" Buck gulped down half a cupful of beer.

Waving his hands in front of him, the man laughed. "No, no, I meant the best."

Someone cranked up the music and more people gyrated to the beat. A line dance formed, boots were kicking in the air, and a lot of beer was spilt. At one point, a conga line snaked around the bonfire. Several people wobbled and fell out of line on the ground, to the delight of those nearby. One man in line pointed at a laughing figure rolling in the grass. "Look. Jake's down again. He never can hold his beer."

After several hours, the music softened. Much of the crowd was still close to the waning bonfire, some folks standing or propped against one another but many asleep on blankets on the ground.

Buck stood alone, leaning against his hot rod, sipping beer and studying the crowd.

He frowned and shook his head, walked to the edge of the trees and flung his half-empty cup of beer into the woods. He was alone here and out of sight of the crowd. Braced against a tree, his head dropped and he rubbed his eyes.

He stood by the tree for hours, lost in thought, facing away from the dying embers of the bonfire, until the faint light of dawn. At times, he heard moaning from deep within the Big Thicket.

"Buck?"

He flinched and looked back. A girl had walked up behind him. "Didn't hear you comin'," he said.

She yawned and stretched her arms. "Sorry."

She put her arm around his waist and laid her head on his chest. "Let's get out of here. Let's get in your car and just drive somewhere far away."

Buck hugged her, looked up to the trees, and sighed.

What the hell should I do with my life?

Chapter 21

Aaron sat bolt upright in bed.

My owl friend is loud this morning. It must be near the house.

Aaron looked around inside, then turned off the house alarm and peeked out the back door, his fists clenched.

All right, machete man. Bring it on.

He ventured out and was swallowed by a thick fog that blanketed his yard and house, and he saw and heard nothing as he tiptoed up to the fence.

Figures emerged from the fog in front of him. "Whoa, I didn't know you were here," he said to the Belkin cattle. Some of the cows looked at him but made no noise. Aaron stood at the fence for several minutes and watched the cattle move around at times. *Funny, I can't hear you.*

A chill rippled down his back. He turned and hurried back to the house.

It was just past dawn on Saturday, and his fingers twitched on the steering wheel as he drove to the hospital. *My head is in a fog. I must be really short of sleep.*

He left the radio off and kept his car window open halfway to feel the wind on his face. Every few seconds, his eyes went to the rearview mirror.

Standing just inside the entrance doors to the hospital, Aaron surveyed the parking lot. No one had followed him.

He found Cristal's room and knocked on the door.

"Come in," Marley said.

Aaron pushed the door open. *Forrester's not here.*

"How is she?" he asked Marley.

"The same. She slept all night."

Aaron studied Cristal and her monitor. "Her vital signs are holding. That's good."

"The nurse said everything is stable."

Aaron touched Marley's shoulder. "Have you heard anything about Forrester?"

"No."

"That can be good."

"I know. That's the way I look at it."

"Your eyes are red. Now you're the one who looks tired," Aaron said.

Marley smiled. "I'll be all right."

"I'll watch her. Do you want to get some sleep?"

"No, I can't sleep just yet."

"I understand. I'll check on you later. If she's doing well, I might go to my first rodeo today with Grant Belkin."

Marley looked up at Aaron. "Your first rodeo? That's great. You should go."

"Cristal is in good hands."

"I know."

Aaron stared at her. "Are you sure—"?

"I'm okay, and I really appreciate your coming to see us."

He turned and left the room.

As Aaron inspected the grass and landscaping around his house that afternoon, small blotches of sweat popped up across the front of his shirt. He was crouching in his yard when Grant Belkin's pickup truck pulled into his driveway. He trotted to the truck and climbed into the passenger seat. "How's the little girl?" Grant said.

"Wow, word gets around."

"It's a small town."

"I just called Marley at the hospital. Cristal is stable. It's just watch and wait now and let the antibiotics do their thing."

Grant's truck bounced down a two-lane road.

"Marley is a good mother to Cristal," Grant said.

"She's married to a fool Lothario, though."

Grant looked at Aaron. "She'll be all right."

Aaron's brow furrowed. *How can he possibly be sure of that?*

After about thirty minutes, Grant pulled into a parking area near an arena with bleachers. A sign in front of the arena said "Tri-County PRCA Rodeo."

They stepped out of the truck. "What's PRCA?" Aaron said.

"It means the rodeo is sanctioned by the Professional Rodeo Cowboys Association."

"I guess that's good?"

"Yep."

They tromped toward the arena. "Something smells good," Aaron said.

"That's the barbecue cook-off. It's a serious competition. We'll have some later."

"I can't wait."

Just inside the arena entrance, Grant bought two beers and led Aaron to seats in the center of the bleachers and two rows back from the arena fence.

"We're sittin' above the chutes where the bulls and broncs come out," Grant said.

"So these are primo seats."

"I like 'em. We can also watch the cowboys gettin' ready to hold on for dear life."

After a short while, a cowboy on horseback rode into the arena holding an American flag.

Grant stood, removed his hat, and placed his hand over his heart. Aaron followed suit, along with everyone else in the arena. As the cowboy circled the infield, a lady with a southern drawl belted out the national anthem. Grant and Aaron sang along.

As Aaron looked around the bleachers at the people singing to the flag, goose bumps popped up on the back of his neck. *I can't help but feel patriotic in here.*

At one point, horses were loaded into the chutes. "Saddle bronc ridin'," Grant said. "This is fun stuff."

Aaron watched cowboy after cowboy climb onto the fidgety horses. When a rider was secured on his horse and ready to romp, he signaled and the chute door was flung open, with the horse bursting out onto the arena dirt surface and bucking in circles with all its might. Dirt clouds billowed up from the horse's hooves as the rider tried his best to anticipate and blend with the jolting motion of the powerful animal below him. If all went well for the cowboy, for a few glorious seconds the horse and rider became one.

Aaron began to see the action in slow motion. *It's like two wrestlers locked in a battle to the finish.*

"I think I'm getting used to the smells of cattle and horse country," Aaron said as he sipped another beer.

Grant chuckled. "You just might grow to love it."

Aaron clapped and hollered along with the other spectators at the barrel racing event, in which riders guided their horses in straightaway sprints followed by tight rounding of barrels placed in a triangle formation in the arena.

"These cowgirls are good with their horses. Is this mainly a women's event?" Aaron said.

"It usually is. It's where the cowgirls shine."

"Even the horses seem to enjoy it."

"They do. It's in their nature to run." Grant adjusted his cowboy hat and cocked his head at Aaron. "Are you lookin' for somebody?"

"What?"

"You keep studyin' the crowd."

"Oh. It's just all new to me."

"It's a unique culture."

"The crowd seems noisier now," Aaron said.

"That's because bull ridin' is next."

"So that's even more exciting than the other events?"

"The most dangerous eight seconds in any sport."

"Eight seconds? That doesn't sound like a long time."

"Ask a cowboy. He'll tell you eight seconds seems like an eternity on the toughest bulls. A lot of cowboys don't last near that long."

They watched bull after bull kick and spin and try to hurl the riders into flight.

Aaron turned to Grant. "These bulls are pure muscle. It hurts me to watch this. I think my back would break."

"They're bred for this. The bull owners are mighty happy if their bulls win the battles."

Only two cowboys lasted the eight seconds.

"The rodeo clowns are great athletes, too," Aaron said.

"They have to be quick, for sure, and they know the animals. The rodeo clowns save the cowboys a lot of injuries."

After the last bull, Aaron heard a commotion in the bleachers to his far right. He saw two men yelling and pushing each other.

Grant leaned toward Aaron. "That's Forrester Brighton, Marley's husband. He's with his new girlfriend."

Aaron spotted a woman with blond, curly hair. Her curls bounced up and down as she struggled to keep the two men apart.

"I guess Forrester is the one to her right? The tall guy?" Aaron said.

"That's him."

"Who's the other guy?"

"Might be her ex-boyfriend."

"He looks mighty angry with Forrester."

Other men ran up to pull the combatants apart. While being escorted away, the second man yelled and pointed his finger at Forrester, who threw his head back and laughed.

Aaron looked at Grant. "If that guy had carried a gun, I'll bet he would've used it on Forrester."

"Maybe not here."

"Or hire someone to do it for him later."

"It's hard for a hit man to find work around these parts."

"You mean, it's do-it-yourself?"

"Yep."

"I'm thinking about getting a gun," Aaron said. "Do you have one?"

"No."

"So you don't hunt?"

"No."

"What about for self-protection?"

Grant turned to him. "I don't need a gun for that."

Chapter 22

Forrester Brighton gazed at his new girlfriend, Eve, across the table for two. They'd left the rodeo after the altercation for this upscale steakhouse restaurant with dark brown and black tones on the walls and in the furniture. Forrester wore pungent cologne, suggestive of leather and horses.

He hadn't noticed much detail around him except for the bright golden curls of Eve's hair and her flashy blue eyes.

She's sure looking good, Forrester thought. *Maybe I should stay with her.*

"What are you smiling at?" she said.

"You." He raised his beer glass for a toast.

"Do you like your new job, sweetie?" Eve said.

"Sure, I like construction work. It's good for my muscles."

"I'll massage those big muscles later."

Forrester flexed his biceps and smiled.

A server stopped at the table. "Can I take your order?"

"I'll have a T-bone, rare, with mashed potatoes," Forrester said. Eve ordered a filet of steak, medium.

After salads, Eve smiled at Forrester. "When are we getting married?"

Forrester was quiet.

She shook her head. "I don't know how long I can wait."

Forrester looked down at his plate.

"Talk to me," Eve said.

"Well, that other guy keeps bothering you, don't he?"

"He calls sometimes."

"He followed us to the rodeo."

"Don't worry about him. He'll cool down and go away."

"Tell him to get lost."

After their entrees were served, Eve leaned toward him. "When are we going to have sex?"

Forrester coughed on a mouthful of steak and potatoes.

"Is something wrong?" Eve said.

"I've got a lot of things on my mind."

Eve threw her napkin down on the table. "You're not going back to her, are you? You said you'd left her for good."

Forrester managed a weak smile and rubbed her hand. "Take it easy. I'll work everything out." He looked away. *I guess it's time for me to move on.*

Eve sighed. "Sometimes, I just can't figure you out."

After dinner, Forrester opened the restaurant door for Eve. She stopped outside and put her hands on her hips. "You're acting different. You didn't finish your steak. Are you not feeling well? Something's wrong, isn't it?"

"I wasn't hungry."

She fanned her face as she followed him across the parking lot toward his car. "It's hot out here. Get me into some air conditioning."

Forrester opened the front passenger door for Eve. As he shut the door, he heard two pops and felt a sharp, burning pain in his back. He groaned and collapsed to the pavement.

Eve jumped out of the car and screamed. Forrester was sprawled on his stomach, and dark splotches appeared on the back of his shirt. Eve fumbled in her purse and pulled out a phone to call 911. Her fingers trembled, and it wasn't until the third attempt that she punched the correct numbers.

Forrester made out some of her words. It sounded to him as if she were speaking from far away. "Hello. Help me. My boyfriend has been shot." Following instructions from the phone, she bent down close to the body. "Forrester, can you hear me? . . . No, he didn't say anything, he just moaned . . . Please help us, somebody help us . . . Okay, I'm sorry, I'll try to calm down . . . I'm taking slow deep breaths . . . Yes, I think he's breathing."

A few minutes later, a police car and an ambulance pulled into the parking lot. Eve waved them over to Forrester's location, past small groups of gawking onlookers. She stood a few feet back as a paramedic kneeled down to assess Forrester's condition, and a policeman began to ask her questions about the shooting.

"He's got a weak pulse," one of the medics said. "He's breathing okay." They bandaged the wounds, rolled Forrester onto a backboard, and lifted the board onto a gurney.

One medic looked up at the other. "His legs are floppy, no muscle tone."

They pushed the gurney into the back of the ambulance. One of the medics placed a face mask for oxygen and an intravenous catheter, and he adjusted the catheter to a rapid IV fluid rate. As the ambulance drove away, a medic radioed a report to the ER.

Forrester woke up in a hospital bed and saw a nurse at his bedside. She adjusted a catheter taped to his forearm and connected to a bag filled with intravenous fluids.

"What happened?" he said.

"You were shot. You were taken to surgery, and you're now in the post-op area."

"Someone shot me? Who shot me?"

"The police are looking into that. They'll talk with you later."

"I can't feel my legs."

She touched his shoulder. "You had some internal injuries."

"Were they able to fix me?"

"They did what they could." She heard a noise, turned and stepped back. "Here's the surgeon now."

A tall man walked up to Forrester's bed and introduced himself.

"You had internal bleeding, and we repaired some damage to your intestines and one of your kidneys. I'm afraid one of the bullets cut your spinal cord. We'll have to wait and see how much function returns over the next few weeks and months."

"This has got to be a bad dream."

"I know it seems that way," the surgeon said.

"Will I ever walk again?"

"Maybe, maybe not. Only time will tell."

Forrester awakened and opened his eyes the next morning. He was in a different bed, and someone was in the room with him.

He raised his head. "Marley."

"They moved you out of post-op this morning. You've been sedated."

"What day is it?"

"Sunday."

"Someone shot me last night?"

"Yes."

"Who did?"

"The police think it was Eve's old boyfriend."

Forrester's eyes widened.

"Yes. I know about Eve," Marley said.

"Where is she?"

Marley put her hands on her hips. "I don't know, and don't ever ask me about her again."

Forrester laid his head back. "Don't worry, I won't." He clenched his teeth. *I really screwed up this time. I hope Marley will have me back.*

His eyes went to the ceiling, and in less than half a minute, he was asleep.

Chapter 23

Aaron heard Dale's pickup truck pull into his driveway at 5:00 a.m. He locked the front door of the house and climbed into the truck.

"Ready for some fun?" Dale said.

"Sure, but this is really early for me."

"Early is good for fishing. We'll be out on the creek when the bass are biting. Maybe we'll hook some catfish, too."

Aaron lowered his window. As the truck picked up speed through patchy fog, the morning air streamed across his face. Along the way, he peered behind the truck several times but spotted no suspicious vehicles.

After a short drive into the country, Dale backed his boat trailer to the water's edge. "This here's one of my favorite fishing spots, and there's almost never anyone else around."

As they unloaded the truck, Dale pointed to the tackle box. "Now, this is Fishing Rule Number One: before you pick up the tackle box, make sure the lid is latched shut."

"That makes sense. What's Rule Number Two?"

Dale looked up and pulled on his earlobe. "Give me a minute. I'll think of something."

Aaron chuckled.

Dale finished packing the boat and launched it into the water.

"What's in the coolers?" Aaron said.

"One's got cold beer. The other has ice for the fish. Don't get 'em mixed up."

Aaron smiled and clambered into the front of the boat. "That must be Rule Number Two."

Dale laughed. "Yeah, and it's just as important as the first rule."

Aaron could see the calm water in the dim light from the early dawn. He turned as Dale pulled a pouch from his pocket.

"You don't mind if I chew, do you?" Dale said.

"Tobacco?"

Dale nodded and thrust a wad of tobacco to the back of his mouth, bulging his cheek out.

"I hope you get your mouth checked," Aaron said.

"Yeah, I know. It's bad for me."

Dale climbed into the back of the boat, started the motor, and steered the boat out into the creek.

He handed a life jacket to Aaron. "Put this on, and don't worry about the fishing poles. I'll bait your hooks for you."

Aaron heard loud plops at times as Dale spat into the water.

Dale stopped the boat after about half a mile. He lowered his voice. "Let's try here first."

He prepared the poles and handed one to Aaron. "Watch me. Here's how you hold it, and follow how I cast the line."

Aaron copied Dale's motions and cast his hook and line into the water.

"Be extra careful with them hooks," Dale said.

"I know. I've extracted a few fishhooks from people. I remember a drunk guy who had a hook in his nose."

"Ouch. I'll bet that hurt."

"It was difficult to remove."

"I brought a guy out here once that hooked his own butt."

Aaron grinned. "Now, that's embarrassing."

"It certainly was. It cut our trip short. He wouldn't even let me try to pull it out."

They sat still in the boat, watching their lines in the water.

Aaron heard birds chirping in the trees along the creek. As the morning light intensified, the remaining fog lifted and more details of the water and its banks came into view.

He turned to Dale. "This brings back memories of my Boy Scout days. I remember how peaceful it was, just floating on the water in an old canoe."

"For me, there's something about being out on the water. It's always been that way. The real world kind of fades away."

In the first hour, each man caught several fish. Dale showed Aaron how to handle and unhook the fish. They released the smaller fish back into the creek.

"Keep your fingers away from these catfish spines, or you're in for quite a painful jab," Dale said as he showed Aaron the sharp fins jutting out from the fish.

Dale finished his chewing session and expectorated his tobacco chaw, which caused an enormous plop in the creek. He opened a beer, rinsed his mouth, and spat one last time into the water, then threw down three beers in rapid succession.

"I bring a few folks in town to this here creek. We always leave with some fish," Dale said.

"Are there lots of avid fishermen around here?"

"It's one reason why people live in the country. Brad Benningham joins me on the creek three or four times a year. Keller Greevy loves to fish here, too."

"A policeman must have a stressful life. Keller is probably able to take his mind off his job while he's fishing."

"That's why a lot of folks fish."

"Have you known Keller long?"

"For years. He keeps the town safe. That's what he's good at."

"He seems capable."

Dale leaned toward Aaron and whispered, "But, he can be influenced."

Aaron's eyes widened. "What do you mean?"

Dale rubbed his index finger and thumb together. "Dinero."

"He can be bribed?" *That's what Brad was talking about.*

Dale sat back. "I don't like to call it that. You can only get away with it if he likes you. If you're a troublemaker, no way it'll work."

168

Aaron gazed out over the creek and its banks and noticed the trees glistening in the morning light. They were alone on this stretch of the creek. Water lapped against the boat, which had a gentle rocking motion.

Aaron yawned and his eyelids grew heavy. A vision of a smiling blond woman appeared before him … He shouted and his head jerked up as the end of his fishing pole was yanked toward the water.

Dale laughed. "You fell asleep, huh? Like I told you, it's relaxing out here."

"You can say that again."

"I fell asleep once and pitched right over into the water."

A few minutes later, Dale put a fish in the cooler and closed the lid. "Well, that'll do it for me. I've got a honey-do list for today." He secured their fishing poles in the boat and motored back to the launch area.

Some of Dale's words were slurred as he drove his truck onto the road by the creek.

"Are you sure you're okay to drive?" Aaron said.

"No problemo. A six-pack is my norm. My body's used to it."

Aaron nodded. "That was good beer."

"I'll let you in on something: a great investment opportunity," Dale said.

Another investment idea. Everyone assumes I'm rich.

"An oil well. An experienced drilling company is looking for investors. I'm fixing to put in a big chunk of change myself."

"I don't know anything about oil."

"That doesn't matter. These investments can pay off huge, I mean really big returns, and this particular opportunity is a sure thing."

"I don't know."

"There ain't much time to get in on this. You're in Texas, in oil country. You should take advantage of that."

"Well, I'll think about it."

"You won't be sorry."

Aaron shook his head. *I guess owners of car dealerships can make a lot of money. I'm not quite there yet.*

Dale turned the truck radio louder. "I like this song." He sang a few lyrics out of tune.

Aaron nodded. " 'Alcohol,' by Brad Paisley. A really funny song."

Dale stopped the truck along the side of the street in front of Aaron's house and touched Aaron on the shoulder. "I can hook you up with a great girl."

"Thanks, but I'm fine. I like to find my own soul mates."

Dale shook his head. "No, I'm not talking about good girls. I'm talking about good-time girls. We've got some of the best around here, and I know where to find 'em."

Aaron's eyes flew open. "You mean prostitutes, out here in East Texas?"

"Sure. The best in the business. Why, I'll get one for you that does some things in a cowgirl outfit that—"

"Hold on, Boots, uh, Dale." Aaron laughed and held his hand up. "I can't go there. Not interested."

"Well, if you ever change your mind, let me know."

Aaron watched Dale drive away. *I don't know about him.*

He chuckled and turned toward his house. *A cowgirl outfit. Now that does sound interesting.*

****

That evening, Buck Bogarty sat with his mother at their dinner table.

"You've been quiet lately," she said. "What are you thinking about?"

"Nothin'." Buck continued eating his meatloaf and turnip greens.

"Is it a girl? You know, you have to figure out what you're going to do before you settle down with anyone."

Buck picked at his food with a fork.

"Do you have any idea about what you want to do to make a living? I can ask around and talk with my friends. I'm sure we can find something."

I don't know anythin' anymore, he thought. *I don't know what the hell I'm doin'.* Buck put down his fork and walked back to his bedroom.

Chapter 24

On Monday morning, Forrester Brighton lay in his hospital bed, staring up at the white ceiling.

I can't move my legs.

Marley knocked and walked into the room.

Forrester raised his head. "Did you find out who shot me?"

"It was Eve's old boyfriend. He tried to get away, but the police tracked him down."

"Good." Forrester lay back and raised his hands. "I'd like to get my hands on him."

They were both quiet for several minutes.

Forrester reached for Marley. "It's time for me to come home."

"Why should I let you?"

He held her hand. "I was ready to come back. I don't know why I left in the first place." He snorted. "I don't even remember leaving you." Forrester pulled her closer to him. "Look at me."

Marley stared at him.

"I'll always love you. You know that, and you love me, too. I know you do."

Marley looked down.

"What?" Forrester said.

"It's nothing."

Forrester squeezed her hand. "I missed you. I need you."

Marley sighed and rubbed her forehead.

Forrester lifted his head. "I want to be with you and Cristal." He looked around the room. "Where is Cristal?"

"She's in this hospital, on another floor."

Forrester's eyes widened. "She's sick?"

"Tick fever. They're calling it Rocky Mountain Spotted Fever. She's getting medicine IV."

"Is she okay?"

Marley sat down in a chair, her head bowed. She stifled a sob. "I don't know. She's in a coma."

Chapter 25

Aaron's eyes opened Monday morning before his alarm sounded. He turned on coffee in the kitchen and walked to the back door. Scanning the landscape outside, he saw no fog and nothing unusual in the yard or in the pasture behind the fence.

While cleaning up for work, he heard snippets of the morning TV news: " . . . ongoing crime coverage . . . reports of young women missing . . . gun violence . . . Forrester Brighton, a local resident, was shot outside a restaurant Saturday night. According to a hospital spokesperson, he was shot in the back . . ."

Aaron shook his head and spoke to the television. "Poor idiot."

At the clinic, Aaron walked into a patient room. "I hear you have a rash," he said to a young woman sitting on the examination table and texting on her cell phone.

"Sorry, I'm just about finished." She punched in a few more words, sent the message, and held out her arms. "It itches really bad, and it's getting worse over the last couple of days."

"It looks like poison ivy or something similar."

"That's what I wondered. I was at a bonfire a few nights ago, in the woods. I must've brushed against some poison ivy in the dark."

Aaron printed a prescription medication and handed it to her. "This should take care of it."

"Thanks." She jumped down from the table.

"So you went to a bonfire. Were you celebrating something?" Aaron said.

She nodded. "I guess you could call it celebrating. We get together with friends a couple of times a year and stay out all night around a big bonfire. It's kind of a tradition."

"Friends from high school?"

"Yes. Most of us grew up together."

"It sounds like fun."

"It's a lot of fun, and it's the only time some of us girls get to see Buck Bogarty, the guy with the awesome hot rod."

Aaron smiled. "I know Mr. Bogarty." He stroked his chin. "There is something about him."

"Oh, yeah. A lot of girls would like to land him, if he'd ever get a job and settle down."

"Some guys take a while to grow up, but most eventually do."

"The word is that Buck is still bitter about his father leaving a few years ago."

"Boys and girls can have a hard time emotionally if their fathers leave the family."

"Well, his father is gone for a reason. He was beating up Buck's mother and she made him leave. I heard that he split and hooked up with another woman." She sighed and looked down. "Buck hasn't been the same since his father left."

That explains a lot, Aaron thought.

They walked into the hall, and she turned to Aaron. "But we keep hoping he'll get over it someday."

After his workday, Aaron ate a light meal of crab-stuffed mushrooms at a local diner and drove to the hospital. His fingers twitched as he walked into Cristal's room. A nurse was at the bedside, tending to her IV line.

"How is she?" Aaron said.

"Her vitals are stable. No fever since this morning."

Aaron exhaled. "That's good news."

"Her mother went to have a snack. She'll be back soon." She snapped off her gloves and left the room.

Aaron examined Cristal. *Her rash has faded.*

"Hi." Marley walked into the room.

Aaron straightened. "I think she's doing better. Has she said anything to you?"

"She just moans sometimes."

"You look exhausted."

"It's been rough." She laid her head on his shoulder.

It's a good fit, he thought as he put his arm around her waist.

They stood together for several minutes.

"I heard on the news that Forrester was shot," Aaron said.

"He's recovering from surgery, in a room in this hospital."

Cristal stirred and then opened her eyes. "Mommy."

Marley jumped and bent down to hug Cristal. "My little angel. Oh, it's so wonderful to hear your voice."

Aaron smiled and clapped his hands. "The crisis is over." *I did good. I got her here in time.*

"Where's Genie?" Cristal said.

Marley picked up the light green plush character from a nearby table. "Here he is."

Cristal smiled and hugged Genie. "Let's go home. I want to see my daddy and Princess."

Marley looked at Aaron, then back at Cristal. She smoothed out Cristal's hair. "We'll all be home together soon."

"Just like Genie told me."

Aaron sighed as the figures of Marley and Cristal faded.

"I think I'll check on Forrester," he said.

"His room is two floors down. He's sleeping most of the time."

"I won't disturb him."

Aaron located Forrester's room and pushed the door open a few inches. Forrester lay asleep on the hospital bed. Aaron stood in the doorway and watched him.

After several minutes, he whispered at Forrester, "You probably don't deserve it, but she forgives you. I hope you never forget that."

Chapter 26

Valerie watched as her husband, Keller, gulped his last bite of rib eye steak, mashed potatoes, and lima beans for Monday dinner.

"I've got to leave for a while," Keller said. "There's something I have to check out."

Valerie perked up. "Check out what? Where are you going?"

"Now, don't you worry about it. I'll be back soon." Keller walked out of the house to his car.

Valerie flung her napkin down on the table. *We'll see about this.*

She locked up the house, hopped in her car, and followed him from a distance. After a few miles and several turns, Keller slowed and stopped on the road shoulder. Valerie parked on an intersecting street, out of Keller's sight. She got out of her car and walked over to the road Keller was on. She saw him open his car door, step out, and walk up the road toward the Taggett's house. After about one-quarter mile, he stopped and leaned against a tree facing the Taggett's front yard.

Valerie walked up the side of the road toward Keller. She kept to the tall pine trees for cover.

What in the world is he up to? she thought. She crept closer to Keller, who stood still with his back to her. She heard a rustle near her, and as she turned, something struck the side of her head.

Valerie Greevy woke up and opened her eyes. She had a pounding headache, and tape was stuck over her mouth. Her wrists and ankles were bound by tape—with her arms behind her—but she managed to sit up after several attempts. She heard a rattle and noticed a heavy chain wound tight around her slim waist and extending several feet to a tree, which stood at the edge of a clearing illuminated by faint moonlight. She spotted a small tent and a campfire pit with a few orange embers smoldering a few feet away from her. On the ground near the pit, she saw glints from an assortment of knives.

Valerie tried to scream, but only a puny blubbering sound came from under the tape on her mouth. She scooted and struggled against the chain to no avail.

What's happening? Where am I? Tears streamed down her cheeks. *Where's Keller?*

After a long quiet period of time, she heard footsteps in the brush and a figure loomed from the tree shadows.

Race Taggett?

Valerie watched as he walked to the campfire pit, poured a liquid over the splintered wood, and then lit a match. A bright yellow fire blazed up. He picked up one of the knives, a large butcher knife, and held it to the flames. He turned and smiled at Valerie, then looked off into the distance. "You remind me of a girl from school," he said. "She was mean to me."

Valerie shook her head, dug her heels into the ground, and tried to push her body away along the ground.

Race gazed at the knife, the gleam from its red-hot surface reflecting on his face.

****

From the cover of the tree shadows, Keller Greevy surveyed the Taggett's property. He remembered Aaron's earnest face when they'd talked about the Taggetts a week before.

I wonder if Doc is onto something. Strange things are happening lately.

At one point, he heard a noise behind him. He turned and listened but saw nothing and heard no strange sounds. *It's probably a stiff breeze in the trees.*

He yawned and checked his cell phone. *I've been watching this house for more than an hour. There's nothing suspicious here.*

Keller walked to his car, made a U-turn, and drove back in the direction of his house.

What? He slowed to a stop at the first intersection. *That looks like Valerie's car. Is she visiting someone over here?*

After parking his car on the road shoulder, he walked up to the other vehicle and glanced around at the articles inside. *It's her car, all right.*

He studied the street and front lawns close to Valerie's car and knocked on the doors of the two houses nearby. No one answered; the houses were dark. He called Valerie's cell phone but got no response.

"What the hell is going on?" he said, throwing his hands up.

Keller walked in the direction of his previous stakeout. *She must've followed me out here.*

"Valerie," he shouted, quickening his pace to a jog along the edge of the trees beside the road.

He skidded to a stop on the road shoulder as he spotted something on top of the grass. He crouched and picked up the object, which was pink and fuzzy.

It looks like one of Valerie's house shoes.

Keller jammed the shoe into his pocket. Nausea gnawed at his stomach as he walked among the nearby trees.

Something's wrong.

Discovering nothing else, he hurried on to the Taggett's house. He could see no lights in the windows and heard no sounds from the house, so he changed directions and plunged into the trees behind the house.

Wheezing and gasping, Keller weaved among the tall pines and stumbled through underbrush in the dim light from the moon. At times, tree trunks and underbrush scraped and jabbed his legs.

After about fifty yards, he exploded into a small open space in the trees. Splotches of sweat covered his shirt. He stopped to catch his breath and wipe the sweat from his forehead and eyes with a handkerchief. His heaving chest calmed as he peered around the area.

I'll be damned. A trail.

He crouched and examined the dirt surface, finding several incomplete shoe prints. *This trail has been used.* He stood and glanced around him. *But, who would use it? No one lives back in this part of the Big Thicket. At least, no one that I know of.*

Since he had approached the opening from the direction of the Taggett's house, and since the neighborhood road was to his right, he turned and walked along the path away from the road. Keller's wide body just fit between the trees along the sides of the trail. At times, he saw ruts in the dirt.

After about ten minutes of walking, he stopped when he heard a noise ahead of him. He walked now with soft footsteps, and another clearing appeared past several trees in front of him. In the clearing, a campfire blazed in front of a tent. A man stood by the campfire sideways to Keller and pulled a knife out of the flames. Its blade was bright red.

Race Taggett, Keller thought.

Keller heard a muffled moan from the other side of the tent. He pulled his gun from its holster and rounded the tent. A woman was bending her knees and scooting away from Race along the ground.

"Valerie," Keller said.

Race jerked upright and turned. He screamed and, in a lightning motion, flung the knife at Keller.

Keller ducked and fired his pistol as the knife bounced off his neck. Race fell to the ground beside the fire.

Keller's neck stung like fire and he smelled burnt flesh. He put a hand on his neck and felt moisture in his palm.

He hurried over to Valerie, then stood and studied Race's limp body on the ground. He returned the pistol to its holster and eased the tape from Valerie's mouth.

"Oh, Keller, what a nightmare."

He crouched and held her to him as she sobbed into his chest.

"Did he hurt you?"

"No, but I think he was about to." She caught her breath. "He almost scared me to death."

Keller peeled the tape from her wrists and ankles and released the metal clasp from the chain around her waist.

"I almost lost you," Keller said. He stroked her hair. "Thank God you're okay."

She looked up at him. "It's not that easy to get rid of me."

Keller smiled. "Good."

He glanced over at Race's body on the ground and saw no movement.

"He's sick. A real psycho," Valerie said, shivering.

"I know that now."

"Do you think he's dead?"

"Well, he's not moving. I'll check him out in a minute. Right now, I want to make sure you're okay. Can you stand up?" Keller helped her to her feet, and the chain rattled to the ground.

"I can't believe this is happening," she said, sobbing on Keller's shoulder as he held her close.

After several minutes, she wiped her eyes and looked up at him. "How did you find me?"

Keller looked off into the trees. "I just felt something wasn't right around the Taggett's house." He pulled the house shoe from his pocket. "And I found this. I'm glad they don't fit too tight."

Valerie smiled at him. "I guess you haven't been following that woman around lately."

Keller shook his head. "I was acting like an idiot." He touched her cheek. "You're the only woman for me."

She hugged him and laid her head on his chest.

Keller sighed. "I don't deserve you."

"Yes, you do. I love you."

"Sometimes I'm not a good person. There are some things I've done—"

Valerie put her finger against his lips. "It's all right. You're everything I need."

Keller kissed her forehead. "I'll be a better man for you."

"You already are."

Keller heard footsteps and looked up. "What . . .?"

Race bounded away through the trees. Keller pulled out his handgun and jogged to the edge of the clearing. He stopped and listened.

"I don't hear anything. He's already gone."

He walked back to Valerie and touched her shoulder. "You're still shivering."

"I'll be okay." She took slow, deep breaths and felt the side of her head. "At least my headache is gone."

"He hit you in the head? Should I take you to a hospital?"

Valerie shook her head. "No. I'll go if anything gets worse. I think I'll be fine. Besides, you know how hardheaded I am."

Keller chuckled. "Amen to that." He embraced her, and then looked over to the clearing. "Race didn't seem to be hurt. I must've just winged him."

"We've got to find him and put him away. He could hurt more people."

Keller nodded. "I'll notify the sheriff. We'll try to track him down. First, I want to get you out of here."

"Keep your gun ready. I'm sticking to you like glue."

"Let's both stay alert for him. I've got plenty of bullets left."

"Why are you holding your neck?"

"His knife bounced off me."

"Let's get home so I can have a look at it." She pulled on her pink house shoe.

Keller grinned. "At least you'll have one foot covered. We'll stay on the dirt trails to protect your feet."

Chapter 27

Brad Benningham woke up to a noise and glanced at his alarm clock. It was 1:50 a.m. early Tuesday morning.

He crept to his bedroom door, peeked out, and saw Preston tiptoeing away down the hall. Brad threw on clothes and shoes and raced to the front door, in time to see Preston step into his car and start the engine. Brad's figure filled the doorway, and his lips were taut across his mouth as he spoke, "Tonight, I cut off the head of the snake."

He closed the door, and after a few seconds, the garage door opened. Brad backed his truck out of the garage and sped away after Preston's taillights.

Preston's car weaved down the road for several miles and screeched through a few turns, before it slowed near a dark alley in town. Preston pulled into the alley and stepped out of his car.

Brad's truck bounced to a stop behind Preston's car, the truck's headlights illuminating the alley. Brad spotted a figure standing against a wall in the shadows.

Preston turned and his eyes widened. "Crap."

"What the hell?" the man in the shadows said. He pulled a handgun from a pocket.

Brad leaped from his truck and then stopped in his tracks. Queasiness seized his stomach. *This is the same alley I was in two years ago.*

He shook his head and ran toward Preston. "Get down, now," Brad yelled.

"What are you doing here?" Preston said, his hands clenched.

Brad fired three rounds from his handgun at the figure running away down the alley. From the shallow cover of a recessed doorway, the man began to shoot at anything that moved or stood upright. Brad crouched behind a trash bin.

Preston screamed as blood sprayed from his left shoulder.

"Get down, Preston," Brad said.

Another person ran out of the far side shadows of the alley, yelling and flailing his arms. He stopped and kneeled down in front of Preston, who was on his knees and moaning. As he put his hands on Preston's shoulders, several bullets struck his back. His body arched twice and collapsed onto the pavement.

"No," Preston said. "No."

Brad walked past Preston and the supine figure, firing into the doorway ahead of him. A man fell out of the doorway, his handgun clattering away along the pavement. Brad crept up to him with his gun pointed. Detecting no movement, Brad kicked his side, rolled him over, and saw that he wasn't breathing. He picked up the man's gun.

Brad jogged back toward Preston, who was wailing and rocking back and forth while holding the arm of a limp body on the ground. A moist hole had appeared in the shirt over Preston's left shoulder.

"You've been shot," Brad said.

Preston moaned and continued rocking.

Brad looked at the face of the limp figure. "It's Rocky Donnigan. The bastard got him." He crouched down beside the body. "He's not breathing. I'll call the ambulance, but it may be too late." He called 911 and started CPR with chest compressions.

"That should've been me," Preston said between sobs. "That should've been me."

An ambulance arrived, and the paramedics swept Rocky up onto a gurney. They continued CPR in the back of the ambulance.

As he was bandaging Preston's shoulder, one of the medical personnel turned to Brad. "I think he needs to be checked out at the hospital."

"Yes, I'll take him," Brad said.

Just after the ambulance screamed away, a police car pulled up behind Brad's truck.

Brad held pressure with his hand over Preston's bandaged shoulder. "What was Rocky even doing here? He liked his alcohol, but I didn't think he used drugs any more," he said.

Preston managed to speak a few words at a time. "He knows the dealers . . . I guess he was worried . . . about me."

"I've got to get you to a hospital."

Preston crumpled to the ground and wailed. "I should be dead. I don't deserve to be alive."

Brad gave a short report to the police officer, and then he helped Preston into his truck and drove him to the hospital.

Chapter 28

Aaron awakened every few hours that night. At one point, he rubbed his eyes and stumbled to the bathroom. He stood in front of the mirror and ran his fingers along the deep scar that deformed his jaw.

Maybe a plastic surgeon can make this look better.

At the clinic registration desk the next morning, Stella dabbed her eyes with tissue.

"What's wrong?" Aaron said.

"Rocky Donnigan died last night."

"Rocky is dead?"

"He was shot. He jumped in front of Preston."

Aaron stared out the window, then he walked back to his office and closed the door.

An hour later, Stella knocked on his door. "Sorry to bother you, but your first patient is here. Do you want me to reschedule today's list?"

"No. Give me a few more minutes."

"No problem."

After a while, he sighed. *Is there anything I could've done to prevent Rocky's death?* He slapped the desk. *Back at my old hospital, someone questioned my medical competence.* He stood and shook his head. *Will this nag at me until I die?*

Near noon, Stella brought Aaron a report that had been faxed from the testing lab. Aaron read the results: the powder from the Taggett's house was thallium sulfate.

He shot out of his desk chair and hopped up and down with his hands in the air. "I got something right."

Stella stepped back. "What in the world are you shouting about?"

"Sorry about that. I just guessed correctly this time, and I'm all in now."

"Okay, good. You guessed right. What's thallium?" Stella said.

"It's a poisonous chemical used to kill rodents, and sometimes people."

"Wait a minute. What do you mean 'you're all in'?"

Aaron pounded his fist into his hand. "I'm into doing some good in this town. That's what I'm here for."

He called Constable Greevy. "I have my proof that Wanda Taggett is poisoning Sid. She's feeding him thallium, and he's dying. She's slowly killing him."

"How did you find that out?"

"I removed some powder from their home."

"Okay. Wanda didn't give it to you. So, you must've broken into the house when Wanda wasn't there. Am I wrong?"

"She wasn't at home, but Sid let me in. Anyway, we've got to figure out what's going on in that house. Maybe I can get him back to the hospital. I'll bet we'll find thallium in his blood and urine."

Keller sighed. "All right. Try to get him to the hospital, but now I've got my own reason for a search warrant." Keller told Aaron about his encounter with Race Taggett.

Several hours later, Stella motioned to Aaron. "Keller Greevy would like to talk to you on the phone. Do you have time?"

"Sure." Aaron walked to his office and picked up the receiver.

"I got a warrant," Keller said. "I'm going to visit the Taggetts. You can come along and get Sid to the treatment he needs."

Constable Greevy and two other officers stopped by the clinic late that afternoon, and Aaron followed the police car to the Taggett's house.

They stepped out of their cars and walked toward the house. Aaron noticed Keller's bandage. "Is that where Race's knife cut you?"

"You got it. Maybe you can take a look at it later?"

"I'd be happy to."

"Any more threatening notes from your machete guy?"

"No."

"We're still looking for him."

As they walked through the straggly front yard, Aaron sighed. "It's sad about Rocky Donnigan."

"Yeah, it is." Keller looked down. "I guess he had some good in him after all, didn't he?"

They climbed the front steps, and the wooden slats creaked under their feet as they crossed the porch to the door.

"Wanda's car is out front, so she's got to be home," Keller said.

"Has Race been found?" Aaron said.

"Not yet."

A shiver shot through Aaron's chest.

Keller punched the front doorbell and then pounded on the door. After a few minutes, the door squeaked open a crack.

Keller held up his search warrant. "You've got to let me in, Wanda."

"No."

"I'll break the door down. Let me in, now."

After a minute, the door opened wide. "Why are you here?"

"I need to search your house. Race assaulted my wife, and we're looking for him. Is he here?"

"No. I haven't seen him."

"Do you know where he is?"

"No. So, you can leave now."

"I want to talk with Sid."

She raised her voice. "You leave him alone."

Keller and his protuberant potbelly pushed sideways past Wanda, his hand poised on his holster. He was followed by the other two officers.

Keller shouted back at Aaron, "The coast is clear. Come on in."

Aaron stepped through the door. *It smells like she's used a room deodorizer.* He stopped and looked around the room. *I wonder if Wanda had new plans for Sid.*

Keller and Aaron walked up to Sid's bed. He was asleep and taking deep, regular breaths. Wanda walked to the other side of the bed, her arms crossed.

She's not giving in, Aaron thought.

"Sid," Keller said as he shook Sid's shoulders.

Sid opened and closed his eyes, and Keller shook him again.

Aaron looked at Wanda. *She must be sedating him, too, with drugs.*

Sid's eyes opened and he tried to lift his head.

"It's me, Constable Greevy. The doc and I want to talk to you."

Keller helped Sid sit up in bed. Sid grabbed his arm. "I'm sick. Take me to the hospital."

"We will. Where's Race?"

"Race? I don't know." He took several breaths. "I haven't seen him in a while."

"Stay here a minute. We'll have a look around."

With gloved hands, the three officers searched the house room by room. Aaron led Keller to the cabinet with the crumpled box. Keller opened the cabinet door and looked in. There was no sign of the box.

Wanda stood behind them with her hands on her hips.

Aaron turned to her. "Will you unlock the kitchen cabinet?"

"Sure, but I don't see why." Wanda went to her purse and pulled out a key chain, then she walked to the cabinet and unlocked it.

She looks smug. She's not worried. "Why do you lock it?" Aaron said.

194

Wanda spat the words at him. "Because it's nobody's business. I want to keep everyone but me away from Sid's medicines."

Keller found several small pill bottles labeled as various vitamins and supplements. He placed the bottles into separate baggies.

It looks like she cleaned up the cabinets, Aaron thought. *Maybe Race came by so she was expecting a visit from us.*

"What in tarnation is this?" Keller stood in a room nearby, staring at an object in his hand. It appeared to be a small, black cloth doll with a frown on its face and a pin stuck through its head.

"Looks like a voodoo doll," one of the officers said.

"Crap." Keller's hands flew back, and the doll fell to the floor.

Leaning over it, the officer nodded. "Yep, I'm sure it is. I had an aunt that was into the voodoo religion, and she had dolls like that."

Wanda snatched up the doll and wagged it at Keller. "I curse you. I curse you."

Keller shook his head and walked away.

After thirty minutes or so, the officers packed their baggies and a few other impounded articles into a briefcase.

Aaron stood at Sid's bed, holding up a cloth pouch he'd pulled out from under Sid's pillow. He turned to Wanda. "What's this?"

Wanda grabbed it from him. "It's my gris-gris. Don't ever touch it again."

Keller stared at the pouch. "So that's what a gris-gris is. I've heard they're used in voodoo, for good or bad."

She held the pouch close to Keller's face. "Like I said, you've been cursed."

Keller snorted and stepped back. "Sure, whatever you say."

He looked at Aaron. "Do you want to check Sid into the hospital?"

"Yes," Aaron said.

Wanda held up her hands. "Wait a minute. You can't just take him from me. I know my rights."

"This man is sick. He needs a hospital checkup," Keller said.

"He's already been there, several times. They can't help him."

"Doc here has some other ideas. Do you want me to call an ambulance, or will you go along in a car?"

Wanda didn't answer, and Keller looked at Aaron.

"He can go by car. I can take him," Aaron said as he made a phone call to a hospitalist at a nearby hospital to arrange for inpatient admission.

Keller turned to Wanda. "I'm done in here for now. We're going to search around outside the house. I expect you'll be going along with Sid."

"I'll follow him to the hospital. Then I have to find my son."

"So, you do know where he is."

"No, I told you no."

Keller shook his finger at her. "You'd better let me know if you find him."

Wanda packed a bag for Sid, and then she and Aaron supported Sid as he stumbled to Aaron's car.

"They'll do a lot of tests, and they still won't know what's wrong," Wanda said.

After Sid was situated in the car, Aaron looked at Wanda. "You've had a lot of stress on you lately. I think you need to see a doctor—a psychiatrist—to help you deal with your stress."

Wanda glared at him. "There's nothing wrong with me." She stormed away to her car.

Aaron drove away to the hospital with Sid lying down in the back seat and Wanda following in her car.

Aaron brought a wheelchair to the car and pushed Sid through the hospital entrance doors and then checked him into an inpatient room. Wanda stood in the room with Aaron and the nurse until Sid was resting comfortably in bed. He fell asleep after a few minutes. Wanda flung her hands at Aaron and stomped out of the room.

"What's wrong with her?" the nurse said to Aaron.

"She's having a bad day."

The nurse nodded and looked up as the hospitalist walked in and introduced himself to Aaron. He then stepped to the bedside and studied Sid. "This man is emaciated, like you told me."

He turned to Aaron. "I've reviewed his recent hospital records. There may be something we're missing. You said you had some ideas?"

"Check for thallium," Aaron said.

"Thallium? That's used sometimes as a poison."

"That's what I'm worried about. We found thallium powder at the house, and his wife may've been feeding it to him."

"Interesting. I've never seen a case of thallium poisoning. I'll research it."

Aaron stepped to the bedside and pointed. "See how he's lost his eyelashes and lateral eyebrows?"

"You're right."

"That's one sign of thallium poisoning."

Soon after Aaron left, the hospitalist started treatment for a presumptive diagnosis of thallium toxicity.

Chapter 29

Constable Greevy locked his briefcase in his car, and then he and the other two officers searched around outside the Taggett's house. They inspected two large garbage cans and sifted through several piles of trash at the edge of the back yard. While walking along the perimeter of the yard, Keller came across a small trailhead between two trees.

Keller motioned to the other officers. "Let's go in. Stay alert. Race Taggett is dangerous." They headed off into the pines along a narrow trail that traveled in the general direction of the path that Keller had followed the day before to find Valerie bound and gagged.

I'll bet Race has used this trail, Keller thought.

By his watch, they'd walked for about twenty minutes when they came to an intersecting path. Sweat dripped from his forehead, and he wiped his burning eyes with a handkerchief to clear his vision.

This looks like the same trail I found yesterday.

They turned on the path in a direction away from the road that ended at the Taggett's house. Soon Keller came to the familiar clearing with the tent and campfire pit. He stopped and listened and heard nothing sinister. The officers looked inside the tent and around the periphery of the clearing. They were alone.

Near the tree to which Valerie had been chained was another small trailhead. Keller merged into the trees and followed this new trail about twenty yards to another clearing, larger than the first one. He stopped and caught his breath. Along the perimeter of the clearing were three trees with chains around their trunks, and the ground had been disturbed in the middle of the clearing. He winced at the smell of rotten meat.

Looks like two graves. Cupping his hand to his mouth, Keller turned and yelled. "I've got something here."

Keller called the medical examiner's office, and the three men, vigilant and with guns drawn, walked back to the Taggett's house. In less than an hour, a forensics van pulled up in the cul-de-sac in front of the house. Keller and the two other officers led the forensics team to the site with the disturbed dirt, where the team arranged their equipment, examined the scene, and began to dig with shovels. Within a short time, two decaying bodies were exposed in their graves.

"Two females," one of the team said.

"The work of Race Taggett," Keller said. He looked toward the trees. "I wonder where the hell he is."

Feeling nauseated from the sight and the stench, Keller turned and walked away.

He returned to the Taggett's house and waited. The forensics team loaded their van with the bodies and other evidence collected from the burial site and then left for the morgue. In the dim moonlight, Keller could see no clear details around the house. He heard the hooting of an owl from trees nearby.

Damn, this place is spooky.

He jumped as his phone rang. "Hello."

"We think we've spotted Race Taggett," a deputy said. "He's running in the direction of his house. He's less than two miles from the house now."

"I'm at the Taggett's house. We'll wait for him. Keep tailing him."

The three officers walked to trees at the perimeter of the yard and close to the street.

After a short while, Keller saw the headlights of a fast-moving vehicle coming from the direction of Dr. Rovsing's clinic. Another car slowed to a stop at the intersection of the Rovsing clinic road and allowed the speeding car to pass in front of it and through the intersection. Flashing lights split the darkness and a siren shriek erupted from the stopped car, which turned left and sped after the first car, and the two vehicles closed in on the Taggett's house.

The three officers stepped out from the trees and walked toward the road and the cars. Keller stopped and caught his breath as he saw something leap out into the road in front of the cars. Tires screeched as the driver of the lead car slammed the brakes and tried to avoid contact. Keller heard a thud as the lead car struck the figure, which was propelled over the hood and into the windshield and then over the vehicle, bouncing and skidding on the road before coming to rest.

201

Swerving and braking, the police car managed to steer clear of the first car. Keller jogged to the scene as people jumped out of the vehicles and into the street. He recognized Wanda's screams.

"No, no." Wanda ran up to the heap in the road. She kneeled and cradled a head and torso in her arms, crying and rocking back and forth.

"Oh, my son, my son. I've killed my son."

Keller crouched next to Wanda. Race took feeble breaths in her arms, his eyes closed. Keller noticed blood splattered over Race's hair, face, and shirt.

"Lay him flat. We may need to breathe for him," Keller said. He called 911 and reported the injury. "An ambulance is on the way," he said to Wanda, who continued to wail and rock back and forth with her son in her arms.

Keller stood and turned to the officer standing next to him. "How did you find him?"

"A report came in. A woman thought someone was acting strange outside a bar. You were busy, so I was dispatched to the scene. When I got there, he ran off."

Keller pointed at Wanda. "I wonder why she's here."

"Maybe she has a police scanner," the officer said.

"I wouldn't be surprised. I know she was out looking for Race."

"Well, she found him all right."

Keller watched Race. He still took feeble breaths and appeared unconscious.

After about ten minutes, Race was still breathing. Keller heard a siren up the street. He and the officers walked past the cars to direct the ambulance with their flashlights.

They led the paramedics to park at the side of the road, and then Keller walked back to Wanda. "What the ..."

Wanda and Race were gone. Keller looked up and spotted Wanda dragging Race around a back corner of their house. He motioned to the paramedics, who ran behind Keller and the other officers toward the back yard.

Keller turned the corner out of breath. Wanda sat on the back steps, and he hurried to her.

Light from the moon cast a grayish pall over her body. She stared up at the moon, and Keller caught a flicker of a smile on her face.

"Where's Race?" he said.

She pointed to the trees, without lowering her eyes from the sky.

"How could he be gone? He looked nearly dead." Keller jogged toward the forest, and he and the others searched around the border trees without finding anything.

Keller returned to Wanda. He heard her giggle and mumble, as she gazed up at the moon.

"Did you say something?" he asked. He leaned toward her.

"Moonie, moonie, doonie, doomie, doom, broom, brebble, pebble, debble, devil, devil."

"What did you say?" Keller bent down closer.

Keller's screams echoed in the forest as Wanda chomped on his ear. Everyone ran out from the trees and back to the house.

Wanda had Keller in a headlock, and he was hitting her with his fist. "Get her off me."

One paramedic grabbed Wanda's arms and pulled them behind her. Another paramedic grabbed her chin and forehead to force her mouth open. Keller moaned and fell to the ground with his hand over his left ear. Blood trickled onto his hand and cheek.

Wanda screamed, blood dripping from her lips. "Give heavy hurt, burt, beat, heat, heal, hill, kill, thrill, rickett, ticket, thicket, thicket."

Keller sat up holding his ear. "Damn, that hurts." He managed to get to his feet. "You guys be careful of her teeth. Can you take her to the hospital?"

Two muscled paramedics struggled to restrain her. One of them turned to Keller. "Sure. She definitely needs help. Is she schizophrenic?"

"She's something strange."

"You need to get that ear looked at," the paramedic said, and then he pointed at Keller's neck bandage. "It looks like you've had a bad week."

"Tell me about it. At least we have a doctor in town now." Keller moaned. "I hope my ear doesn't fall off." He nodded at Wanda. "That crazy woman put a voodoo curse on me."

Chapter 30

Aaron paced around his house that evening and felt his wrist pulse at times. It was more rapid than usual.

One hundred and ten beats a minute. What's going on with my heart?

As he settled into bed for the night, he winced at the buzzing in his ears.

It must be stress getting to me.

A vision popped into his head: a silver machete poised in the air.

Aaron and Stella walked into a patient room the next morning, Wednesday. Constable Greevy sat in a chair. Stella had removed the bandages from his head and neck.

"You've got another injury. What happened?" Aaron said.

Keller updated Aaron about his recent encounters with Race and Wanda.

Aaron examined the wounds and prescribed an antibiotic to prevent infection. Stella cleaned and bandaged the injuries.

Keller shook his head. "I thought Wanda would bite my ear clean off. Are you sure it'll be all right?"

"I think you'll be fine," Aaron said.

"I'm worried. I've never been voodoo cursed before."

Stella laughed. "Wanda cursed you?"

Keller nodded. "With her voodoo doll and a gris-gris."

"I wouldn't worry about that. I don't think she's for real," Stella said.

"I agree," Aaron said. "Wanda has a serious mental illness, and I wouldn't be surprised if she spouts bizarre curses all the time."

"I'll bet she's cursing up a storm now," Keller said.

Aaron sighed. "So Wanda is hospitalized and Race, a serial killer, is on the loose." He shivered as he saw Race's eyes. *I guess I'm not surprised he's a killer.*

Keller grimaced when he turned his head, holding the ear bandage. "Catching that guy is like trying to corner an angry mountain lion."

"He might show up in a hospital ER somewhere," Aaron said.

"We're checking all that."

A man stopped Aaron outside a patient room. "I'm Daniel's father," the man said. "You saw him recently. He's in the Army."

"Oh, yes." Aaron shook his hand. "How's he doing?"

"He's getting more sleep now thanks to your prescription, but I don't think his mental health is good."

"He's going to counseling, right?"

"I make sure of that, but the wife and I are worried sick about him. He's not getting better."

"It can take time."

"We just found out that a soldier from his unit committed suicide. That makes two suicides of guys he knew and fought alongside."

Aaron shook his head. "That's tragic."

"That's our worst fear since he came back. We keep a close eye on him."

"Try to get him involved with the community in some way."

"That's really why I'm here. I wondered if you could give us any advice. He wanted to be a paramedic. He was always helping others. He'd give the shirt off his back to help someone."

"I'll bet the ambulance or firefighter guys would help him out. They like soldiers. Maybe he could hang out around their quarters and get to know them."

"I'll look into that."

"Let me know if I can help."

As Aaron pulled into his driveway that evening, he spotted a vehicle in the shadows at the side of the road, in front of the grove of trees next to his house. He stopped in the garage and watched the rearview and side view mirrors as the garage door closed behind him. Seeing nothing suspicious, he sighed and stepped out.

After closing the car door, he heard a noise behind him and something struck the side of his head.

Aaron gasped and opened his eyes. Swaying branches of tall trees came into focus, and he felt grass and hard ground beneath him. He lifted his head and looked around, and a pounding ache in his head intensified. A thick cloth filled his mouth and wrapped around the back of his neck. His arms were behind him, his wrists and ankles bound with what felt like twine or rope. After several attempts, he managed to sit up with his back against a tree. He heard a rustle in the grass, and a bald man walked up to him.

"Hello, Doc. I hope you got your beauty rest. It'll be your last."

The bald man kneeled in front of Aaron and grabbed his chin. "Do you know who I am?"

Aaron nodded, his eyes wide.

"You ruined my life, you know. Or maybe you don't know. Maybe you don't give a damn."

Aaron tried to talk but could only groan.

"Yep. Everyone knows about pill mills and prescription drug ODs, and you did that to my daughter. You killed her. The only person I had in the world. Now, nothing matters. My life isn't worth crap." He stood and smiled at Aaron. "And neither is yours."

He walked over to a backpack on the ground and pulled out a coil of rope. Aaron moved his back from the tree and flopped flat on the ground, bent his knees, and pushed himself away along the grass.

"No, you don't," the man said as he ran over to Aaron, dragged him back, and slammed him against the tree trunk. He wrapped the rope again and again around Aaron's chest, securing him to the tree. Aaron had to take shallow breaths, as he couldn't fully inhale against the tight rope.

How can I get out of this?

The man returned to the backpack, and Aaron saw a glint from the machete as the man turned around.

"I missed last time. But now, you're a sitting duck. You don't know how much I've been looking forward to this." His eyes gleamed as he crept closer.

Aaron moaned and shook his head, his heart thumping and skipping beats.

I'm not ready to die.

He stood over Aaron and raised the machete. Aaron looked up at the shiny metal and squinted his eyes.

Holding the machete in midair, the man hesitated and sighed.

Aaron heard a rustle in the brush. Something smashed into the side of the man, knocking him off his feet and onto the ground. The machete skidded away and bounced off a tree. Aaron watched the struggle in the grass and saw a flicker of rope.

A figure stood and walked over to Aaron.

Damn. Race Taggett? Aaron thought. *Now what?*

Race frowned as he untied Aaron from the tree and loosened his ankle and wrist bindings. He shook his finger at Aaron. "Can't stay away from the Taggetts, can you?" He unwrapped the cloth from Aaron's mouth and neck. "Well, you're lucky. It's not your time yet."

Aaron coughed and took deep breaths, and his voice croaked. "How did you find . . .?" Race whirled around and vanished into the trees.

Aaron removed the ropes from his arms and legs, and he trotted over to the trees at the edge of the clearing. *What am I doing? I don't really expect to find Race.*

He took more deep breaths, stretched his arms, and massaged his head. *Calm down. At least I'm still alive.*

Aaron walked over to the man lying on the ground on his side. His wrists were tied behind him and his ankles were bound together.

It's like Race was roping a calf.

The man rolled over on his back and looked up. He scowled at Aaron as he spoke, "I guess you can butcher me now. Go ahead, get it over with."

Aaron coughed. "I'm not a killer." He sat down on the ground beside the man.

"It's okay. Put me out of my misery." He glanced at the sky. "I want to go where she is."

"Listen. I'm very sorry about what happened to your daughter. I'm sure you miss her."

"You have no idea."

"I made a mistake. I'm not perfect. I was only trying to help her."

Aaron heard a breeze in the trees.

"I don't think you're a killer, either," Aaron said.

"She was a beautiful little girl. I used to take her swimming, and we hiked in the hills when she was a Girl Scout." He talked more about his daughter's childhood and teen years. "Then my job got crazy, and I wasn't at home much anymore. I don't know when she got into drugs. I should've been there for her." His voice broke and his eyes were moist. "I want to see her and tell her that I love her."

"I'm not going to hurt you."

He raised his head. "Do you have a daughter?"

"No."

"Then you can't know what it's like."

They were quiet for several minutes. Aaron heard soft sloshing from a stream nearby.

He untied the man's ankles and wrists.

"Who the hell hog-tied me?" the man said.

Aaron chuckled. "A local guy. Very athletic."

"I didn't think anyone would bother us out here."

"Where are we?"

"Deep in the Big Thicket. I tied you up and dragged you out here in a tarp."

"I might've never been found."

"That was the idea. I researched this place, but I didn't count on your athletic guardian angel."

An angel? No way, Aaron thought. *But why would Race Taggett, of all people, save my life?* He recalled the hurt he'd seen before in Race's eyes.

Is there any hope for him?

Aaron helped the man to his feet. As the machete guy walked around in the clearing, he favored the right side of his chest. He picked up the long knife and stared at it, turning it in his hands, then he looked at Aaron and shook his head. With a yell that reverberated through the forest, he arched his arm back and heaved the machete through an opening in the trees. He flinched and held a hand against his chest.

"Why a machete?" Aaron said.

He walked over to Aaron. "A long time ago, a friend of mine sold me his, when I needed to clear some brush around my house. I got mighty good at swinging it. I still had it in my garage." He glanced at Aaron's scar. "It's great for slicing things up, and the handle knocked you out cold."

Aaron felt the scar on his jaw. *It sure did a number on me.*

"I thought revenge would be sweet, even after my sister got you fired."

Aaron's eyes flew open. "What're you talking about?"

"My sister is a doctor at the hospital you were at. After my daughter died, she complained about you to the higher-ups. She told me she got you fired."

Aaron nodded. "Thanks for letting me know." *So, that charge against me of patient endangerment may've been a big fat lie.*

"Let's get out of here," the man said. He pulled a compass from his backpack and studied it, then swung the backpack onto his shoulders. "Follow me out."

"I was wondering. What color were her eyes?" Aaron said.

The bald man stopped and smiled. "Green. Bright green."

Aaron walked behind him for what seemed like thirty minutes or more. Branches from low brush jabbed his pants and scraped his lower legs. They sloshed around several shallow marshes, and at times, Aaron heard critters darting away. They stopped at the edge of a rutted road. An SUV was parked a few feet away.

"I'll drop you off at your house."

They were quiet on the return trip. In his driveway, Aaron opened the passenger door. He hesitated and turned to the man. "Where are you going?" he said.

"Out west somewhere. Alaska maybe. My wife left me after our daughter's death, so I'll try to start over. I have friends that might help me."

Aaron took a deep breath. "What about the lawsuit?"

He snorted. "There's no lawsuit. Those things take too long. My lawyer said you might win anyway. That's why I came after you. I couldn't wait."

As Aaron stepped out of the SUV, the man leaned toward him. He grimaced and held his right chest. "If you call the police, they won't find me. I know how to stay out of sight."

"I'm sure you're right." Aaron pointed at the man's chest. "You might need to get that injury checked out."

"I'll be fine. I've been through worse."

Aaron shut the door and watched the man drive away. He took in a deep breath of fresh night air. His headache was gone, but when he was still, the buzzing in his head was deafening. It sounded like bees were flying around inside his ears.

Chapter 31

Aaron stopped just inside the front door of his clinic the next morning. He took a deep breath and spread his arms. "It's great to be here."

"You look terrible," Stella said. "Are you sick?"

"No, but I am lucky to be alive."

"Were you in an accident? You've got bruises on your face."

Aaron grimaced. His lower legs burned from numerous abrasions. "I had a battle with the Big Thicket last night."

"What in the world happened in the Big Thicket?"

Aaron sighed. "I'll tell you all about it someday. Right now, it hurts to talk, so I'll speak in a soft voice today. If anyone asks, tell them I had a minor accident and that I'm okay."

"Are you sure you're all right?"

Aaron nodded. "Oh, yeah. Things are much better now."

"And just how are things better? You don't look better."

"Let me put it this way. Some bad things in my life are over and behind me now."

Back in his office, Aaron counted on his fingers his good fortunes.

One, I probably didn't endanger any patients back in Connecticut after all. Two, my lawsuit is over and my would-be killer has gone away.

He leaned back in his chair with his fingers together. *Three, I'm still alive.*

A shiver passed over him as he walked to his window and looked out to the Big Thicket trees across the road. *But how do I deal with Race Taggett?*

A swirling breeze flushed a flock of birds from the trees. *Maybe I won't have to deal with him at all. Maybe he'll just go away, or the police will catch him.*

Race's frowning face appeared before Aaron. *Why did he say to me, "It's not your time yet"?*

Near noon, Aaron heard loud talking in the waiting room.

"Our Cajun patient, Tucker Boudreaux, is in the lobby talking with the other patients," Stella said. "I think they're getting annoyed with him. His bipolar mania must be worse today."

Aaron walked to the front of the clinic. Tucker stood and held a poster in front of him as he addressed the four people in the lobby. His words were rapid fire and his short hair danced on his head. From their chairs, the patients looked at Aaron with wide eyes.

Aaron walked up to Tucker. "Will you come back to my office where we can talk?"

"Sure, Doc. I want you to hear this, too. I've created a design for a rocket that can carry people into orbit and even to the moon. I'm looking for investors ..." His words tumbled into each other and the sentences didn't always make sense.

Aaron stepped toward Stella. "Try to find his mother."

He led Tucker to his office in the back. Tucker paced around the room, flailing his arms and pouring out his theories about rocket fuel and hull construction.

I've never heard a person talk so fast, Aaron thought. *He can't get some of the words out. His brain is moving faster than his mouth can.*

After a short while, Stella opened the office door and Tucker's mother hurried into the room.

She clasped her hands in front of her. "I'm so sorry. I can't control him. His psychiatrist added a new medication last week, and it seemed to help at first. Since yesterday, though, he's been like this."

Tucker slammed his hands on Aaron's desk. "What are you guys worried about? I'll build the first colony on the moon, I know what food will grow there, I'll organize moon sports leagues, . . ."

His mother stepped closer to Aaron and raised her voice so she could be heard over Tucker's monologue. "He's washed our car every day this week, and yesterday he came home with over twenty pairs of shoes. I had to freeze his credit card." She took hold of Tucker's arm. "As soon as we leave here, I'll call his psychiatrist and drive Tucker over to see him."

"*Lune, Lune,* moon, moon, lagoon, baboon. I wonder if baboons could live on the moon . . ."

She led Tucker out of the office and then stopped in the hallway and leaned toward Aaron behind her.

"Sometimes . . ."

"Yes," Aaron said.

"I feel strange saying this to you, but sometimes when he rants on and on like this, he says something that makes sense."

Aaron nodded and waited.

"What I mean is, sometimes he says something . . . that comes true later."

"Like a prediction?"

She scratched her cheek. "Well, a prediction, or a warning, and he might remember what he said and he might not." She cocked her head. "Have you ever heard of that?"

"No, but that is interesting."

She hurried to catch up with Tucker near the registration desk.

Tucker darted over to Juliana, who sat behind the counter.

"Do you want to have sex?" Tucker said, a broad grin on his face.

Juliana's eyes widened, and she pushed her chair back. "*Que diablos?*"

"Tucker, that is not appropriate," his mother said as she grabbed his arm. "Come with me now."

After they left, Aaron collapsed into his desk chair. Stella walked into his office.

"Oh, my goodness," she said. "He needs help."

Aaron wiped his forehead with a handkerchief. "I imagine he'll crash at some point. Probably sometime after I do. My brain hurts."

Stella chuckled. "I've heard he can be like this for days at a time."

"I hope his psychiatrist can calm him down," Aaron said.

After work, Aaron drove to his happy hour bar for dinner and drinks. Red straightened the chair next to him and waved Aaron over.

"I've become a real happy hour fan of this place," Aaron said.

Red smiled. "Just like me."

"I think of it as my 'sane' place."

"It's my sanctuary, for sure."

Aaron glanced up at a TV near him on the wall behind the bar. Someone had just homered and was rounding the bases in a Major League baseball game.

He turned to Red. "Are there any other decent bars like this?"

"Sure, but I like this one best."

Aaron ordered broccoli cheese soup and wine.

"You never order much food," Red said.

"I snack at the office and eat larger dinners most days when I'm off work."

"Sensible." Red sipped his brandy. "I had to patch up my fence. My dog got out for a while, and I like to keep him in the yard. My previous dog loved to roam around in the Big Thicket."

"I'll bet he had a field day in there catching critters."

"Yep. He brought a few of them back. Sometimes I couldn't even figure out what kind of animal it was. Strange things live in that place."

"So I've heard."

Aaron sampled his wine. *My taste buds must be learning. I can taste hints of blackberry and licorice, I think.*

He leaned toward Red. "I've been reading up a bit about World War Two. I didn't realize it sure could've gone the other way."

"You're right about that. Why, I was on a ship at the surrender of the Japanese. We expected they'd pull something funny and start another battle right there. But they surrendered all right."

"I guess you guys were happy with that."

"We celebrated, big time." Red studied his brandy. "There aren't many happy people in war these days. No one surrenders anymore. Everyone loses."

At least some of my battles are over, Aaron thought. A vision of Race Taggett's glinting eyes appeared to him.

Chapter 32

Constable Keller Greevy winced with certain movements of his head. He sat in his office chair, sipping from a mug of steaming hot coffee, a large white bandage on the right side of his neck and a head wrap securing another bandage over his left ear.

He glanced at caller ID as the phone rang. It was the ME's office.

"Those pills from the Taggett's house look so far to be just vitamins and nutritional supplements, nothing unusual."

"That was quick work. Anything else?"

"We have some preliminary autopsy results for you."

Keller sat up and put his mug down on the desk. "Go ahead."

"It seems the two women died from strangulation. There were bruises on their necks consistent with choking."

"Were they sexually assaulted?"

"There is no evidence of that."

"Well, at least he's not a rapist."

"There was something strange. Both corpses had the letter 'W' cut into their upper chests, apparently with a knife."

"So Race did torture them."

"I don't think so. The condition of the blood in the wounds and the appearance of the wound edges indicate that the knife was used after they were dead."

Chapter 33

Buck Bogarty jumped as the doorbell rang. He and his mother, Sandra, were lounging in their living room, watching evening TV.

Sandra went to the door and peered through the peephole. "It's a policeman." Buck walked up beside her as she opened the door.

"I'm Officer Perkins. Is Lee Bogarty here?"

"No, he doesn't live here anymore," Sandra said. "Why do you ask?"

"We need to speak with him."

"What about?"

"The death of a woman."

Sandra put her hand over her mouth.

"He's on the run, and he might show up here," the officer said. "We think he's armed."

"If he comes, you'll be the first to know," Sandra said. She closed and locked the door.

Buck collapsed back onto the living room couch. Sandra sat beside him and put her hand on his shoulder.

Buck rubbed his eyes. "What really happened to him?"

"Your father was a good man once, until he lost his job. He always blamed some of the people he worked with. He never got over that, and he wasn't able to get decent work again."

Buck shook his head. "You've told me all that before, but I know there's something else." He looked at Sandra. "He was like his father, wasn't he?"

Sandra dropped her head and covered her eyes to hold back the tears. "I'm . . . so sorry," she said between sobs.

"Why did they beat up women?"

She shook her head and blotted her eyes with tissue. "I don't know."

Chapter 34

Aaron's patient list was growing, and his Friday clinic schedule was packed. Folks with diabetes, hypertension, heart disease, arthritis, obesity and other ailments were added weekly. A litany of the common afflictions of the American way of life showed up at Aaron's door . . . including mental illness.

Near noon, as Aaron was about to open the door to a patient room, he stopped and smiled as he heard the strumming of a guitar. *Ah, Cam, my schizophrenic guitarist.*

"How can I help you today, Mr. Fillmore?"

Cam's hair swayed as he strummed a few chords on his guitar, then he looked up. "I can't find my medicine. I must've pitched it out by accident."

"So you've not taken your medicine recently?"

"Not for a while."

"Well, I'm glad you're here for a refill."

Aaron checked Cam's heart, lungs, and pupils and performed a mental status exam. "That's good. You seem to be thinking clearly."

He handed Cam a prescription. "Take care of yourself. Remember to take this as directed."

"Thanks, Doc. You've been good to me, so I'm watching out for you."

"What do you mean?"

"I'll let you know of any enemies closing in."

"Your beam blockers signal you, right?"

"That's right. They help me spot any suspicious folks driving around."

As Cam strolled through the clinic, he stopped to play his guitar a few minutes for the surprised patients in the waiting room.

Aaron lifted his head. "That sounds a little like 'Friends in Low Places,' by Garth Brooks."

Early in the afternoon, Aaron closed his clinic, and he and Stella drove to a small Baptist church nearby to attend the funeral of Rocky Donnigan. Brad Benningham had organized the funeral.

Stella turned to Aaron in the car. "I made some phone calls. At the hospital, they found thallium in Sid Taggett, and Wanda was charged with his attempted murder."

"I guess we could say she's guilty by reason of insanity?" Aaron said.

"That's what they thought at the hospital. She was diagnosed with severe chronic schizophrenia and transferred to a long-term state psych facility."

Aaron nodded. "Good. I guess the DA made a quick deal. Anyway, that's where she needs to be."

Aaron approached the church. *Wow, no empty parking spaces.*

He pulled his car onto the grass next to the paved parking lot. They walked into the church just in time for the start of the service. Several people scooted and squished together in a rear pew to make room for Aaron and Stella.

A minister talked about Rocky's attributes: his marvelous mechanical skills and the quality of his friendship to those who were close to him.

After the minister's prayer, Rocky's coworker at the garage stepped up to the podium. "As most of you know, Rocky was real good with cars."

"Amen," several people said from the audience.

He said he felt lucky to have worked with Rocky, and he gave a few examples of Rocky's expertise. "I could go on for hours. Everyone in town knew they could trust their cars to Rocky. He was also one of the nicest people I've ever known. He had a kind heart."

Next, Preston Benningham walked up to the podium. He read from a piece of paper, mumbling his first few words. He looked up and saw that some people had leaned forward and cupped their ears to hear him. With a strengthened voice, he started over again.

"I've had trouble the last few years with drug addiction. It almost ruined my life. Rocky talked with me all the time about it, offering me hope, giving me support. He wanted to help me recover." His voice broke. "And then he gave me . . . the ultimate sacrifice . . . the greatest gift of all . . ." He took a deep breath. "A few nights ago, he shielded me . . . and he died instead of me; he saved my life." Tears rolled down his cheeks. "He died for me . . . I'll never forget him, and I'll think of him every day . . . for the rest of my life." He wiped his eyes and face with a handkerchief and looked out over the audience. "And thanks to Rocky, the addiction demon is gone from me, forever."

"Amens" erupted from the audience, and Aaron saw many people in the pews blotting their eyes with tissue.

After the service, Aaron motioned to Brad outside the church.

"I looked around for any of Rocky's family. Did his ex-wife come today?" Aaron said.

"No. She wasn't interested."

Chapter 35

Buck Bogarty wiped his eyes to hold back the tears.

He's my dad. Why doesn't he talk to me?

He floored the hot rod's accelerator. Headlights illuminated only a short span of the winding country road in front of the car. Three guys rode along with him in the car, and they howled with delight as Buck would negotiate tight turns with squealing tires and then accelerate down straightaways.

"Let her rip, Buck."

"Take it to the limit."

"Let's see what she can do."

They didn't notice the frown on Buck's face.

A low hill appeared in the headlights, a hump in the road. Buck's hot rod hit the bump and went airborne, then slammed back down on the road. He didn't anticipate the sharp turn a few yards away from the hill. As he strained with the steering wheel to follow the road, the car lurched onto the two right tires and then began to roll and bounce off the road and into the trees. Buck's vision went black.

Several minutes later, Buck opened his eyes and coughed. He lay in shallow water, and he spat and cleared his mouth then raised his body up into a sitting position. As he stood up, he felt stiffness in his neck and lower back.

Buck looked around and spotted his car perched on its side against some trees. "Hello," he said.

He heard moaning, and two heads appeared from the grass near the car. "Buck, are you okay?" someone said.

Two figures stood up from the grass and brushed off their clothes. Buck walked over to them. "Ever'one all right?"

"I think so," one of the guys said. "I guess we had a wreck."

"Where's Spike?" Buck said.

They searched the area for several minutes.

"Over here." One of the guys kneeled down and shook a body in the grass. "Hey, I don't think he's breathing."

Buck ran over and dropped to his knees at the other side of Spike's limp body.

After shaking the body again, the guy looked up at Buck. "He's not breathing. What do we do? Buck, what do we do?"

Buck stared at Spike and started to speak.

"C'mon, Buck. We've got to do something."

Buck bent down and began to breathe into Spike's mouth.

Don't die, Spike. Please, don't die.

Buck pulled Spike's jaw down to open his mouth more, and his second breath was more forceful. He saw Spike's chest rise out of the corner of his eye. *Damn it, Spike. Wake up.*

After several seconds, Spike coughed once and took several breaths. Buck shook him, and Spike opened his eyes.

Buck sat back and exhaled. "Thank God."

Spike raised his head. "What happened?"

"I wrecked my hot rod. Does anything hurt?"

Spike considered the question. "Not too bad." Buck and the other two guys helped Spike stand up. He stretched his arms and legs, and felt his head and chest. "I don't think anything's broke." He looked up. "Why are you shaking, Buck?"

Buck thrust his hands into his pockets, dropped his head, and walked away.

****

Aaron lay stretched out on his bed late that night. Various body parts ached from his Big Thicket ordeal, and he hadn't slept well for the last several nights.

He sat up in bed and slammed his fist into his palm. *I know I can make this job work. I've done some good here already.*

He peered into the painting on the wall across from his bed.

At the end of that dirt trail, those people in the trees are warning me about something. That must be one heck of a dangerous path.

Chapter 36

After Forrester Brighton was shot, Aaron saw Marley only by happenstance.

Around noon on a sunny Saturday, he spotted Marley and Cristal in their front yard and pulled his car to a stop at the side of the road. He waved from the car and walked up to them.

"You look well, Cristal." He looked at Marley. "Is she back to normal?"

"Yes, as if nothing had happened. She doesn't remember much about her time in the hospital. And as you can see, the tick rash is all gone."

"It's great to see her healthy again." He patted Cristal's shoulder.

Cristal held her forearm up to him. "I have a sore."

Aaron noticed a red spot where an intravenous catheter had penetrated the skin. Yellow coloring surrounded the spot.

"She's proud of that sore," Marley said. "She painted a sun around it."

Cristal nodded. "That's how I got my medicine."

Aaron leaned down and examined the colorful spot. "Nice job. The medicine helped you, like the sun does."

He stepped back and looked at Marley. "Now, we all have our battle wounds."

Marley met his gaze.

Aaron crossed his arms. "How's Forrester?"

Marley smiled. "It's rough, but he's learning to live with the injury. He's going to the rehab center tomorrow."

Cristal tugged on Aaron's arm. "Genie made my wish come true. My daddy's coming home."

Aaron sighed, and he nodded at Cristal. "I'm happy for you."

Marley touched his arm. "Thanks for helping out with the Taggett family."

Aaron nodded. "That's worked out well." He looked down. "So far anyway."

"Keep at it. I have faith in you."

He reached out and squeezed her hand. She squeezed back for a moment, then she let go.

"Goodbye," Aaron said.

He turned and walked away, stepped into his car, and looked back.

Marley hadn't moved. A breeze lifted her hair. She held her head high and smiled at him.

Later that afternoon, Aaron lounged in his living room and stared at the front windows. He hadn't switched on the TV or the stereo, and the house was dark and quiet.

He slapped his thighs. "Snap out of it. I've got things to do."

Aaron backed his car out of the driveway and headed for a grocery store to restock his kitchen. As he turned right onto the road to his clinic, he spotted someone walking in the front yard of Rocky Donnigan's trailer home. As far as Aaron knew, the fate of Rocky's home and possessions was yet to be determined after his untimely death.

Aaron pulled his car to the side of the road. A man looked up as Aaron stepped out of the car.

"Preston." Aaron hiked over to him through the tall grass.

"Hi, Doc."

"You look good. Is the shoulder healing well?"

Preston wore a sling to support his left shoulder. "It's coming along."

"Stop by the clinic in a few days and let me check you out."

"I'll do that."

Aaron glanced at the trailer home. "I guess someone will dismantle this place. I don't think it's worth much."

"I'm looking for his bike. Have you seen it?"

"Maybe it's around back." They walked to Rocky's back yard and spotted the bike propped up against the back of the trailer.

Preston ran his hand over the handlebars. "Can I take it with me? I'll take good care of it."

Aaron put his hand on Preston's back. "I don't think anyone will mind. I can't think of a better place for it."

Preston stared at the bike. "Sometimes I feel like Rocky is still watching out for me."

"Maybe he is. That can give you strength."

Aaron lay in bed that night and stared at the ceiling. His body aches were less intense today, but all evening, his heart had raced and pounded off and on.

He sat up on the side of the bed and felt his pulse. *Heart rate about 100 beats a minute. It's not my thyroid; I've had that checked, and I stopped drinking caffeine late in the day.*

He sighed. *I know stress can kill. Maybe it's stress from all this craziness going on around me.*

He relaxed back on his pillow. *At least, I haven't had a nightmare for a while.*

As he closed his eyes, Marley's smiling face appeared. After a few seconds, her face dissolved into blackness.

Aaron tossed and turned for hours, drifting off to sleep at about 3:00 a.m.

Chapter 37

Stella connected with the Sunday morning sermon; it was about the power of forgiveness.

She found herself walking toward the exit next to Myra Benningham.

"How's Preston doing?" Stella said.

"Much better, thanks."

"Is he here?"

"No, he and his dad are at the movies."

"They're doing things together. That's good."

Myra stopped and turned to Stella. "I'm headed out for a meal, along with most everybody else. Why don't we have lunch together?"

"Sure. I'd like that."

Stella followed Myra's car to a restaurant not far away. Soon they sat at a table across from each other with their food from the Sunday brunch buffet.

"Can you tell me more about Preston?" Stella said. "I have a special interest in his progress as he's one of our patients."

Myra sipped her iced tea. "Preston is in a twelve-step program, and he's been going to the meetings. He seems committed to recovering." She smiled. "For the first time in years, we have real hope."

"I'm so glad to hear that he's improving." Stella shook her head. "He's had such a tough road."

"He talks with me again, like the old days. He's eating healthy. It's wonderful. He even asked us to give his gun away."

"I'm sure glad he didn't squeeze the trigger that day in our clinic."

"Me, too. We've had it locked up since then." Myra cocked her head. "I think he shot his gun only one time that I heard about."

"He shot his gun? You mean, at someone?"

"I don't know. I don't think so."

"When was that?"

"I think about two years ago or so. Brad refuses to talk to me about it."

Stella gulped her bite of ham and cheese omelette and coughed. "Two years ago?"

"I think that's about right."

"Where did this happen?"

"I don't know for certain. I think it was close by, in town. I just have a vague impression of the whole thing."

Stella stood up. An image of her dead son's smiling face floated across her vision. She was breathing fast, and she fanned her face with her napkin.

"Stella, are you all right?"

"I'm sorry. I have to go now." Stella turned and stumbled out of the restaurant. She sat on a bench outside for several minutes, then walked to her car and drove away.

****

Late that afternoon, Brad and Myra Benningham sat in their living room, sipping coffee.

"We had a great day at the movies. He's different this time," Brad said, his arm around Myra's shoulders.

Myra smiled. "Yes, he is. He seems more like the old Preston to me."

They were silent for several minutes, gazing out the front window.

Brad sighed. "I have to make up for lost time."

"That will be good for him and you."

Myra turned to him. "After church today, I had lunch with Stella. I told her about Preston, that he's doing better and he wanted us to give his gun away."

"I'll bet that made her happy. He really scared her with his gun in the clinic that day."

"She got upset about something. I told her I seemed to remember that Preston shot his gun once."

Brad lifted his arm from Myra and sat up. "Why did you tell her that? She doesn't need to know that."

"So, I'm right? He did shoot his gun? Was anyone hurt?"

Brad stood up and pointed at her. "It's of no concern to you or anyone. Don't mention it again." He whirled around and walked away.

He struck his fist into the palm of his hand. *I have to make this go away. It can't come out.*

Chapter 38

On Sunday afternoon, eight days after his spinal injury, Forrester Brighton was transferred to the rehabilitation center. Marley helped Cristal sing every song they could think of during their drive to visit Forrester at the center.

Cristal was first into Forrester's room. He smiled and held out his arms. "Good morning, my little princess."

She hugged his arm. "Daddy. I'm glad you're coming home."

Marley walked up to the bed and Forrester hugged her with his other arm. "It'll be so good to be back with you," he said.

Marley had arranged their home to accommodate the new Forrester. She felt a renewed excitement because Forrester was back with her, for good. At times, when she wasn't busy with this new challenge, images of a smiling or an embarrassed Aaron would pop into her mind.

You'll be a good man for some lucky woman, she thought. *It just wasn't meant to be for us.*

During the next few months, Forrester spent many hours in rehab, learning to maneuver with his arms, use a wheelchair, and catheterize his bladder. Cristal was at his side whenever she could manage to be. Marley would patiently reorient him during his periodic memory lapses.

Forrester never asked about Eve again.

Chapter 39

Aaron's hands twitched on the steering wheel on his way to work Monday morning. *I've got to be sleep-deprived. Maybe I should think about a sleep medicine.*

He opened the door of a room to see his first patient of the day.

"Hi, Dale. Are you going fishing anytime soon?"

"No, but I'll sure 'nuf let you know when I do."

Dale McCorkindale sighed and looked at Aaron with wide eyes. "I think I've got VD. There's a discharge and it hurts to pee."

Aaron examined Dale's abdomen and genitals and nodded. "Yep, gonorrhea or chlamydia, or both. I'll culture it and find out. In the meantime, I'll start antibiotics."

"You don't think I could get HIV, too, do you?"

"I'll order tests for the other STDs. We'll check it all out."

"I've been thinking. You can pick this up from toilet seats, right? Tell me you can."

"Ah, the wife doesn't know," Aaron said.

"She's already suspicious, but she'll believe the toilet seat story. So, what do you say?"

"I don't think it ever happens that way, but I guess anything's possible."

Dale hopped up and pumped Aaron's hand. "I'm beholden to you, Doc."

"I advise that you contact your recent liaisons and let them know so they can get checked out."

Dale beamed his best salesman's glistening-teeth smile and released his grip. "Sure. Anything you say."

Aaron motioned at the chair. "Wait in here. You'll need a shot and then I'll get you a prescription for oral antibiotics and an order for lab tests."

Aaron turned around at the door of the room. "I've been thinking about a pickup truck."

Dale gave Aaron a thumbs-up. "Now you're talking."

"I'm looking at classic trucks online."

"A classic. Good. I follow the classics market. What got you interested?"

"Oh, a friend of mine." Aaron looked up. He saw an image of a smiling Rocky Donnigan standing in his auto shop. *Thanks, Rocky. I'll make it a good one.*

"Do you have anything in mind?" Dale said.

"What are your favorites?"

Dale pulled on his earlobe. "Well, if you want a real classic, you can't go wrong with the very first Ford F-1 truck, 1948, a beauty. The first in the F-Series."

"I'm interested."

"I'll see what I can find."

I'll study the market, too. So, don't try to rip me off.

"Stop by the dealership any ol' time. I'm there more than ever now, since I had to kick my CFO's butt out the door."

Aaron's eyes widened. "What happened?"

Dale crossed his arms. "Oh, he and I didn't see eye to eye on the books."

Aaron walked out into the hallway. *I wonder what he meant by that.*

Late afternoon, Aaron opened the door of a patient room and stopped in the doorway.

"Rachel. From the hospital, right? I visited your office a few weeks ago and you helped me with medical information about the Taggett family."

She nodded. "You remember me." She was seated in a chair along the wall.

Aaron closed the door. "What can I do for you today?"

Rachel held out her right hand. "Something bit me on my hand a couple of days ago. Do you think it's a spider bite?"

Aaron examined her skin and saw a small red lesion surrounded by mild swelling on the back of her hand. "It looks like you're having a local allergic reaction to an insect bite. It doesn't appear to be one of the spider bites that we worry about."

Rachel sighed. "Good."

"Just put cool compresses on the bite off and on and take Benadryl, and elevate your hand when you can. You should be fine."

Rachel stood and smiled at Aaron. "Thank you."

He hesitated before he opened the door for her. *I remember those dimples.*

"How's the hospital business?" he said.

"Challenging, as always." She stopped and looked up at him. "I was wondering . . ."

"Yes?"

She looked away. "Oh, it's nothing."

Aaron watched her walk out. *And, I remember those bright green eyes.*

He was smiling after her when the clinic door burst open. Constable Greevy stumbled into the waiting room.

"Doc, you've got to help me." His eyes were wide.

"What's happened?" Aaron said.

"I haven't slept in days. I think Wanda's voodoo curse is driving me batty."

Stella walked over to him and held up her hand. "Wait a minute. Remember, people can get sick from worrying about a voodoo curse and not from any real effect of the curse itself."

Aaron nodded. "That makes sense. You're just stressing yourself over that curse."

"Well, that may be, but I'm not taking any chances." Keller pulled a doll out of his pocket. "I made a felt poppet to break the curse." He held up a white doll with eyes and a smile painted on its face. Irregular lumps distorted the body of the doll.

"You put something inside it?" Stella said.

"Black onyx and coffee grounds. They help the poppet break the curse on me." He read from a sheet of paper. "But I need vetivert herb to put in the poppet, and patchouli oil, garlic powder, and a purple candle. It says to break a curse once and for all, I should write my name on a purple candle, and pour the oil over the candle and garlic powder over the poppet, then let the candle burn all the way down." He looked up at Aaron. "Do you know anything about this stuff? Can you prescribe any of it for me?"

Stella shook her head. "You don't need a prescription. You can usually find those things online or in a store that sells herbs and essential oils."

"Okay, then. That's my next stop. Wish me luck." Keller started for the door and then turned to Aaron. "Heard anything from your machete guy?"

"Don't worry. That's all behind me now."

Keller cocked his head. "Is that so? Want to tell me about it?"

"Not especially. It's all good."

Keller stared at Aaron, and then shook his head. "All right. One less thing for me to worry about. We haven't found him anyway." He pushed the door open and left.

At the end of their workday, Stella locked the front door and stood outside with Aaron.

He touched her shoulder. "Are you not feeling well? You look down."

"I'm trying to solve a mystery."

"A mystery? What—"

Stella held up her hand. "Don't ask." She walked away.

Aaron put his hand to his eyes. He had felt dizzy spells off and on all day.

Aaron stood outside his house and inspected the nearby trees for the hooting owl. *Hello up there. I haven't heard you for a while.*

He fired up his Volvo. *I'm in need of my happy hour wine, especially with all the craziness around here. Wine always smooths me out.*

Aaron spotted Red at the corner of the bar, swirling his brandy. He sat beside him and ordered a tomato and avocado salad and cabernet wine. "Is everything all right?" Aaron said.

Red sipped his brandy. "I imagine."

Aaron sampled his wine and nodded his approval to the bartender.

"Are you settling in here okay?" Red said.

"I'm not sure. I'm still trying to get my bearings."

"Some things take time."

Aaron sighed. "You may be right." He drank from his wine glass and turned to Red. "I hope you don't mind me asking, but what did you do after the war?"

"I went to college."

"What was your major?"

"Biology."

Aaron nodded. "That was my major, too. So what did you do with a biology degree?"

Red smiled at Aaron. "Same as you."

"You went to medical school?"

"Yes, I did."

"What kind of doctor were you?"

Red stared at his brandy. "Psychiatrist."

"That must have been a challenging career."

"It was."

"I've met only a couple of psychiatrists. Did you do office and hospital practice?"

"I did just about everything. I got heavy into forensics in the last years. Most of the lawyers and judges that deal with mental health in these parts know me pretty well."

Aaron leaned toward him. "We've needed forensics around here recently. I've just met my first serial killer."

Red turned to him. "Welcome to the club."

Aaron raised his eyebrows. "Sure, I imagine in forensics, you dealt a lot with the work of crazy murderers."

Red stopped swirling his brandy. His head dropped and he closed his eyes.

Aaron looked down and took a bite of salad. *Oh, boy. I touched a raw nerve.*

Aaron glanced at Red a few times out of the corner of his eye. Red's eyes were closed.

After several minutes, Red lifted his head and looked ahead of him. "I went out in a bad way. There was a patient I had treated for years. His family and I were friends. One day, he was confiding in me his thoughts and fantasies. It was a typical session, part of his usual therapy." Red shook his head. "I didn't catch on to one particular fantasy he talked about. At the time, it didn't seem any different from the way his mind always worked. But as it turned out, it was different."

"What happened?"

"He told me he dreamed about killing people, and he heard voices that commanded him to murder. That was a fantasy he often had. We'd work through it over time in therapy and with medication. Only this time, he didn't let go of it." Red closed his eyes. "Two days after the last session, he shot and killed everyone in his family."

Aaron put down his fork. "How could anyone have prevented that? How's a psychiatrist to know?"

"It's hard. I keep going over it. I don't know if I did anything wrong." Red rubbed his forehead. "I just don't know, but I think I may have missed something, a warning signal. Maybe my guard was down."

"When did it happen?"

"A few years ago. I retired a year later." Red sighed. "It wasn't the same after that. I wasn't the same." He swallowed the last drop of brandy. "No one is perfect. But doctors like us aren't supposed to make mistakes."

Aaron snorted. "How well do I know that."

"When they do, they have a veneer, a shell, that usually shields them from the pain." Red pushed his chair back. "My shell didn't protect me that time." He stood and put a shaky hand on Aaron's shoulder. "Thanks for listening."

Red hesitated on his way out and looked back at Aaron. He waved his hand and gave a slight nod, and then he was gone.

Chapter 40

Aaron stopped as he was about to open the front door of his clinic. No birds were chirping this morning, and the air was heavy and still. He turned as he heard a faint moaning behind him.

It came from deep within the Big Thicket forest across the road. *It's the trees,* Aaron thought. *And Race Taggett is in there, somewhere.*

A chill shot down his spine. He opened the door and hurried inside.

Stella looked up from behind the registration counter. "Is anything wrong? Your eyes are bloodshot."

Aaron took a few deep breaths. "This has been a rough couple of weeks for me."

Later in the morning, Stella directed Preston Benningham into a patient room. He was no longer wearing the shoulder sling.

Stella paused at the door, her lips taut. "Can I talk with you before you leave?"

Preston nodded. "Sure."

Stella moved away as Aaron walked into the room. "How's the shoulder?"

"It's getting better."

Aaron examined Preston and the shoulder injury. "You do look different somehow."

"I've been to all my support sessions. I'm going to kick this addiction thing."

"I think you can."

"I'm lucky to be alive. To have parents like I do. I'm not going to blow it this time."

Aaron touched his arm. "I believe you."

A smile covered Preston's face. "Dad's taking me deer hunting."

Aaron gave him a thumbs-up.

Preston slid down from the table and walked toward the door. He stopped and turned to Aaron, his eyes moistened with tears. "Rocky died for me. He tried to help me. I think about him all the time."

"Rocky had a good heart."

"I'll never forget the way his face looked when they lifted him into the ambulance."

"What about his face?"

"He was smiling."

Aaron sighed. "That's a good memory. He was already in a better place."

Preston stopped as he walked toward the front door of the clinic. Stella stared at him from a chair behind the registration counter.

He turned to her. "You wanted to talk to me?"

Stella nodded. She held a tissue over her eyes.

Preston walked up to the counter. "Are you okay?"

Stella's voice croaked. "Did you shoot someone, about two years ago?"

Preston hesitated. "I . . . I don't think so. My mind is hazy about that night. I remember hearing some gunshots. I think I might have shot at someone. Why?"

"Were you in town, nearby?"

"I believe I was. I remember I was in bad shape that night."

"You needed drugs."

"Yeah, I did, and I didn't trust the dealer."

"Which is why you had a gun."

Preston nodded.

"Did you talk to the police?"

Preston shook his head. "No. Not that I remember."

"Did you read about the shooting later? Or did your father tell you anything about it?"

"He asked me a lot of questions. Then he put me in rehab."

Stella sighed and stood up. "Okay."

Preston walked out of the clinic, frowning. *Sometimes I get the feeling that my father was there with me.*

Chapter 41

"Gee whiz, my eyes really are bloodshot." Aaron stared into a mirror later that morning. "It's got to be lack of sleep."

He walked down the hallway to see a patient, passing by a room with an open door. Out of the corner of his eye, he caught a glimpse of a woman sitting on the edge of the examination table with long, white hair falling over her shoulders.

I guess I'll see her after this next patient.

Stella stopped Aaron in the hall. "You'll hardly recognize this guy. It's Sid Taggett, just recovered from his thallium poisoning."

Aaron opened the door and his jaw dropped. "Sid, is it really you?"

"It's really me, Doc. I wanted you to see the new Sid."

"You look great."

"I feel so much better. I've got my old body back, most of it anyway."

"Are you having any problems?"

Sid glanced down at his legs. "Just this burning pain in my legs, but the medicine makes it better."

"Good."

"I'm eating real food again."

"You're gaining weight."

Sid shook his head. "I can't believe I almost died. Wanda had me fooled real good."

"She had everyone fooled."

"It's strange. There are holes in my memory over the last six months. It's like part of my life was erased."

"You don't need to remember most of it."

"I remember you came to see me. Thanks."

A warm flush coursed through Aaron's body. "It's what I'm here for."

"I hope I never see her again for the rest of my life," Sid said.

"She'll be in the state hospital for a while."

"I hope until she dies. No one deserves her."

"She might improve with medication."

"It doesn't matter. I could never trust her anymore."

"Even if she was back to the old Wanda, like when you first met her?"

Sid shook his head. "It was her eyes. They turned pure evil. It gives me chills thinking about those eyes." He looked down. "Besides, she wouldn't trust me either. I wasn't the most faithful husband in the world."

Sid cocked his head. "Can you believe she even tried to voodoo curse me?"

Aaron chuckled. "I don't think she was seriously into the voodoo religion. I'm sure that was just one of her delusions."

"She went off her rocker, all right."

"What about Race?" Aaron said.

Sid snorted. "I heard about him. The police questioned me. He always was a wild one, but I had no idea he was that sick in the head."

"He's disappeared. No one has seen him."

"I'm sure he's somewhere in the Big Thicket. He told me before that he likes it in there. He's got special places where he can hide out, and no one can find him."

"No one's found him yet."

Sid hopped off the table. "Well, good luck with that. I'm moving to Nevada. I have a brother there."

"Are you selling your house?"

"I'm gonna try to. With what's happened, I can't stay around here."

Aaron nodded. "I don't blame you."

"Why don't you come to visit me after I settle in? Las Vegas has the National Finals Rodeo every year. We could go. It would be great fun."

Aaron shook Sid's hand. "Count me in."

He watched Sid walk out and then turned into the adjoining patient room. He stopped and scanned the room. No one was there; the woman with the white hair was gone. *I guess she couldn't wait.*

Aaron approached Stella in the registration area. "What happened to the lady in Room Two? Did she leave?"

Stella studied the computer screen. "I don't see any female patients scheduled for this time." She turned to Aaron and shrugged her shoulders. "Maybe she got an emergency call and had to go."

Later that afternoon, Stella signaled to Aaron. "A nurse from the hospital is on the phone. She has a question."

He walked to the phone. "Hello."

"Dr. Rovsing, this . . . this is Rachel. I was at your clinic yesterday."

Aaron nodded. *Rachel, with the dimples and bright green eyes.*

"Well, hello again. How is your hand?" he said.

"It's fine. No problems."

"I'm glad to hear that."

"I'm . . . I'm sorry to bother you, but I thought I'd ask if you're coming to the hospital social tonight."

"I'd forgotten about that, and you're not bothering me at all. I'll be there." Aaron grinned and sat down. "Can I look for you?"

"Please do. I'll save you a seat."

Aaron stood outside with Stella as she locked up the clinic. She hesitated at the door and looked up at Aaron.

"Are you okay?" Aaron said.

"I have to talk to Brad Benningham, Preston's father. Can you come with me to his house? I need your help."

"Sure. What's this about?"

"I'm not one hundred percent sure, but I think Preston might be the one who shot my son two years ago."

Aaron stepped back. "Preston? Oh, no."

"I want to find out for myself, but I may lose it. I need you there."

Aaron followed Stella's car to Brad's mansion.

Stella's finger twitched as she rang the front doorbell. In less than a minute, Myra swung the door open.

"Hi. An unexpected surprise," Myra said.

"Is Brad here?" Stella said.

"He'll be home in a few minutes. He's probably on his way home now."

"Can we come in?"

"Sure." Myra stepped back and directed Stella and Aaron to the living room chairs and couches.

"Is this about our conversation a few days ago, after church?" Myra said.

Stella crossed her arms. "If you don't mind."

Myra straightened as the doorbell chimed again.

"That's probably Keller Greevy," Stella said. "I talked to him about this and asked him to come."

"Wow, this is getting serious," Myra said with a giggle. She led Keller to the living room and then sat down near Stella. Keller remained standing with arms crossed. His ear and neck wounds were covered with small Band-Aids.

Interesting, Aaron thought. *Brad told me he's kept Preston out of jail because of an "understanding" he has with the law, and on our fishing trip, Dale*

McCorkindale told me that Keller can be bribed. And now, these guys will stand face to face.

Myra looked up at Keller. "Stella seems concerned that my son, Preston, shot his gun in town two years ago. Is that why you're here?"

"Yes, ma'am."

"I'm pretty sure I heard that Preston did shoot his gun. I think he was trying to get drugs and something went wrong. Brad took him to rehab the next day."

"Did the police investigate?" Stella said.

Keller nodded. "There was an investigation."

"I don't think anyone was actually hurt," Myra said. "We'd have heard about that, right? If someone had been hurt?"

Aaron heard noises from the back of the house.

"Brad's home. I'll tell him you're here." Myra stood and walked out of the living room.

Aaron heard indistinct conversation, and then Brad's voice was louder.

Brad's boots clomped into the living room. "What the hell is going on here?"

Stella stood and glared at him. "About two years ago, Preston shot his gun in town one night. He wanted drugs."

"So what? There were several gunshots that night. Nothing happened. I sent him to rehab the next day."

"Two years ago, my son was shot and killed, in town, at night." Her lips quivered.

"Oh, my," Myra said, her hands over her temples.

Brad stood facing Stella. He put his hands on his hips. "Are you suggesting that Preston shot your son?"

Stella looked down. Her eyelids were wet. "I don't know what I'm suggesting. I just want to know why my son died."

"It was on the news. Keller here looked into it. They couldn't trace any reason for your son's death. It was a shootout. The reporters said it was a drug deal gone bad."

"I'd like to see if the bullet that killed my son—"

"Hold on a minute. You can't drag all that up now."

Stella stomped her foot. "I can, and I will."

Brad glared at Keller. "This has got to stop here." He pointed toward the floor.

Keller met his stare for a few seconds, and then shook his head. "I don't think so." He turned to Stella. "I'll reopen the case."

Way to go, Keller, Aaron thought.

Brad clenched his fists and snorted at Keller, who didn't flinch or blink.

Brad's shoulders drooped, and he plopped down on a couch. He motioned to Stella. "Please sit down."

Brad leaned back on the couch. His head was bowed, and his hands were clasped across his waist. Stella sat down in her chair.

No one spoke for several minutes. Brad shook his head several times.

Stella broke the silence. "I want to know how my son died. I want justice for him."

Brad sighed and looked up. "Justice. Everyone wants justice. For so long, I've wanted a just life for my only son. We're almost there now, almost. It's the closest we've been in a long time to a decent future for him."

Brad stood and paced around the room. "Preston doesn't even remember that night. He's been living in hell these last few years." He stopped and took a deep breath. "Then Rocky died in his arms. It's like he's got a new life now."

He turned to Stella. "I don't think he could take it. He'd go right back in the gutter, back to that addiction hell." Myra frowned and walked over to Brad.

Everyone looked up as Preston jogged into the living room. He held his cell phone up in front of him. "Mom, Dad, I got the call. They hired me."

He ran up between Brad and Myra and draped his arms over their shoulders. "I got the job." A grin spread across his flushed face.

"Outstanding," Brad said, pumping his fist. "This is great news."

Myra put her hand to her mouth and squealed.

Preston glanced around at Aaron, Stella, and Keller. "I'm sorry. Did I interrupt something?"

Stella stared at the family embrace. Brad smiled at his son and held his fist in the air. Myra still had her hand over her mouth, and her eyes were teary.

Stella sighed. "We were just hashing out old stories."

Preston cocked his head. "Is this about that time when I might've shot my—"

Stella stood up. "Yes, it is. That shot might've hurt someone. It's possible you shot my son."

Preston dropped to his knees, his hands over his ears. "Oh, God. I've always had a feeling something bad happened that night." He moaned and began to sob. Myra put her hands on his shoulders.

This isn't going well, Aaron thought. He watched as Brad strolled over to Keller and lowered his voice. "Let's you and I talk in private about this. I think we can come to an understanding. Come with me." Brad turned around.

Keller didn't move. "No. No more of that. I'm reopening the case."

Brad stiffened and leaned back to Keller. "I can make it worth—"

"I said I'm reopening the case."

Brad's face tightened. "Damn."

All eyes turned to Preston, who stood straight and faced Brad and Keller. "I'm okay, I'm okay." Preston wiped his eyes. "I want to know what happened."

Aaron's jaw dropped. *Good for you, Preston.*

Preston nodded. "Don't worry about me. I can take it now, wherever it leads."

Stella turned to Aaron. "Let's go."

She stopped outside at her car.

"Maybe Keller can find out the truth now," Aaron said.

"I think I know the truth, but . . ." She sighed.

"But what?" Aaron said.

"Punishing Preston won't bring my son back."

"No, but you might feel better knowing for sure."

Her eyes were moist. "I wonder if I can ever forgive. To escape this . . . pain, this misery." She looked at Aaron. "Can forgiveness help me do that?"

Aaron took a deep breath of the muggy air. "I don't know."

During Aaron's drive to a local country club that evening, the car radio blared a series of country songs. He sang along with the lyrics to several of them.

He parked in front of the club, stepped out of his Volvo, and looked over the cars in the parking lot. *These hospital socials must be popular.*

Aaron walked through the front entrance and was directed to a ballroom filled with small square tables covered with white tablecloths. At one end of the room, long tables displayed buffet food in silver chafing dishes identified by labels. People were milling about engaged in shifting two or three-person conversations. Many cradled wine or beer or cocktails.

Aaron scanned the room and spotted Rachel sitting in a chair at one of the small tables. She waved at him and he strolled toward her table.

As she came into sharper view, he caught his breath. She wore a silky black dress, which hugged her lean figure like a gift wrap.

Aaron's heart pounded faster as he pulled a chair out and sat down. He couldn't suppress a broad grin. "Hello again."

"It's great to see you," she said.

Now I know why cowboys sing about angel eyes, he thought.

Rachel stood. "Let me show you the buffet. The food is usually good."

They brought back plates heaped with steaming vegetables, chicken, and fish.

Aaron and Rachel chatted for the next hour. They mostly discussed hospital issues, and she pointed out various doctors, nurses, and administrators in the room. After dinner, the hospital CEO gave a short presentation on future plans for improvement.

"Who's that tall guy in the expensive suit standing in the corner?" Aaron said.

She glanced over at a man who was fond of smoothing his hair. "That's Dr. Sterling, the head of orthopedics."

"He's been alone in that same spot for a while."

"He's a respected surgeon here, but I don't think he's very popular. I know he's turned off more than one female in this room. I hear he thinks all women are attracted to him."

Aaron chuckled. "Some doctors get inflated egos."

At one point, Aaron looked around at the other tables. "People are leaving." He turned to Rachel. "Is it already time to go?"

Rachel smiled. "How time flies."

Aaron took a deep breath and pulled his cell phone from his pocket. "I hope you don't mind, but you don't have to call me at my office—"

Rachel nodded. "Yes. Let's exchange numbers."

After the social, Aaron pulled into his garage and sat in the car for several minutes letting his thoughts flow.

He slapped the dashboard with his palm, jumped out, and hopped up and down, pumping his arms.

Go for it, dude. He pulled out his phone and searched his contact list.

"Hello?" a woman's voice said.

"Rachel, it's me, Aaron."

"Well, hi. Is everything okay?"

"Everything is terrific. I wanted to tell you it was great seeing you tonight."

"I feel the same way."

"Do you want to go on a dinner date Saturday?" He held his breath.

"Yes, I'd love to."

Aaron exhaled. "Wonderful. I'll pick you up about six o'clock? Is that all right?"

"Six o'clock is fine." Her voice softened. "I need to let you know something."

"Sure." *Oh, no. Here we go,* Aaron thought.

"I like animals. I have lots of animals in my house."

"Lots of animals?"

"I help rehabilitate injured and abused animals."

Aaron smiled. "I think that's awesome."

Chapter 42

Aaron switched on a light in his kitchen and stopped in mid-stride. Curtains fluttered near the back door, and he heard a noise from another room.

Someone is in here.

He held his breath as he peered around a corner of the wall toward his bedroom. He saw a flash and lurched back as a gunshot rang out.

His heart racing, Aaron sprinted to the garage, punched the garage door control button, and rolled out under the rising door.

On his hands and knees, Aaron saw a man running across his front yard with a bag under one arm and waving at an approaching van. In his waving hand was a gun. As the van screeched to a stop, the man jumped in through the rear door.

Flashing lights and a siren erupted at the end of Aaron's street, and a police car sped toward the van. Aaron trotted to the street as the van burned rubber down the road ahead of the police car. He watched the two vehicles squeal into sharp turns at the nearby intersecting road.

Aaron's mouth gaped open at the scene before him, which seemed to play out in slow motion. Tipping over onto its left tires, the van lost stability and slammed down on its left side. Sparks flew up from the pavement as the van skidded down the road with a horrific shriek and crashed into a light pole. Aaron ran back to his car and drove to the area of the wreck.

Constable Keller Greevy pulled a man out of the rear of the van. "Take a look at him, Doc," he said as Aaron jogged over to them. "I'll check on the driver and anyone else in the van."

Keller held his gun in front of him as he crept toward the front of the van. He stopped and looked back at Aaron. "Don't come too close. I think it's on fire."

Aaron backpedaled as he saw flames shooting out of a window of the van and held up his hand toward Keller. "Maybe we should wait for the firefighters."

Keller crept back toward the rear of the van. Smoke billowed from the rear doors. "I don't know if I can get back in—"

Aaron jumped as the van exploded, knocking Keller off his feet and onto his back. After several seconds, he rolled over and crawled back to Aaron.

"Are you all right?" Aaron said. "Let me check you over."

Keller managed to stand upright, his eyes wide open. "That was close." He checked out his body parts. "I guess I should've waited."

"Does anything hurt? I don't see any burns or gashes."

"I'm okay, just a little shook up."

Aaron wiped off Keller's back. "You've got some scrapes back here. You're lucky; I don't smell any burned clothing."

Keller pointed to the man on the street. "How's he doing?"

"I think his neck is broken. Anyway, he's dead."

"Let's stand farther away from the fire." Keller called the fire department and EMS.

He exited his phone and stepped closer to Aaron. "These guys had a string of robberies going. One guy would rob a house, and the van would pull up just in time to pick up the loot."

"Do you know them?"

Keller looked at the prostrate man lying on the ground. "I've seen him. He was a drug dealer and probably a user, too."

Aaron's stomach tightened as he walked over to the inert body. He recognized the clothing and pointed at the man. "He shot at me."

An image of his smiling parents flashed into his mind, followed by a vision of a drugged robber standing with a gun over their bloody dead bodies. His head swam and he gasped for air, then his vision went black.

Aaron felt arms around his waist, and he was pulled back.

"Doc, snap out of it."

Aaron blinked and put his hand to his forehead. "What happened?"

Keller released his grip. "You started yelling and kicking the guy. If he wasn't dead before, he sure is now. It even hurt me to watch, and I'm hurting more than enough already."

Aaron pulled a handkerchief from his pocket and wiped sweat from his eyes and off his face.

Keller leaned toward him. "It must've been something real personal."

Aaron took a deep breath and looked up at the sky. "Yeah. It was."

"Are you okay?"

"I'm better now, thanks."

A fire truck and an ambulance arrived, and Aaron and Keller watched as the firefighters doused the fire and the paramedics examined the victims.

Aaron turned to Keller. "What about Wanda's voodoo curse on you? Did the poppet work?"

Keller grinned. "Like a charm. There's no curse on me now."

One of the medics walked over to Keller. "I don't think we need to transport them to the hospital. CPR won't help. They're both dead, one traumatic cardiac arrest and the driver burnt to a crisp."

"I'll call the ME," Keller said.

"How did you happen to be right behind the van?" Aaron said.

"We got a call that a robbery was going down in your neighborhood."

"One of my neighbors called? That's interesting. Our houses aren't that close together, and trees block the views. I wonder how they knew?"

"I don't think the caller was one of the neighbors on your street."

Aaron cocked his head. "Who was it then?"

"He didn't leave his name, but the dispatcher said it sounded like Grant Belkin, the rancher behind you."

****

Grant Belkin sat at his kitchen table and spoke to an empty chair. "Your hair looks good today. Soft and bright."

Grant sighed and nodded. "I know I look stressed. A lot has been happenin' around here. Things that needed to happen."

He listened for several seconds.

"Yeah, I know. The doctor is havin' a rough time."

Chapter 43

Aaron skipped around puddles in the parking area as he caught up with Stella outside the front door of the clinic Wednesday morning.

"How did you sleep last night?"

Stella sighed. "Not well."

She stopped inside the door. "What happened to your hand?"

Aaron looked at the bandages on his right palm. "I surprised a robber in my house last night. He had a gun, and I scraped my hand while I was crawling out of my garage to get away."

"Are you okay?"

"I'm not hurt. They're just abrasions."

"Did the robber steal anything?"

"Not much. An old watch and some money I'd left out on my bathroom counter. I don't think he'd been inside for very long."

"So, he got away?"

Aaron shook his head. "No, he didn't. He died when his getaway van crashed."

Stella's eyes widened. "I heard about that on the news. What a night you had."

"He shot at me. I'm lucky he missed. I felt the bullet whiz by my ear."

"Honey, with all that's been happening to you lately, you must have a guardian angel."

Aaron nodded and looked up. "I think I do."

Later that morning, Aaron strutted down the hall toward a patient room.

"Okay, Doc," Stella said. "What's up with you? Since you got here today, you've been acting like a cowboy who's just lassoed a cowgirl."

Aaron stopped and smiled. "Is it that obvious?"

"Something has perked you up."

"I think I'm in cowgirl heaven."

"Is it anyone in particular? Maybe that nice lady who called a few days ago?"

"You're sharp."

"A woman knows when love is in the air."

"Love?" He scratched his chin. "I don't know."

"You're blushing, so it must be love."

Aaron smiled. "We'll see."

Aaron drove to a nearby store in the early evening to pick up toothpaste, shaving cream, and a few other personal necessities, and then he guided his car through a drizzling rain to his happy hour place. After shaking water from his umbrella at the front door, he entered the bar and looked for Red, but the corner chairs were empty.

Aaron sat down in his usual place.

"Did you hear about Red?" the bartender said.

"No. What about him?"

"He died in his sleep two nights ago. His son flew in and stopped by here yesterday."

Aaron shook his head. "That's too bad. I was just getting to know him. I'll sure miss him."

"So will all of us. His son said Red used to talk about our bar all the time."

"I know he liked it here."

They looked at Red's empty space.

"We're thinking about putting a plaque on the chair, in memory of him," the bartender said.

"That's a great idea. I'll contribute to that."

"Thanks. His son asked about you. I think Red really liked your company."

Aaron sipped his cabernet and sat in silence at the bar.

So maybe Red's shell didn't protect him. I guess he never got over that misdiagnosis, that patient of his who went berserk and killed his own family.

Aaron looked down and sighed. *I wonder how my shell is doing.*

He nodded and pounded his thigh with his fist.

I'm going to do my best with this job, even if it kills me.

He stayed for several hours, thinking of Red and the parade of recent strange events in East Texas.

Steven Gossington

It's like I'm in the twilight zone.

Chapter 44

Stella knocked on Aaron's office door the next morning. "Marley Brighton is here. She'd like a prescription refill for Forrester."

"I'll be right out."

Aaron scanned the last page of a patient's medical record and walked out into the hallway. He saw Marley and cleared his throat. "Good afternoon. How's Forrester?"

"He's adjusting. It's hard, day by day."

"I can only imagine."

"I'm sorry to bother you, but can you refill this prescription for him? I figured since I was in the neighborhood . . ."

Aaron looked at the pill bottle. It had contained a muscle relaxant. "Sure, no problem."

Marley leaned in closer to him. "I'm sorry it didn't work out between us."

Aaron shrugged his shoulders. "It wasn't meant to be." *I'm already moving on,* he thought.

He wrote a prescription for a muscle relaxant and handed it to Marley.

"Forrester and I appreciate this." She smiled at him and put the prescription in her purse. "And thanks again for helping out with the Taggett family."

"I feel good about that, but there's still a big question mark: Race." Aaron sighed. "I can't figure him."

Marley's eyes were bright like lasers. "You'll be fine."

Aaron looked down. *I wish I could be sure of that.*

Just after Marley left, a tall man walked through the front door of the clinic.

"Is Dr. Rovsing here?" he said to Juliana at the registration desk.

"Yes. Who shall I say wants to see him?"

"I'm Red Relford's son."

"Is Mr. Relford one of our patients?"

"No. He was a friend of Dr. Rovsing's. He died three days ago."

"I'm so sorry. Wait here and I'll let him know."

A few minutes later, Aaron followed Juliana to the waiting area.

"I'm happy to meet you," Aaron said as the two men shook hands.

"Same here. Thanks for being a good friend for Dad. He talked about you."

Aaron nodded. "I enjoyed my evenings with him at the bar. I'll miss him."

"He lived a long, good life. I wish I could've seen him more. My job keeps me in Oregon."

"He told me stories about his life, his experiences. I enjoyed those stories. I'll never forget them."

"He was a psychiatrist. He helped a lot of people."

"I'm sure he did." Aaron put his hand on the man's shoulder. "He had a kindness about him."

"He was happy with his work, until the last few years of his practice." He sighed and looked down. "We were close to this family, and my dad treated one of the sons. One day, the son flipped out and killed everyone in the family. Dad was never the same after that. He always felt he should've done something."

"Red told me about that. I'm sorry that happened to him. Unfortunately, doctors can't predict everything."

"We kept telling him that. Anyway, I'm glad he met you. He seemed happier in the last few weeks."

Aaron smiled. "Thanks for letting me know."

Red's son pulled an envelope from his pocket. "He wrote you a letter. I guess he might've known he was dying."

Aaron opened the envelope and smiled as he scanned the letter. "I'll keep this letter safe."

"He'll be cremated. He wants you and me to spread his ashes in the Big Thicket."

"Interesting. He never talked to me about that. Ashes in the Big Thicket."

"Don't you think it's a strange request? I mean, I hear that it's a weird place."

"You heard right."

"Why would he want his ashes in there?"

Aaron stared out the front window across the road at the trees in the Big Thicket. "Maybe he felt it would be a good place to dispose of the baggage he left behind."

"Like bad memories?"

Aaron nodded. "That's a thought." He contemplated the trees swaying in the breeze.

Red's son turned to Aaron. "Oh, one more favor. I wonder if you could take his dog."

Aaron laughed. "Now that you mention it, I've been thinking about getting a dog. Sure, I'll take him."

Aaron walked into a patient room, and a woman extended her hand. "I'm Sandra Bogarty. My son is Buck."

"I remember Buck. Did his hand heal?"

"Oh, yes. That's all fine." She looked down. "He wrecked his hot rod a week ago."

"Is he okay?"

"No bad injuries, but other boys were in the car, and they told me what happened. One of them was on the ground and not breathing at first."

"They were ejected? Is everyone all right now?"

"Yes, thank goodness, but the wreck really affected Buck. He won't come out of his bedroom. He barely eats at all, and he won't talk to me."

"It sounds like the experience traumatized him emotionally."

She massaged her temple. "He's never been like this. He won't even see his friends when they come over. Should I worry about him?"

"Maybe I can come over and talk with him."

"Oh, thank you. I would so appreciate it if you did."

She and Aaron worked out a time for his visit to Buck.

A man sat in a chair in the hallway.

Aaron saw him and stopped. "Tucker Boudreaux. Is it you today?"

Tucker stood and approached Aaron. "It sure is." His short hair was combed and he wore a dress shirt.

Aaron smiled. "You're looking well."

"I feel good. Sometimes I feel even better when I don't take my medicine, but everyone says the pills help me."

"Yes, they do. Please remember that."

"I saw you in the store yesterday, and I had an idea about you."

Here we go, Aaron thought.

"You looked so happy. A thought came into my head: if it's a *fille,* a girl, then you should go for it."

Aaron grinned and put his hands on Tucker's shoulders. "I might just do that."

"Trust me. I can tell. You won't be sorry."

"That's right. Sometimes you can predict things."

Tucker nodded. "And when I do, you'd best pay attention."

In the lounge, Aaron poured coffee into his and Stella's cups. "This has been a crazy month," he said.

Stella sipped from her cup. "That's a good word for it. Crazy people have been a challenge to you since you got here. Do you think you attract them?"

Aaron laughed. "Maybe I do."

They walked out into the hall, and Stella turned to him. "Speaking of this crazy month, it seems that we really do have more than our fair share of addiction and mental illness in this town. What do you think?"

"It's a problem everywhere, not just here."

Stella furrowed her brow. "Are you sure about that?"

Aaron nodded. "There aren't enough behavioral health specialists in this country, and even if there were, we don't have cures for every mind gone haywire."

Stella shook her head. "What a world. Maybe all of us will end up someday in the Big Thicket, right along with Race Taggett."

Aaron frowned. *Is that my fate?*

"By the way, I wonder if Keller still feels Wanda's voodoo curse," Stella said.

"He told me his poppet broke the spell."

Stella chuckled. "Maybe it did, but what's important is that he believes the curse is gone."

After their workday, Stella held on to Aaron's elbow and escorted him into the parking area. "You've got that look in your eyes. Is there a romantic weekend ahead?"

"I hope so. I've got my best boots on," Aaron said.

Stella laughed. "Good luck. I'll be cheering for you, cowboy."

Back home, Aaron sat at his desk and unfolded the letter from Red Relford: "It was nice chatting with you, Aaron. You helped me reconnect with good memories. I've been thinking about the Great War. You remind me of a sergeant I served with. A good man, like you. The world needs more good people."

Aaron sat back in his chair and looked up at the ceiling. *Thanks, Red, I needed that.*

Chapter 45

With windows down and radio blaring, Aaron sped to Rachel's house early Saturday evening. She lived out in the country, about ten miles from Aaron's town, on the edge of the Big Thicket. He passed only one other house on her road, about one-half mile back.

Aaron hopped out of his car humming a song and turned around in a circle. *I don't see any other houses.*

Rachel walked out onto her front porch and waved. "I'm kind of isolated way out here."

"It's a beautiful area."

"Do you want to have a look around?"

Aaron nodded. "Sure." He stepped up to the porch and followed her into the living room. *It smells like a vet's office.*

She led him back through her kitchen and into a family room. Two dogs barked at him from behind a fence, and a few cats roamed in other areas of the spacious room.

"I have some wild things outside." She led Aaron out the back door and up to a tall fence. "Take a look around the yard. A couple of raccoons might be wandering about."

They walked to one side of the fence. She pointed to a section of the yard with a caged-in area. "There's a young bald eagle in the aviary part."

"This is impressive. It's your own little private zoo. Where do you get these animals?"

"From the rehabilitation group I belong to. I'm trained and licensed to care for certain wild mammals and birds of prey. They're usually found injured in the Big Thicket and need a place to rest and recover."

"Do you handle them and get close to them?"

"Not too close. You have to maintain your distance. If they become accustomed to humans, they might not last long back in the wild."

"Raccoons can carry rabies, but I'll bet you knew that."

"Don't worry. I got my shots. I'm safe."

Rachel's cell phone rang as they walked back into the house.

She checked the caller ID and looked at Aaron. "It's my sister. I'd better take the call."

Aaron waved his hand. "No problem." They stood in the kitchen.

"Hello, Diana . . . Dad wandered away? . . . Three hours? . . . A barn? . . ." Rachel put a hand to her forehead. She ended the call and Aaron waited.

"My father is in a nursing home about one hour from here. He's got dementia and it's worsening. This is the first time he's wandered off." She took a deep breath. "Thank heavens they found him in a barn, and not in the middle of a street somewhere. He was curled up asleep in the hay."

"They may need to move him to a more secure area," Aaron said.

"That's what their plan is." Rachel sighed. "He worked on a farm as a young boy. Maybe he still has those memories of his past, but he doesn't know me or my sister most of the time now."

"It's painful to watch that happen to someone."

Rachel nodded. "He was such an active, intelligent man. He rarely got sick."

"Maybe someday we'll have an effective treatment or prevention for dementia. Everyone fears that fate in their final years."

"I hope my end is quick and painless."

They walked outside. "Are you still up for dinner?" Aaron said.

"Yes. It'll lift my spirits."

Aaron started the car, but then hesitated. "I made reservations at a steak place. Is that okay?"

Rachel smiled. "Sure. I'm looking forward to it."

Aaron's car radio was on low volume in the background.

"Do you like country music?" Rachel said.

Aaron recognized the song and turned up the volume. "I'm getting into it. I have a list of my favorite country songs in my head."

Rachel laughed. "That's wonderful. I've been a country music fan since I was a young girl."

A wave of warmth coursed through Aaron's body. *Everything is good.*

At the restaurant, they strolled into dim lighting and muted music and were ushered to cushioned chairs at a table for two.

"When did you get interested in helping injured animals?" Aaron said.

"One of my college biology professors was into animal rehab as a hobby. We'd visit her home, and she'd teach us about it." Rachel touched his hand. "I hope you like animals."

Aaron smiled and grabbed her hand. "Have no fear. I do."

"Then all is well."

Rachel ordered merlot and Aaron his cabernet.

"How long have you worked at the hospital?" Aaron said.

"Almost six years. I graduated from nursing school eight years ago, so I've been around here most of my career so far."

"I'm sure you see a lot of pathology in that hospital."

"Yes, we do."

Rachel ordered Steak Diane, and Aaron grilled shrimp. After the server walked away, Rachel looked up. "Speaking of pathology, whatever happened to that strange family you were asking me about?"

"The Taggetts. Wanda is in a psychiatric hospital for a long stay. She was poisoning her husband, Sid. He was treated and he's much better now, feeling healthy. He's moving to Las Vegas."

"Vegas." Rachel laughed. "He's feeling good, all right. What about the son? I heard on the news that he's a serial killer?"

Aaron's voice was hoarse. "Yes. Race Taggett. He's still at large."

"That's scary." Rachel sipped her merlot. "Isn't their house near the Belkin Ranch?"

"Yes, right across the road."

"Did you know Mr. Belkin?"

"Grant Belkin? Sure, I know him well. He's a patient of mine. Why do you ask?"

Rachel sat forward. "You mean, he's still alive?"

Aaron coughed and put down his water glass. "As far as I know. Did something happen that I don't know about?"

"Since you're his doctor, I suppose it's okay for me to share: he was at the hospital sometime last year. I heard the doctors say he had a brain tumor."

"A brain tumor?"

"They said it was inoperable. He wasn't supposed to last a year, and I'm sure it's been more than a year now."

"I had no idea. I'll talk with him about it."

They listened to country music during the drive back to Rachel's house. Aaron kept time drumming his fingers on the steering wheel as they sang along.

During a commercial break, Aaron turned to Rachel. "Do you work out?"

"I jog. Do you?"

"I'm getting back into it. I just need to stick to a routine. My life has been so crazy lately."

"There's a 5K run in a couple of months. Let's do it together. It'll be good for you."

Aaron gave her a high five. "It's a date."

Aaron walked Rachel to her front door. They stood under the porch light. "Have you read 'The Great Gatsby'?" Aaron said.

Rachel turned to him. "That takes me back. I've read it, but it's been a while." Rachel gazed past Aaron, a faraway look in her eyes. "I remember the woman that cheated on her husband, and that led to big problems."

Aaron smiled and nodded. *This is going really well.*

Rachel touched her lower lip. "Do I have something on my lip?"

Aaron's face reddened. "I'm sorry. I was staring. No, your lips are just fine."

Rachel laughed. "Well then, you can stare at me all you want, and you don't have to feel embarrassed."

Aaron leaned toward her. "The reason I was staring . . ."

"Yes."

"I really like your dimples."

She touched his elbow. "Do you want to talk more inside?"

Aaron sighed. "I'd love to."

Two dogs barked at them from the family room at the back. Aaron followed Rachel to her living room. He sat down on a couch as Rachel turned the television to a country station for background music. "Can I offer you a glass of wine?"

"I never turn down wine."

Rachel poured two glasses of merlot and brought them into the living room. She sat down next to him on the couch. "You've got me thinking. I want to read 'The Great Gatsby' again."

Aaron leaned near to her. "I can't believe you're unattached."

Rachel smiled. "Oh, I was attached, a few years ago."

"Was he a doctor?"

"Yes, but not anymore. He's in jail. Medicare insurance fraud."

Aaron's eyes widened and he sat back. "I don't think I've ever known anybody involved with that. At least, I didn't know it if they were." He sipped his wine. "How did he commit fraud?"

Rachel hesitated and looked away from Aaron. "He overcharged Medicare for equipment and patient care that he didn't provide, so he could line his pockets."

"Sometimes, I guess you really don't know people."

They sat for a short time drinking their wine, and then Rachel grinned at him. "You don't have any dark secrets, do you?"

Aaron blushed. "Nothing important."

Rachel touched his hand. "Oh, I've embarrassed you again. I'm sorry."

Aaron chuckled. "That's okay. When you mentioned dark secrets, a vision popped into my head. I was drunk and hooting it up with some college buddies in a topless bar. That wasn't one of my stellar moments."

Rachel nodded. "Everyone has their not-so-stellar moments. I've had a few of my own."

Later that night, Aaron walked into his house and was greeted by his new best friend, Red, a black Labrador retriever, named for Aaron's recently deceased happy hour comrade. Red was hyperactive in his new environment, jumping and barking and turning in circles.

Aaron stared into Red's eyes and rubbed his head. "I'm sure you miss our friend like I do, but I think you'll be happy here."

Outside, Red completed a thorough inspection of the back yard and adjacent pasture. Aaron looked over at the trees and listened for the owl. *I guess owls have to sleep, too.* With a series of barks, his dog announced that all was well at the Rovsing property.

As he prepared for bed, Aaron's cheeks were tiring from a continuous grin on his face.

Chapter 46

Monday evening arrived, ten days after Buck Bogarty's hot rod accident. As agreed, Aaron drove to the Bogarty's house to check on Buck.

As he approached the house, Aaron saw a man barge in through the front door.

Aaron hopped out of his car, heard shouting from inside the house, and sprinted to the open door.

In the living room, a muscular man dragged a struggling Sandra toward the front door. He whipped around, pointing a gun at Aaron's chest.

Aaron gasped, stepped back, and held up his hands.

"Who are you?" the man said. "You're not a cop, are you?"

Aaron's voice squeaked. "No."

A bare-chested Buck jogged into the room and stopped. "Dad. What's goin' on?"

"I need your mother to be with me. I'm on the run, and I've got to get out of here. They might be watching the house."

"Let go of me," Sandra yelled. "Go away and leave us alone."

"You be still, or I'll shoot somebody." He motioned his gun at Aaron. "Who's this guy?"

"He's a doctor, Lee," Sandra said. "He's here to help Buck." She was short of breath. "Don't shoot. Just leave, please."

"What do you need Mom for? Let her go and take me." Buck stepped toward his father.

"Stay away. You don't understand."

"I need to talk to you," Buck said.

With his gun, Lee motioned Aaron over to Buck. "Stay right there. I don't want to hurt anybody, but I will if I have to." He pulled Sandra toward the front door.

Buck extended his hands toward his father. "I have to talk—"

"Drop your weapon." A man in a police uniform leaned into the front doorway, his handgun pointed at Buck's father. "Drop it. Now."

Sandra screamed, twisted out of his hold, and fell to the floor. Lee straightened up and raised his gun toward the officer.

Aaron saw a flash and heard a pop. Lee groaned and fell to the floor on his back, the gun tumbling from his hand.

"Dad." Buck ran to his father, with Aaron right behind him. He kneeled and lifted his head. "Dad. Talk to me."

A red stain was spreading at the center of Lee's chest. Opening his eyes, he focused on Buck and wheezed as he tried to breath. "I don't think . . . we're going . . . to have that talk." He struggled to breathe.

"Hang on. Stay with me, please."

"I'm sorry, Son." Lee coughed and gurgled as blood trickled out of his mouth. "I made . . . a mess of things."

"Don't die. I'm not ready."

"Be better than me . . . like your mom . . . not like me." Staring at Buck, he gasped for air and blood gushed out over his chin and neck. His eyes glazed over after one final chest rattle, and his head fell back, limp in Buck's hand.

Buck looked up at Aaron. "No. He can't be dead."

Aaron felt for a carotid pulse in the neck. "His heart's stopped. Let me do CPR." He looked up at the officer. "Can you call 911?"

Buck moaned as he eased his father to the floor.

Aaron began CPR.

"It's not goin' to work, is it?" Buck asked Aaron.

Aaron shook his head as he compressed the chest. "CPR rarely works in this situation. His heart's already gone."

Buck rocked back and forth, his hand on his forehead, until the paramedics arrived.

Buck's father was declared dead, there on the living room floor.

****

Just after sunset the next evening, Buck walked out the back door of his house and sat down in a chair on the patio. He'd been in his bedroom all day.

Sandra came up behind him and put her hands on his shoulders. "I'm sorry you had to see that. You've been through so much."

Buck was quiet.

291

Sandra leaned closer. "He was a wicked man. You're not like him."

Buck shook his head. "I don't understand."

"I don't either. I never understood him."

Buck looked up at her. "I don't understand what's happenin' to me."

Sandra stood up straight and let out a breath. *What can I do for him?* she thought. She massaged his shoulders. *Maybe Dr. Rovsing can help.*

Chapter 47

Across town that Tuesday, Constable Keller Greevy stopped when he heard a noise.

It was seven days after Keller had announced that he was reopening the case of the death of Stella's son. He was about to open the door to the interview room near his office when Brad Benningham stepped in front of him.

Brad pointed his finger at Keller. "This is your last chance. We should come to an agreement and avoid all this trouble. Like our prior arrangements."

Keller glared at Brad. "No. No more. The next time you try to pull that, I'll arrest you for attempting to bribe an officer of the law."

Brad snorted. "That'd just get both of us into trouble."

"I guess it would."

Keller pushed past Brad and walked into the room.

After a short while, five people sat around a square table. Keller presided from the largest plush chair at the head of the table. To Keller's right: Stella, then Myra, Brad, and Preston Benningham. Brad sat next to Preston at one side of the table.

Brad fidgeted in his chair. Stella was calm, with a faint smile.

Keller opened a folder in front of him. "I've reviewed all the reports filed concerning the death of Stella's son two years ago. Apparently, a drug deal was in progress in an alley in town. One of the parties became confrontational, and several shots were fired. Witnesses say the shots were from handguns. The group dispersed in different directions, and Stella's son was found down close to the alley. He'd been shot, and he died from his wound."

Keller glanced at Brad and Preston. "Do you have any details to add?"

Brad shook his head. "No. That jives with what the news said."

"I don't remember much about that night. I did hear some gunshots," Preston said.

Keller crossed his arms. "I'd like to clear up an inconsistency."

"Ask me anything," Brad said.

"One of the witnesses thought that you were there."

Brad's eyes flew open. "Me? No way."

Preston looked at Brad. "I get flashback memories of that night, and sometimes I think you're behind me."

Brad dropped his head.

Preston's eyes widened. "Yes, I see you behind me just before my gun fired."

Brad looked at Keller and raised his palms. "All right. All right. I was there. I often followed Preston when I was worried about him."

Preston lifted his hand. "Dad, I remember now. You tried to take my gun from me, and then it went off."

Brad pounded the table and shot up out of his chair. "I was trying to help you, to get you out of there." He leaned on the table and glared at Keller and then Stella. "Why do we have to dredge all this up? Why?" His chest heaved and his fists were clenched.

Preston sat back and looked down. Myra's hands covered her cheeks.

Stella stared back at Brad, who put his hand to his forehead. He had trouble voicing his words. "I can't imagine losing a child, an only child."

Preston stood and put his hand on Brad's arm. "Dad, it's okay."

Brad bowed his head and moaned. "I don't know if it is."

"We can get through this. I can help you."

Brad sat down with his head on his forearms. "I'm so sorry."

Keller met Stella's eyes. "Now, we know the truth," he said.

"Yes."

"What was your son doing there?"

She sighed. "I think to buy drugs, just like Preston."

Keller scanned the group. "Does anyone have anything else to add?"

Preston and Stella shook their heads.

"Stella, do you want to pursue this further?"

She looked down at the table. "No."

Keller turned to Preston. "Do you still have a handgun?"

Preston shook his head. "No, and I never will again."

"You had a weapon in your hand and it was discharged in the setting of an illegal drug deal. I could arrest you for manslaughter."

Preston nodded. "I know."

Keller stared at Preston, then he sighed and slapped the table. "My judgment is homicide by misadventure, accidental homicide." He scribbled the verdict on paper and shut the folder. "This case is closed."

He stood and glanced at Preston. "You're free to go."

Chapter 48

Something caught the corner of Aaron's eye as he walked down the hallway toward a patient room. He spotted a moving figure in the waiting area, a woman with long, bright white hair passing through the front door. *I've seen her before.*

Aaron backtracked to the registration desk and motioned to Stella. "I saw a woman just leave. Who is she?"

Stella furrowed her brow and glanced at the front door. "I don't recall anyone just now." She studied the patient list on her computer screen. "No, I've put the last two patients scheduled for today into rooms, and they're both men, and we've had no recent walk-ins."

Aaron stood with his mouth half open, closed his eyes, and shook his head to clear the fuzziness.

"Are you sure about that?" Stella said.

Aaron took a deep breath and exhaled. "I must've been mistaken."

Stella locked the front door of the clinic and stood outside with Aaron. Dark clouds were gathering above them.

"You haven't mentioned your meeting with Constable Keller and Preston Benningham," Aaron said.

Stella sighed. "We found out what really happened."

"What?"

"Brad tried to grab Preston's gun, and it went off. He was trying to save his son."

Aaron whistled. "So that's the way it was."

"I've been thinking about it, and if I'd been in his shoes, I might've done the same thing."

Rain pelted Aaron's car as he drove home from work that Thursday afternoon. "A tornado watch is in effect for the following counties . . .," a voice from the radio said.

Aaron peered out his car windows at dark clouds hovering in the sky. He pulled into his garage and Red, his new dog, greeted him at the door, though with less than his usual exuberance. Aaron let him out in the bushes near the front door to do his business, which didn't take long. Red shook his wet body and stayed glued to Aaron as they went up to the living room window. Aaron caught his breath. An enormous black cloud blanketed the sky across from his house.

His eyes widened. Not far away, a funnel stretched from the cloud to the ground.

Aaron jogged toward the bedroom. "Come on, Red. Let's get in the bathtub." He pulled a mattress off his bed and dragged it into the bathroom. *I'll take one more look.*

He ran to the living room and gasped. The tornado had at least doubled in width and seemed closer.

Oh, man. This looks bad. Debris whirled around outside the funnel. *It must be right over the town. I'll bet people are videoing this monster.*

"Let's get to cover." He and Red ran back and settled into the bathtub, and Aaron yanked the mattress over the two of them.

He hugged his shivering dog. "It's okay, buddy. We'll be all right." Noise from the tornado was faint at first but soon swelled to a deafening howl.

****

Grant Belkin stood with his cows at Aaron's backyard fence. He pressed his hat against the top of his head and shielded his eyes from the rain as he watched the tornado swirl and blast its way toward Aaron's house.

When it reached the Benningham property across Aaron's street, the twister hesitated and then veered west away from the Benningham mansion, avoiding Aaron's neighborhood and carving a path straight into the Big Thicket.

Chapter 49

Aaron waited until the noise faded, then he and Red climbed out of the bathtub and hurried to the living room window. Aaron no longer heard the freight train sound of the tornado, and the rain had stopped. He walked around inside the house and out to the front yard, finding no damage to his house or property. He stepped into the street, looking both ways, and saw no sign of damage to the neighborhood trees or front yards of the four houses.

"Stay, Red. You're safe now," Aaron said as he walked back through the house to the garage. Jumping into his car with his medical bag, he heard sirens of rescue vehicles in the distance.

He called Rachel on his cell phone. "Did you hear about our tornado?" Aaron said.

"I heard on the news about a tornado watch. Did you see one?"

"Yes. A big one. It just missed my neighborhood, but it tore up the area near me. Are you okay?"

"I'm fine. It's just raining at my house."

"Good. I think the tornado is moving away from your area. I'm off to see if I can help the rescue folks. I'll talk with you later."

Aaron drove away in a direction that was generally parallel with the swath of destruction left by the tornado. He first encountered an area covered with mountainous piles of debris.

This used to be part of a neighborhood. I can't see where the streets are.

Aaron stopped his car in a clearing and walked among piles of wreckage where houses once stood. He joined two paramedics pulling and lifting splintered slabs of wood.

"We heard a voice in there," one of the men said, pointing at a mound of rubble. After several minutes of straining and lifting, the men exposed part of a bed, and they crouched and peered under it. Aaron saw two small wide eyes staring back at him.

"It's okay, little one. We're here to help you." They cleared a path and pulled the child out from under the bed. She was able to stand.

"Are you all right?" one of the medics said, kneeling in front of her.

She hugged a cloth doll. "Where's my mommy?"

"I don't know. We'll look for her." He touched her shoulder. "What's your name?"

"Kaley."

"How old are you?"

She held up three fingers.

"We need to take you somewhere safe, okay?"

Aaron watched as the paramedic carried the girl toward a nearby ambulance.

Aaron heard a loud cry from another pile of debris about twenty yards away. "Help, help."

He walked toward the voice and spotted a familiar face running from another direction. "Daniel, is that you?"

"Hi, Doc." Daniel ran up to him. "I was visiting my brother in a neighborhood over there." He pointed toward the setting sun. "We had no damage in there at all, but just look at this mess."

"I know. It looks like bombs went off around us."

They heard the voice again. "Help."

Aaron and Daniel strained at heavy fragments of brick wall and sheetrock. Sweat dripped from Aaron's face. At one point, he stopped and stared at Daniel, who had a grin on his face.

Daniel nodded. "This is what I live for, sir." He dove back into the rubble and began to throw off slabs of wood.

They grappled with one particular piece of marble and stucco. "It looks like part of a fireplace," Daniel said. "It won't budge."

"Let me help y'all with that," a man said behind them.

Aaron turned. "Buck Bogarty. Good. We need your muscles."

Buck toiled with Daniel and Aaron until they exposed a frightened young woman lying on her side under a sturdy wooden table.

"Ma'am, can you stand up?" Buck said.

"I can try."

"Why, you're pregnant."

"Eight months." She stood up, her eyes glazed over and she collapsed against Buck.

"I'll carry you out of here and get you to a hospital." Buck laid her across his forearms. He hesitated and looked at Aaron.

Aaron stretched out his hand to Buck's shoulder. "We're glad you're here."

Buck nodded. "Thanks." He stepped over debris and toward the flashing lights of an ambulance.

"Doc, over there." Daniel pointed to a mound of debris more than twenty yards away. "I heard something."

Aaron zigzagged with him toward a faint, moaning sound at one edge of the pile.

As they cleared splintered wood away, a shoe appeared. Then they uncovered the legs, torso, and head of a man lying on the muddy ground. One of the larger pieces of wood wouldn't budge.

Aaron held up his hand. "Don't try to move it."

A jagged shard was impaled through the man's mid abdomen and stuck into something underneath him. He took shallow, rapid breaths.

Daniel kneeled down close to him. "Jed, is that you?"

Jed opened his eyes and stared, focusing on Daniel's face. He managed a smile and a whisper. "Daniel . . . my old buddy."

"We've got to get you to a hospital. Hold on."

Jed tried in vain to lift his head. "Remember . . . our solemn oath?"

"Sure I do."

"Well, you've done good." He gasped for air. "You're my soldier hero."

"Hold on. You're not done yet."

"It's okay, my friend . . . Remember the oath." He breathed in, exhaled with a frothy sound, and his eyes closed. His chest stopped moving.

Daniel shook Jed's shoulders. "Wake up, Jed. You can't die."

Aaron crouched and felt Jed's neck for a carotid pulse, and then he turned to Daniel. "He had a bad injury. Too much internal bleeding. He's gone."

Daniel withdrew his hands, sat back, and hung his head.

"There's nothing we could've done," Aaron said.

Daniel was still, gazing at Jed's face.

Aaron notified 911 of the location of the body.

After several minutes, Daniel dried his eyes with a handkerchief and then crossed his arms. "I don't know if I can handle all this."

Aaron walked with him to a nearby grove of trees, out of the tornado zone of destruction.

"I'm sorry about your friend," Aaron said.

"We were part of a great group of guys. We were like brothers."

"All of you took an oath?"

Daniel nodded. " 'Follow your dreams and live with courage, so you can die with dignity.' "

"That's a cool oath. Where did you find it?"

"We made it up." Daniel sobbed into his handkerchief.

Aaron stood with him for a while.

Daniel sighed. "We were a bunch of clueless teenagers. The oath just seemed right for us. I don't remember which one of us thought of it first, but we worked on it and adopted it as our own. It was one of our better moments."

Aaron put his hand on Daniel's shoulder. "You have a lot to offer. There's good to be done."

"Jed didn't deserve to die."

"No, but I'm glad he saw you before he passed."

Daniel nodded. "He was thinking of the oath." He clenched his teeth and looked away into the trees, then he took several deep breaths and returned the handkerchief to his pocket.

"Hey, can you guys help us over here?" a man shouted from near a bright spotlight inside the debris field.

Daniel straightened his back and glanced toward the spotlighted area, then he turned to Aaron. "Let's go, sir," he said.

Aaron smiled. *He has that look in his eyes. That's got to be good.*

He followed Daniel to join the paramedics.

One hour later, Aaron and Daniel were searching along the debris field for any signs of people or animals.

Buck walked up to them. "Hey, Doc, can I join you guys?"

"Sure. It's good to see you again," Aaron said. "There's plenty of work to be done out here."

As the three men lifted a heavy slab of wood, Aaron looked at Buck. "Is the pregnant lady okay?"

"I think so." Buck grinned. "She thanked me."

Aaron nodded. "That's what it's all about."

They continued their search in another pile of debris. Buck touched Daniel's back. "You're a soldier, right?"

"Yes, I am."

"I think I want to be a soldier, too. Like you."

Daniel stood straight. "You'd make a good soldier. Let's talk about it after we finish up here."

For the rest of the night, they toiled alongside the medics to clear rubble and search for the injured.

At one point close to midnight, Daniel and Buck had marched away carrying patients to the ambulances. Aaron was alone at the edge of the forest, standing with his medical bag.

"Hey, you."

Aaron shouted, stumbled back several steps, and splashed down on his buttocks. Race Taggett leaned against a tree nearby, his eyes glowing like hot coals.

Aaron's chest tightened. *Oh, crap.*

"You must be in heaven, with all these moaning people around."

Aaron stood up, put a hand over his heart, and slowed his breathing. "Oh, this isn't heaven."

Race grinned. "No, you're right. It's more like hell."

"Why do you dislike me?"

Race spat on the ground. "That's not it. Hospitals and doctors. They wouldn't touch me. Nobody touches me." He sneered at Aaron. "I'm a freak."

"I'm sorry you feel that way."

Race's face contorted and he raised his hands toward Aaron. "Do you have any idea what it's like? Nobody wanting to touch you?"

Aaron stared at him. "I can't even imagine how painful that must feel."

Race snorted and put his hands on his hips. "It doesn't matter anymore. I found a way to get over all that."

"Look, there's hope for you. Turn yourself in—"

"Haven't you figured it out? I only feel good when I'm killing, when I see the fear." He smiled and looked past Aaron. "When I smell the fear."

Race spat again. "Otherwise, my life ain't worth living." Muscles bulged in Race's forearms. He stepped forward and pointed at Aaron. "That's why I've been watching you. At a time I choose, I'm going to hurt you."

Aaron's heart pounded so hard that his chest hurt. "Why?"

"Because you and me, we're really the same. Only you're good, and I'm bad." He snickered. "So which one do you think will win?"

"There doesn't have to be a battle. You're still young. You can try to do better."

"I knew you'd keep trying to help me, but can't you see? So what if I'm a freak? I'm already better than everybody. I've always been better. I can beat anyone."

Race stepped away from the trees and looked off into the distance. "I could've been a hell of an athlete."

"I believe that," Aaron said.

For a few seconds, Race stood still, his head held high.

He turned and leaned toward Aaron. "That's all dead and gone. Now it's you and me. I need to have you with me, so I have to beat you, and I will because I'm better than you. I'll prove it, soon enough." He laughed and vanished into the blackness.

Aaron shivered so hard that his bones felt like they would break.

He braced himself against a tree for a while until he stopped shaking, then he stumbled toward the lights and ambulances, seeking more uplifting company. Alongside Buck and Daniel, Aaron sweated and plugged away with the rescue folks until dawn.

****

Before his clinic opened that morning, Aaron treated Buck and Daniel to breakfast at a local diner. Aaron sat across from them at the table.

"You guys look beat," Aaron said.

Buck looked out of a window of the diner. "People died yesterday."

Daniel leaned toward Buck. "We did what we could."

They were silent for a while as they picked at eggs, bacon, and potatoes.

Daniel turned to Buck. "So, you're thinking about joining the military?"

Buck nodded. "Sure am. I want to make somethin' of myself." He sipped steaming coffee. "What's it like to be a soldier?"

Daniel sighed. "It changes you."

"Yeah, I figured that. For the better, I hope."

Daniel hesitated and then gave Buck a faint nod. "Yes. Mostly for the better."

As they walked out of the restaurant, Daniel turned to Aaron. "Are you feeling okay?"

Aaron sighed. "I'm just tired." He waved them off. "I'll stay around here a while."

He called Stella, Marley, Grant, and Rachel. Everyone was well and uninjured. He'd ask Stella and Juliana at the clinic to phone their patients and check on them.

That night, Aaron jerked awake to the owl hooting outside. His fingers trembled, and he heard sharp buzzing in his ears. He recalled a dream about that final meeting in Connecticut when a sneering chief of staff with glinting eyes demanded that Aaron resign from the hospital.

There's going to be a showdown between Race and me, and I've got to stand tall.

He got out of bed and roamed the house, ending up in his office desk chair, where he sat staring into space. He woke up several hours later, slumped in the chair, with Red's head in his lap.

Chapter 50

Five days later, on his way home from work, Aaron spotted activity at the Taggett's old house. As he approached the property, he saw a brown SUV parked out front and then a "sold" sign came into view. He drove to the cul-de-sac and parked near the dirt driveway.

A woman walked around a corner of the house and stopped. Aaron stepped out and waved. "I'm a neighbor," he shouted. He walked onto a lawn recently covered with soft green St. Augustine grass. They rendezvoused in the front yard and shook hands.

"I'm Emily. We just moved in."

"I'm the family doctor in town. I haven't been here long myself."

Emily smiled. "It's good for us that a doctor is close by. It's me, my husband, and two kids."

"Welcome, and I hope you'll be comfortable here."

"They tell me you don't get tornadoes that often around here. Is that right?"

Aaron nodded. "That's true. You probably heard about the big one that came through here recently."

"While I was driving around town, I saw some of the damaged areas."

"We're not likely to have another one like that for a long time."

Aaron paced around his house later that evening. After a while, Red stopped following him. Aaron stopped and shook his head.

Sometimes I can't even hear because of the buzzing in my ears.

Aaron's arms and legs tingled as he crawled into bed for the night. Several hours later, his body jerked awake. He was breathing fast, and his skin dripped with sweat. He remembered fragments of a dream, a woman with shining white hair that flowed down her body and two other faces that floated before him.

Mom and Dad.

They screamed for help as a wild-eyed, scruffy man pumped bullets into their bodies. With a husky laugh and a contorted mouth, the man pulled his trigger, again and again.

Aaron rolled out of bed and walked to his office. He picked up the framed photograph of his parents, and his eyes filled with tears as he stared at their happy faces.

He looked toward the ceiling. "I've got to let go of this. Mom and Dad, help me let go of this."

Aaron plopped down in his desk chair. He put his hands over his ears to smother the buzzing sound, and he closed his eyes to cover up the wavy lines in his vision.

Several minutes later, an idea popped into his head and his eyes flew open. He bolted to his bedroom and pulled on running clothes and shoes. Aaron heard Red barking, but he didn't stop to pet him as he dashed out of the house, slamming the front door behind him. An owl hooted from a nearby tree.

Aaron hurried along his street and soon passed by Marley Brighton's house, turning right at the intersection. In a short while, he made it to the front door of his clinic and peered inside. He pounded several times on the door.

He was supposed to meet me, but no one is in there. Aaron shrugged his shoulders, turned and walked away.

Funny, how my shoes sometimes don't touch the ground.

Someone directed him back down the road. Aaron gasped as he saw a faint light hovering over Rocky Donnigan's trailer home. He ran faster, away from the light, following the voice's instructions. Eventually, he left the road and climbed over fences and trotted through fields and sprinted down a driveway to a house. He banged on the front door and then lurched back and ran away toward the trees.

Aaron flinched as another voice shouted at him, and he stopped and looked around but didn't see anyone. "Who yelled at me?" he said.

No one answered.

I'm trying to do what I'm told.

He sprinted into the Big Thicket, stopped, and turned around. "Stop talking to me like that. That's not fair. Why are you cursing at me and calling me a worthless doctor?"

Ripping off his shirt, soggy with sweat, he turned in circles and watched the trees dancing and swaying around him. *I've got to find a place to hide. I'll look for a big hole in a tree trunk to crawl into.*

After weaving through the pines for several minutes, he spotted a bench and stumbled over to it. *I'll sit here for a while and think about where to hide.*

He crossed his arms and rocked back and forth. All the images around him, the bench, the trees, the ground, were blurred and wavy, as if he were looking through translucent glass. People he didn't recognize began to float out from the trees and across his vision. Faces bobbing and drifting in front of him dissolved into the heads of animals and into unrecognizable, snarling mouths with glistening fangs that dripped with blood. As Aaron waved his hands to swat away the menacing teeth, his head began to spin and he fell off the bench and rolled around on the ground.

A huge face appeared before him. It was covered with saggy skin and draining sores, and the mouth was sending out commands to him, with words and letters materializing in the air. "Go to the middle of the Big Thicket and find the evil one, Race Taggett. Kill him. Kill him."

Aaron sat up and struck at the face with his fists. His body began to whirl and tumble, and he slid into a deep black hole and fell headlong into empty space, hurtling down, the grotesque faces yelling at him and flying after him deeper and deeper into the abyss . . .

Aaron's eyes flew open. Above him was a white ceiling with bright fluorescent lights. He tried to lift a hand to scratch his nose, but his arm wouldn't budge, so he raised his head and glanced around. "What the . . ." His wrists and legs were tied down to a stretcher.

Aaron's eyes focused on a person standing at his bedside. "Daniel, is that you?" he said.

"Ah, you're back with us. Yes, it's me, sir," Daniel said. "We brought you to the hospital."

"What for? What happened to me?"

Daniel looked down. "Grant Belkin called EMS."

"Was I in a car wreck?"

"No. Mr. Belkin found you wandering around."

"Wandering?"

"Out of your head."

Aaron's vision blurred as he stared at Daniel. "Out of my head?"

"You were in the Big Thicket."

Aaron sighed, closed his eyes, and fell back to sleep.

Aaron awakened several hours later and took note of the same ceiling and stretcher. Daniel sat in a chair near his bed.

"Hello again. You've been snoozing," Daniel said.

Aaron lay quiet for several minutes and then looked at Daniel. "You said that you brought me here. In an ambulance?"

"Yes, sir." Daniel stepped to the bedside as a male nurse walked into the room.

"So, he's awake now?" the nurse said.

Daniel nodded. "He just woke up."

"How do you feel?" the nurse said to Aaron.

"I'm confused about what's going on with me."

"Well, at least you're coherent again. Let's get these restraints off. I'll tell the doctor you're awake."

Aaron stretched his arms, propped his pillow, and sat up. He turned to the nurse. "I guess I was incoherent?"

"You were, but you're better now. Try to relax," he said.

"Thanks for taking care of me."

"That's what we're here for." He patted Aaron's shoulder, noted his vital signs, and left the room.

"I'm glad you pulled out of it," Daniel said.

"So am I, whatever it was." Aaron took a deep breath. "Incoherent in the Big Thicket. I have a bad feeling about this."

"The doctors here will sort it all out."

"Yeah, I suppose you're right." Aaron read the tag on Daniel's shirt. "So, you're riding with EMS now. Are you training to be a paramedic?"

Daniel grinned. "Yes, sir. I'm in school now. The EMS company lets me help them out."

Aaron shook hands with Daniel. "I appreciate all you've done for me."

"It's the least I could do." Daniel stared at Aaron for a few seconds. "Good luck to you, Doc." He gave Aaron a thumbs-up as he walked out of the room.

Several hours later, Aaron looked up as Grant Belkin and Rachel appeared at the door.

"Come on in," Aaron said. He blushed and shrugged his shoulders as they approached his bedside.

Aaron held hands with Rachel. "I'm sorry—"

"Don't worry about a thing. You're okay now."

Aaron squeezed Rachel's hand and then turned to Grant. "You found me?"

"You made a ruckus at my front door, then you ran off. It took me a while to track you down."

Aaron gazed past him. "I remember a loud buzzing in my ears and my eyes went blurry. I heard people giving me orders and then I started seeing things, hideous creatures floating in front of me."

Grant nodded. "You were hallucinatin'."

Aaron's eyes widened. "It was very real. Like a horror movie, except that I thought it was actually happening to me."

Rachel patted his hand. "I'm glad it's over."

Aaron shook his head. "I never want to go through that again. I wouldn't wish that on my worst enemy."

"They gave you medication when you got here. I think it's workin'," Grant said.

"At least the buzzing and weird visions are gone now. What the heck happened to me?"

Grant scratched his cheek. "The doctor will be here soon."

Aaron sighed. "Then I'll get the scoop."

"A lot has been happenin' to you lately. People can become ill with all that stress."

A doctor entered the room and introduced herself as a psychiatrist.

"What do you think is wrong with me?" Aaron said.

"It appears that you had a breakdown, a psychotic episode."

"That's what I figured."

"We gave you an antipsychotic medication when you arrived here. It seems to have helped. At first, you were hallucinating."

"Am I schizophrenic?"

"Not necessarily. If you've never had an episode before, this could be the only psychotic break you'll ever have, but now we know you're susceptible. It could happen again."

Aaron shook his head. "I surely hope not. Do you think something led to my breakdown?"

She leaned toward him. "They tell me you've had plenty of shocks to your system recently."

"That's true. So, you're saying maybe I had a breakdown from post-traumatic stress?"

"Not maybe. I think that's your main problem. Anyway, I'll prescribe medication to help prevent it happening again, then I'll see you in my office in one week and we can adjust your therapy from there."

"I can still practice medicine, right?"

"Of course you can, but you may need to remain on medication."

"Oh, how well do I know that mantra: 'Sir, remember to take your medicine.' "

She nodded. "Good. I don't believe you'll be a problem patient."

"I appreciate your help."

"I think you're going to be fine." She smiled at Aaron and left the room.

Grant touched Aaron's arm. "You're back to the Aaron we all know."

Aaron laughed. "I guess that's good. I'll try to be a better Aaron now."

"Take it from me, you're better already. It's all for the good."

He looked up at Grant. "You say that like you really mean it."

"I do."

Aaron grabbed his hand. "Thanks for finding me."

"I did what anyone else would do. We've got to keep you healthy. This town needs a good doctor like you." Grant nestled his cowboy hat back on his head. "See you back at the ranch."

After Grant left, Aaron held Rachel's hand and looked at her. "You didn't know this about me before. I didn't know this about me."

Rachel shook her head. "It doesn't change anything."

"I must have a genetic flaw—"

"No one is perfect. All of us have flaws."

"Think about it for a while." Aaron swallowed. "I'd understand if you—"

Rachel squeezed his hand. "I want to be with you."

Aaron grinned and looked at her eyes and dimples. A familiar warm flush coursed over him.

"I've got to check on things at my house," she said.

"Sure. I'll be all right."

Alone again, Aaron stared out of the window of his room at the morning sky.

I wonder why Race Taggett didn't find me out there.

Chapter 51

I've got to get back to work, Aaron thought. *Taking more time off wouldn't be good for me.*

It was Monday, four days after his psychotic breakdown. He lay awake in his own bed well before the alarm clock was set to ring.

I wonder how everyone will treat me.

As he opened the front door of the clinic, he heard a familiar voice.

"Good morning, Doc," Stella said.

Aaron stopped, took a deep breath, and scanned the waiting room and the hallway. "It's good to be back."

Stella walked out from behind the registration desk. "Good for us, too. Otherwise, we don't make a living. You look great."

"Thanks. I feel good. Not just good. I feel better today than I've felt in a long time."

"Wonderful. Let's fire this place up again."

"Did you change the light bulbs? It looks a lot brighter in here now."

Stella smiled and put her hand on his shoulder. "No. The light bulbs are the same. I think you're the one that's been changed."

Aaron sighed. "For the better I hope." *Everything feels fine.*

An hour later, Aaron entered a patient room and saw an adolescent boy sitting on the examination table, rocking back and forth. A woman stood and greeted Aaron. "I'm Owen's mother."

"What can I do for you today?" Aaron said.

"Owen has had problems in school for a while, but recently he's been acting very strange."

Owen stared ahead of him as he rocked.

"How has his behavior been strange?" Aaron said.

"Sometimes when he talks, he doesn't make sense, and he's been disappearing from the house. We find him outside, usually hiding in bushes. He acts like he's afraid of something, and he won't leave the bushes. We have a hard time getting him back into the house."

Aaron stood beside Owen. "Why do you hide outside?"

Owen looked down. "Because they yell at me."

"That's what he tells us," Owen's mother said. "But we certainly never yell at him. Do you think he's imagining these things?"

"That's possible." *I know exactly what he's going through. He's trying to get away from the cruel voices.*

Aaron turned to Owen's mother. "I'd like to refer him to a local psychiatrist. I think he needs a thorough evaluation."

"Can he be helped?"

Aaron nodded. "Absolutely he can." *Believe me, I know.*

Just after closing time, Aaron sat in a chair across from Stella at the registration desk. He leaned toward her. "How have you been sleeping?"

"You're wondering how I'm doing after—"

Aaron nodded. "After we found out Brad was the one who accidentally caused your son's death."

Stella smiled. "I'm feeling much better about things."

"You're letting go of the anger?"

She swelled her chest. "Does it look that way?"

Aaron smiled. "Yes, it does."

"I'm glad it shows."

"I think you answered your own burning question."

Stella looked puzzled, and then she nodded. "Oh, you mean about forgiveness."

"Clearing out the pain with forgiveness."

"I guess I did answer it."

"Come on, let's dance," Aaron said.

Stella laughed. "Dance? Whatever for?"

"We're both feeling good. Let's do it." He walked over to her and escorted her to the waiting room.

Aaron waltzed with her in circles.

"Stop a minute. If we're going to do a happy dance, I'll teach you the Cajun jig," Stella said. "Follow my steps."

As she hummed a festive Cajun song beat, they held hands and pushed and pulled their arms back and forth, with an up and down movement of their bodies combined with twirls and spins and any other variations around the floor that Stella could think of.

"Where did you learn a Cajun dance?"

"In the early years of our marriage, we'd spend a weekend now and then in Louisiana, and we'd go to Cajun dancehalls after dinner. You should try it."

"I might do that."

After several minutes, Stella stopped, out of breath. "You learn fast."

Aaron laughed and walked her to the front door. "Thanks. That was fun. I could hear the Cajun accordion and fiddle playing as we danced."

"It's a great way to celebrate." Stella's jolly face beamed. "You brought back good memories for me."

That evening, Aaron drove to Rachel's house for dinner. A pleasant aroma of tomato sauce with a hint of garlic greeted Aaron at the front door.

They sat down close to each other at the dining room table, toasted their wine glasses, and dove into the savory meal.

"This lasagna is terrific," Aaron said through a mouthful of pasta.

Rachel smiled. "It's one of my specialties."

After dinner, Rachel stood and walked over to a window that looked out to the trees behind her house. "I got some weird news today."

Aaron joined her. "What?"

"Remember I told you about my ex-fiance?"

"How could I forget? The doctor in prison for Medicare fraud, right?"

"That's him. A friend at the hospital called me and said he's not in prison anymore."

"Maybe they released him for good behavior or some other reason?"

"I don't know why he's out. But I wonder if he's still mad at me."

"Why would he be mad at you?"

Rachel sighed. "I'll tell you the whole story someday."

Chapter 52

Aaron felt less stressed since starting his new antipsychotic medication, and he experienced no significant side effects. Even his anxiety over Race calmed down a bit.

One afternoon—nine days after Aaron's return to work—his new neighbor Emily knocked on his front door.

"Hello, Em—"

"We're moving out tomorrow." Emily's wide eyes were bloodshot. "I haven't slept in a week."

"What's wrong?"

"I think that house is haunted."

"The Taggett's old house? Haunted?"

"Our kids told us about a light moving around deep in the woods in back of the house. And I saw it, too, a few nights ago."

"A light? Like a flashlight?"

"No, not really. It's a faint light, and it floats around."

"That's weird."

"We hear strange noises at night. Sometimes it sounds like moaning, from deep in the forest. It's too creepy."

"I don't think I could sleep in that house, either."

Emily shivered. "I heard stories about that crazy guy who killed girls. He used to live in that house."

"Race Taggett."

"What happened to him? Is he in prison?"

"No. They haven't found him. The police think he's hiding out somewhere in the Big Thicket."

"We're staying in a motel tonight." She looked back at the trees across the road. "We've got to get away from here."

"I don't blame you."

Aaron closed and locked the door. He felt tightness in his throat.

Race is still roaming out there, somewhere.

Chapter 53

Tucker Boudreaux rushed into the clinic near closing time the next day, his hair ruffled with a cowlick jutting straight up.

Aaron hurried over to him. "What's wrong?"

"I've been worried sick. Mama told me about something I'd said."

Aaron smiled. "Now, what are you worried about? Did you say something about me?"

"Not you, your *bele*, your girlfriend."

"Rachel? What about her?"

"I'm afraid for her. Somebody is going to hurt her, soon."

Aaron's eyes widened. "What do you mean?"

"Just please keep a close eye on her. I'll feel better."

"Okay, I will. Thanks for letting me know."

Aaron frowned as he watched Tucker leave.

A short time later in the parking lot, Aaron called Rachel on his cell phone.

"Hi, Aaron."

"I just called to say hello. Is everything all right?" he said.

"Sure. It's nice of you to think about me."

"Nothing unusual has happened recently?"

"No . . ." Rachel paused.

"What? Rachel?"

"Well, now that you mention it, I thought I saw someone in the woods behind my house a few days ago. I'd forgotten about it."

"Keep your house locked up at night."

"I don't think you need to worry. I'll stay safe and secure."

"Maybe I should come over and check it out."

"You know you're welcome anytime, but I think all is well here."

"I'll visit you now. It'll make me feel better to see you."

"Wonderful. I'll rustle up some food for dinner."

Aaron's stomach knotted up as he started up the Volvo. *It's probably nothing.*

He called her again on the way. "I'm almost to your house. I should've offered to bring some food or drink."

"That's okay. I've got everything we . . ."

"Rachel? Are you there?"

"My eagle is making quite a ruckus out back. I'll see you in a minute." She ended the call.

Aaron gunned his car along the last stretch to Rachel's house. He whipped into her driveway, jumped out of the car, and sprinted to the back yard.

Pulling up at the rear edge of the sanctuary fence, he spotted a figure jogging toward the edge of the forest with long hair flapping. Something was draped over the figure's shoulder.

Aaron cupped his hands around his mouth. "Race, stop."

Just shy of the trees, the figure slowed and turned around. Aaron ran up closer and stopped about ten feet away. Race's eyes studied him, like a big cat examining its prey.

Aaron shook his head. "Please, don't do this."

Aaron didn't blink as he focused on Race's eyes, and the two men faced each other as still as statues. Aaron heard a whistling breeze from deep in the forest.

Race took several deep breaths, his eyes softening as his face furrowed into a frown. He crouched and laid Rachel on the ground.

Race cocked his head and studied the limp Rachel. "She's not like the others, the ones that laughed at me."

"Then why did you hurt her? Why?"

Race shot up and jabbed his finger at Aaron. "To get at you. To make you suffer, like I've suffered." He snickered. "And I'm having a lot of fun doing it."

A tremor passed over Aaron's body.

Race sneered at Aaron. "I saw you were crazy for a while in the Big Thicket. But I want you as sane as me the next time we meet." He cackled and fled into the trees.

Aaron put a hand to his forehead. *What am I doing in this bizarre place? Maybe I should get the hell out of here.*

Aaron hurried to Rachel and kneeled down beside her. "Rachel?" he said, but she didn't respond. He noticed that her breathing was regular.

He hoisted her up in his arms, then he stared into the trees and listened. *There's no way I could catch that guy. I'll let Constable Greevy know.*

Aaron carried Rachel back to the house and laid her on the living room couch to look her over. *That's a nasty hematoma on her temple.*

Aaron eased her into the back seat of his car and sped toward the hospital ER. En route, she moaned a few times and then opened her eyes and managed to sit up.

"What is happening? I have a pounding headache."

"You were conked over the head. I want to get a CT scan to make sure you're okay. Just try to relax now."

After a few minutes, he looked back. Rachel was curled up on her side, asleep again.

"Rachel?" Aaron shook her foot. She didn't respond. He pressed the accelerator. *At least she's breathing okay.*

Aaron screeched to a stop in a parking space near the ER entrance. "Rachel?" he said as he turned to the back seat.

She was still unresponsive.

"Oh, boy. We need a CT scan stat."

Several hours later, Aaron paced in a waiting room in the postoperative area.

He stopped as a surgeon walked up to him.

"We drilled a hole in her skull and drained a small epidural hematoma," he said.

"So, she's likely to recover all right?"

"Yes. These patients have a good prognosis, especially otherwise healthy patients like her that had a lucid interval after the injury. She had no other significant brain trauma."

Aaron smiled. *That's what I hoped he'd say.*

Later, Rachel was transferred to a private room. For the rest of the night, Aaron slept off and on in the chair beside her bed.

Aaron was awakened the next morning when a nurse entered the room. She checked Rachel's monitors and touched her arm. Rachel opened her eyes, and the nurse smiled. "How are you feeling this morning, my dear?"

"Groggy," Rachel said.

"She's recovering well from the surgery," the nurse said to Aaron, and then she patted Rachel's arm and left the room. Aaron stepped over to the bedside.

"What happened to me?" Rachel said.

"Do you remember anything?"

"I was staring at my eagle. He was upset about something, flapping his wings and squawking like crazy. Then everything went black."

"Race Taggett hit you over the head."

Rachel's eyes widened. "Race Taggett?"

"I stopped him at the edge of the Big Thicket. He was carrying you away."

She shook her head. "What a nightmare." She lifted her head. "I had to have surgery?"

Aaron leaned toward her. "You had bleeding outside the brain but inside your skull. It's all over now. All is well. There was no injury to your brain tissue."

"Whew. I'm glad to hear that. I do remember you were worried about me. I sure owe you one." She laid her head back and sighed. "He must be really psycho. Do you think he'll try again?"

Aaron looked out of the window. Appearing before him were Race's face and eyes with that last mocking expression. "I don't know. I don't think so."

"Why did he do that to me?"

"To hurt me. He wants me, not you."

Rachel lifted her head. "Why on earth does he want you?"

"For some crazy reason, he's chosen me as someone he has to defeat."

"Surely the police or the Texas Rangers can catch him and put him away for good."

"Maybe they can."

Aaron stood at the window as trees in the distance swayed in a stiff breeze.

After the tornado, Race said he needs to have me with him. What the heck did he mean by that?

Chapter 54

Earlier that night, someone was screaming outside. Buck Bogarty opened his eyes. *Was that a nightmare?*

He sat up in bed and listened. *No, it's not a dream.*

Buck got out of bed, threw on clothes and shoes, and met his mother in the living room.

"Someone's outside," Buck said.

Sandra pulled her robe tight. "Are you going out there?"

"I'll check it out."

"Please be careful."

Buck opened the front door and peered out. "Somebody help us," a woman yelled.

Buck ran out into the front yard and saw two women standing in the street, several houses away. As he sprinted toward them, he saw one of the women gesturing and talking on a cell phone, and then he spotted flames shooting through the roof of a house.

"Please help me. My child and husband are in there," a woman said to Buck. She coughed after she spoke. Her nightgown was burned black in several places and her hair was singed.

Buck ran to the house, stopped at the front door, and turned to the woman behind him. "Where are they?"

"To the right and down the hallway," the woman said between coughs. "The two rooms off the hallway."

Buck took a deep breath, lifted the bottom of his shirt over his mouth and nose, and ran in through the front door. He danced around a burning couch and avoided falling chunks of ceiling. His eyes burned from the hot smoke, and he coughed as he made it to the hallway at the right of the living room. Holding his breath, he turned into the first room, which was filled with smoke. Feeling his way to a bed, his hand came across a small leg on the mattress. He forced his arms under the body of a child and jogged out of the room, bouncing off walls along the way. He dodged falling flames and weaved his way back to the front door and outside to the yard, where he stopped and gasped for air. As the woman took her child from Buck, the second woman ran up behind him and beat his back with her hands.

"Your shirt is on fire," she said.

"Thanks." He turned to the woman with the child. "You said someone else is in there?"

"My husband, in the next room over." Buck jogged back to the front door.

"God bless you," she said.

Buck took a deep breath, covered his mouth and nose with his shirttail, and plunged once more into the house. Smoke now filled the living room, and he could no longer make out objects in the room. An acrid smell burned his nose and eyes. Squeezing the shirt over his mouth and nose, he charged forward, trying to follow from memory his previous route. He banged against furniture and walls several times before feeling the doorway opening to the child's room. Groping his way further along the wall, he tripped and fell through another doorway and landed on the floor on his stomach. He heard a siren outside approaching the house.

I need to breathe.

He rolled over on his back. Through watery eyes, he saw a flame falling toward him and then he felt a heavy weight crushing his chest . . .

Chapter 55

Aaron knocked on the door of Sandra Bogarty's house the day after the fire. Several other cars were parked outside along the street.

"Come in," she said and opened the door wide. Her eyes were red from crying.

Aaron stepped inside. "I'm so sorry about Buck."

She started to sob into a tissue, and Aaron put his arm around her shoulders. They walked to a couch nearby.

"He had just joined the Army." She could speak only a few words at a time between sobs. "He was so proud . . . He didn't want to be like his father . . . He wanted to do good."

"He was an amazing young man. He will be missed."

"The firefighters said . . . they're going to give him . . . give me . . . a medal for his courage."

"He so deserves that honor. He was a true hero. He saved a child's life."

She nodded and smiled. "That's just like Buck. He was my hero."

Aaron leaned closer to her. "I think a lot of people are better for having known Buck Bogarty."

Aaron walked out to his car through a light rain with his head down. *Could I ever do anything brave like what Buck did?*

Race Taggett's eyes appeared before him, and a chill went through his chest.

Can I possibly be brave against him?

That night, Aaron lay wide awake on his bed. At times, he sat up and paced around the room. An owl hooted outside.

Why am I doing this? I should clear out of here. He nodded. *I'll take Rachel with me. We'll start a new life.*

He sat on the edge of the bed with his head in his hands. *Face the truth, you idiot. You're not brave like Buck Bogarty.*

He slapped his thighs. *Damn it, I went to medical school to be a doctor. I just want to be a doctor.*

He moaned and clenched his fists.

What did I get myself into? I don't want to die here.

Chapter 56

Two days later, Aaron had made his decision. He called Rachel, who was home from the hospital.

"How are you recovering?" Aaron said.

"I feel fine, just a little weak still."

"I've made a decision. I have to get out of here."

Rachel was quiet.

"Since I moved here, I've been shot at and almost killed with a machete, and I even lost my mind for a while. Then you almost died because of me, and that was the last straw. This place isn't good for me."

"You must do what you think is right," Rachel said.

"It's not about being right or not. I just don't want to die. I'm not a match for Race Taggett. You understand that, don't you?"

"I understand that many people would react the same way."

"Please come with me, or join me later."

Rachel paused. "No. I can't do that. My place is here. This is where I belong."

"But I want to be with you."

"I know."

Aaron sighed. "All right, but I'm coming back for you. I'll call you later."

That afternoon, Aaron left a voicemail message for Stella that he wouldn't be in to his clinic the next day and that he'd call her later with an update. After boarding his dog, Red, at a pet hotel, Aaron fled from East Texas in his packed car, heading in the general direction of Connecticut. In the rearview mirror, he saw the Piney Woods recede and then disappear.

"Goodbye, Big Thicket, and good riddance."

He left the radio off, as his mind was preoccupied.

I'm doing the right thing. I'm okay. Even Rachel said this may be something I should do. Isn't that what she said?

He shook his head. *She didn't sound exactly excited for me. Maybe that's because she'll miss me?*

After sunset, when the Big Thicket was far behind him, Aaron pulled into a roadside motel somewhere in the Midwest. His head was in a fog from recent sleepless nights as he jogged through a misty rain to the lobby door,

"Are you checking in for the night?" the registration clerk said.

"Yes, one night."

The clerk studied Aaron as she typed on her computer screen. She leaned over the counter toward him.

"Can I ask you a question?"

Aaron glanced up. "Sure."

"What are you running from?"

Aaron's eyes flew open. *Wow, I've heard that question before. It must be obvious.*

He coughed into his hand. "A bad situation."

"In my years here, I've seen many a person running from something."

"I'll bet you have."

"Do you want to know what I've learned?"

Aaron cocked his head. *What if I said no?*

"Sometimes it's for the best. Most of the time it's not."

Aaron checked into his room and fell onto the bed. He lay there for hours, staring at the ceiling. Faces of people he'd met in East Texas floated across his vision.

He sat up and placed his hands over his ears. *But I can't go up against Race. There's no way I could win.*

His thoughts kept coming back to Buck Bogarty, dying in the fire to save a life, and Rocky Donnigan, shielding Preston Benningham from a hail of bullets.

After staring at his reflection in the bathroom mirror for a while, his legs wobbled, his head started to spin, and he fainted onto the floor.

Aaron opened his eyes to the morning housekeeper shaking his body. "Sir, are you okay?"

He raised his head from a pool of clotted blood that spread over most of the tile floor in front of the toilet.

"I need to get you to the hospital," she said.

Aaron stood and looked around the bathroom and felt his pulse. "No, I think I'm all right." In the mirror, he saw the scar on his jaw oozing blood and pressed his hand against it. "I must've passed out and hit my face on the toilet. At least, the bleeding has slowed."

"Don't worry about the blood. I'll clean everything up. Stay here, and I'll bring you a bandage."

Aaron changed into clean clothes, and the housekeeper returned in several minutes with a first aid kit and bandaged his jaw wound.

"You might need to see a doctor. I can call the ambulance for you, no problem," she said.

Aaron studied the look of concern in her eyes. He smiled and shook his head. "That won't be necessary. It's not an emergency. You see, I'm a doctor. I know it looks like a lot of blood, but the bleeding has stopped and I feel all right. I'll drink a lot of liquids today."

She led him to the bed. "Well, you rest here while I clean up the room."

Aaron watched as she mopped and wiped down the bathroom. She brought him water and checked on him at intervals.

When she was done, she gathered her supplies and stopped in front of him. "I don't know what happened to you last night, but if you're in trouble, I pray you'll be okay."

Aaron nodded. "Thanks for helping me. You didn't panic or wimp out or run away. You did the right thing, didn't you? You did what needed to be done."

She smiled. "I always try to." She stepped toward the door and then turned back to him. "You take care. If you need anything, call the front desk and ask for me, Hazel." She pointed to her nametag.

After the housekeeper left, Aaron paced around the room for a while and then sat down on the edge of the bed. He mumbled and groaned and rocked his body.

As time passed, he nodded or shook his head at intervals. Then his body became still, his head bowed.

Aaron slapped his thighs and walked to the bathroom mirror. *All right. Running away won't help. It would just make everything worse, for me, for my life, maybe even for Rachel.*

He sighed. *Besides, my enemies always seem to find me anyway.*

Aaron stared at the man in the mirror. "I know what I have to do."

Chapter 57

Later that afternoon, Aaron arrived early to Buck Bogarty's funeral.

He surveyed the crowd and chose a spot on a pew toward the back of the church sanctuary. So many people showed up, the church had standing room only, and some folks couldn't get in through the entrance doors. As Aaron had expected, the service was moving and many people cried.

At the end of the service, Aaron bowed his head and tightened his jaw. *I'll be strong like you, Buck Bogarty.*

As he filed out with the crowd, someone tapped his shoulder from behind.

"Were you in a fight?" It was Grant Belkin.

Aaron touched his jaw bandage. "Oh, no. Just a minor accident."

Grant walked with him along a short stretch of the sidewalk. He touched Aaron's arm again and they stopped.

"There's somethin' different about you, Doc."

Aaron nodded. "I hope so."

"Well, I sure wouldn't want to get into a battle with you." Grant smiled and walked away.

Daniel walked past Aaron, staring at the ground.

"Daniel," Aaron said as he caught up with him. "This has got to be hard on you."

Daniel stopped and looked at Aaron. His eyes were reddened. "It's just not fair. So much isn't fair.

"You can carry on for him."

Daniel put his hands into his pockets. "Do you believe in God?"

"Sure, I do. That's the only way things make sense to me."

Daniel threw out his hands in front of him. "What about any of this makes sense?"

Aaron sighed. "I don't pretend to have the answers." He leaned toward Daniel. "But I do know this: you've got to carry on for Buck, to honor his memory."

Daniel gazed up at the sky. As people filed past them, the two men stood side by side.

After several minutes, Daniel turned to Aaron and straightened his back. "You're right, sir, and I will."

Aaron thought of the oath Daniel had sworn with his boyhood friends. "Remember: 'Follow your dreams and live with courage, so you can die with dignity.' "

Daniel saluted.

Aaron smiled at him. *Daniel will follow his dreams with courage, all right. I don't think PTSD will hold him back.*

He watched Daniel walk away. "I want to honor Buck's memory, too," Aaron said under his breath.

That evening, Aaron knocked on Rachel's door. He'd decided to pay her a surprise visit.

His heart raced as heard her dogs barking. *I hope she doesn't boot me out of here.*

Rachel opened the door and her jaw dropped. "Aaron."

He took a deep breath. "Will you have me back?"

She smiled, her dimples deepening. "Come on in." She closed the door after him. "You're hurt. Are you all right?"

He swelled his chest. "Never been better."

"How did you get injured?"

"I had a fall. I think it knocked some sense into me."

She grabbed his arm. "I'm glad you're back. I like that look in your eyes."

"There's something I have to do."

"I know." She leaned closer to him. "We'll both be ready."

"Remember, he wants me, not you, but we have to wait it out." Aaron sighed. "Race Taggett is playing games with me."

"We'll just live like normal until it's time."

Aaron looked down. "I might not live through it."

Rachel shook his arm. "Don't think about that. I can tell; you're stronger now."

Aaron nodded. "I feel that way, but I'll need some help, from deep inside me, and from outside me, too."

Rachel hugged him. "I have faith in you and your outside help. And anyway, there's still hope that the Texas Rangers will get him first."

"I'm not holding my breath."

Chapter 58

Stella's voice was hoarse and her eyes wide open.

It was early afternoon the next day and several patients waited in the exam rooms. Stella fanned her face with a clipboard and signaled to Aaron in the hallway. She leaned toward him and whispered in his ear.

"There's a guy at the registration desk. He's never been here before. I think he wants drugs."

Aaron's face tightened. "What's his complaint?"

"Back pain."

"Go ahead and bring him to a room after he's registered."

Aaron walked back to his office. He took several slow deep breaths. *Keep calm. Stay in control.*

Several minutes later, Aaron opened the door to a patient room and saw a man pacing and grimacing. He wore a rumpled white dress shirt with a red tie, and his hand was flat on his hunched lower back.

"How can I help you, sir?" Aaron said with a husky voice.

"My back is killing me, since this morning. My lumbar herniated disk has been flaring up recently." Some of the man's words were slurred, and he didn't look at Aaron.

"Did you take anything for it?"

"Not yet. When it gets this bad, the only thing that works is Percocet, ten milligrams. I'm out of it." He moaned and rubbed his back. "I need at least thirty Percocets, but if you can give me sixty, I'd really appreciate it."

Stella knocked and opened the door. "Can I come in?"

Aaron turned to her. "Are you sure?"

She nodded, and Aaron motioned her to enter the room. She closed the door and stood just inside.

Aaron examined the patient and noticed that his pupils were small.

He stepped away from the patient and close to Stella. Aaron's eyes were wide and his lower lip quivered.

She leaned close to his ear. "It's okay. We can do this," she said.

Aaron took a deep breath. "We'd better leave the door open," he whispered to her.

"Good idea."

"Can you please help me, Doc?" the man said.

Aaron turned to the moaning patient. "Sir."

He looked up at Aaron with glassy eyes.

"Sir, I understand that you're in pain. But, I also believe that you might have a problem using Percocet. I cannot support your need for Percocet."

The man's moaning stopped and he raised his voice. "You won't help me? You're a doctor, and I need help."

"I can give you a shot of an anti-inflammatory medicine and prescribe a muscle relaxant."

"No, no." His face flushed and he straightened up and put his hands on his hips. "Listen to me. I've already told you, only Percocet works," he said through taut lips.

Aaron could feel his chest wall vibrate with his pounding heart. He heard a buzzing in his ears and his head began to spin. Aaron backed out into the hall. The man—his shoulders squared—followed him.

Aaron talked to himself. *You're doing the right thing. Keep your mind focused.*

He stopped in the middle of the hall and Stella, with clenched fists, walked to his side. Standing tall in his boots, Aaron's vision cleared and he looked the man straight in the eyes. "I will not prescribe Percocet for you. I can try to help you in other ways."

Pointing a finger at Aaron, the man's lips sputtered. "I'm going to tell everyone what a rip-off this place is. You're not doing your job. Pain is a vital sign, and I'm in pain."

He's been searching on the internet, Aaron thought.

He moved closer to Aaron. "Can't you see I'm suffering? It's your duty to help me."

Aaron felt Stella's quivering shoulder against his arm.

"Let's try physical therapy, or I can refer you to a pain management specialist," Aaron said, emphasizing each word.

"No, you're not paying attention to what I'm saying," the man said, raising his hands in front of him.

Aaron shook his head. "No Percocet, sir."

The man closed in to about three inches from Aaron's face. Aaron saw a flash of teeth behind snarling lips and smelled musty breath.

Aaron stared into the man's eyes. He focused on one of the pupils and imagined he could see all the way back to the retina. He visualized how the optic disk and retinal blood vessels might appear.

Just when the air was as stale as Aaron could stand, the man slapped his hands down against his hips and stomped away. "I'm never coming back to this place."

He spoke at several patients in the waiting room. "You won't get any help here. I'm going to shut this place down." He slammed the front door on his way out.

Aaron took a deep breath and turned to Stella.

"You did real well, Doc," Stella said.

He put his hand on Stella's shoulder. "So did you. You look surprisingly calm."

"I kept talking to myself, to keep my mind focused," she said.

"That's what I did, too, and neither one of us lost our heads."

"I'm learning how to handle myself around addicts. I repeated in my mind that they need understanding and forgiveness, just like everyone else. I'm not all the way there yet, but right now I feel better about myself."

"I feel better, too. You think we've been exorcised?"

Stella laughed. "I like that idea. So, now there are two fewer demons in this town."

Chapter 59

Two days after Buck Bogarty's funeral, Aaron and Rachel sat for an early dinner at one of their favorite Tex-Mex restaurants.

Before ordering chicken fajitas for two, they lingered for a while over drinks. Aaron motioned to the server for another margarita.

He looked at Rachel. "How's the bald eagle doing?"

"He's growing and acting well. He should be ready for release soon, back to his home in the Big Thicket."

"You certainly have a knack with animals."

"Well, I haven't lost one in a while."

"If you did, I'll bet the poor creature was too far gone to begin with. By the way, I've been reading a book and studying online about animal rehab."

"Wonderful. Do you want to get into the field?"

"No, I just want to be able to help you if you ever need me to." Aaron sighed. "And I'm trying to occupy my mind with something fun."

Rachel leaned toward him. "I know what you're thinking about."

"I'm ready for whatever comes."

She touched his hand. "I'm worried sick about you. I can't sleep thinking about Race Taggett, so I know it's got to be tough for you."

Aaron grabbed her hand. "I've felt a change in me. Before I lost my head and bolted, I was afraid. Now, it's something different, but it's not fear."

"I guess that's good."

"I've never felt this way before. I think it must be what Daniel, a patient of mine, felt before he charged into a dangerous situation with his Army buddies. Or, what Constable Greevy feels sometimes when he walks into the unknown with his gun drawn. It's my fate, it's something I must do, and I'll give it my all when it happens."

"I know you will, and I'll be rooting for you."

Aaron took a deep breath. "You see, I understand Race Taggett now. I know the pain in his eyes, the pain of his childhood and school years. I know where he came from. I think that understanding will help me when I'm against him. I'll trust my instincts to guide me through it."

Rachel shuddered. "What do you think he'll do?"

Aaron sipped his margarita. "I don't know, but whatever he does, it'll be a surprise."

He turned as a sizzling plate covered with steaming chicken for their fajitas appeared on the table.

After dinner, they walked out into the night air and across a quiet parking lot. Their shoes crunched across the gravelly surface.

"What's that song you're humming?" Rachel said.

Aaron squeezed her hand. " 'If You're Going Through Hell.' "

"I know that one, by Rodney Atkins."

"Somehow it seems appropriate."

Rachel shook her head. "Since I met you, I feel like my life has turned into a wild adventure movie." She stopped and hugged him. "I sure want you around me when times are tough. And I know my hero will save the day again."

Aaron swelled his chest. "I'll admit, I am rather proud of myself."

"You have every right to be."

Chapter 60

"You look stressed," Rachel said.

Three days later, on a Saturday in early October, Aaron and Rachel sat for breakfast in a diner at the edge of the Big Thicket.

Aaron had beads of sweat on his forehead. "I had a horrible nightmare last night; it was so real."

"Can you tell me about it?"

He took a deep breath. "I saw images of faces, many different ones, in front of me as I walked through a forest. They would dart out from behind trees and laugh at me. I recognized several of them as people I once knew, like the medical chief of staff at my old hospital, and another was one of my medical school professors."

"I take it these were unpleasant people?"

"They were people that I disliked, for sure. I was afraid and kept trying to run away but I would trip and fall. I couldn't get away."

"That would make it a nightmare all right. I sure get a creepy feeling when I think of some people from my past."

"The last person I saw before I woke up was Race Taggett."

Rachel shook her head. "I don't think anyone can rest easy around here until he's dealt with, once and for all."

They polished off their eggs and potatoes, walked out of the diner, and stepped into the car. Just after Aaron fired up the engine, Rachel screamed and Aaron jumped, hitting his head on the roof.

A man's face was outside Rachel's window, and he pointed a handgun at her. "Get out of the car," he said. "You'll pay for what you did to me."

Aaron jammed the car in reverse and floored the accelerator. He heard pops and Rachel ducked as her window shattered. They squealed backward and Aaron maneuvered the car at full speed away from the shooter and back onto the road in front of the diner.

"That guy is shooting at us," Aaron said. "Are you all right?"

Rachel checked her chest and arms. "I think so."

"Is that your ex-fiance?"

"It must be." Rachel was breathing fast.

After a few minutes, Aaron clenched the steering wheel. "I believe a car is following us."

Rachel whipped her head around. "It's probably him." She grabbed her phone and began to dial 911.

"I could be wrong, but he may be waiting for the right time and place to catch up with us." He glanced at the rearview mirror. "He's closing in fast."

Rachel's voice shook as she described to the dispatcher their current location a few miles east of the Big Thicket and heading south.

Aaron sped along a slight curve in the road. "He's going to pass us." Aaron caught a glimpse of another fast-moving vehicle, a white pickup truck, behind the car chasing him.

A car pulled up alongside Aaron, and the driver pointed a gun at him. Aaron ducked as his driver-side window shattered.

Rachel screamed and Aaron jerked the steering wheel to the right and veered off the road. Plumes of grass and dirt shot up on both sides of the car as Aaron and Rachel bounced in their seats across a narrow strip of land.

Aaron spotted an opening in the trees in front of him. "Maybe some shelter will help."

He managed to steer the car and stop without smashing into a tree.

"Are you all right?" Aaron said.

She slowed her breathing, her hand over her chest. "I think so." She managed a weak smile. "I'm sure glad I had my seat belt on."

"Then the shot missed both of us, thank goodness."

Aaron and Rachel looked back and saw a man leave his car and walk toward them. He appeared to have a gun in his right hand.

"It doesn't look like Mick, but it must be him," Rachel said. She turned to Aaron, her hands on her temples. "What do we do?"

"He's on foot, and we're still in the car." Aaron put the car in reverse and gunned the accelerator. "Get down."

As he backed out, he heard several pops and his rear window shattered.

Aaron slammed the brakes and glanced back over the top of his seat. A scowling man approached Aaron's car from the side with his gun hand extended, but someone else was near the trees, and a white pickup truck sat behind the pursuer's car.

Aaron and Rachel watched a man close in behind the gunman, toss a rope over him, and yank it back. The gunman's eyes flew open and he yelped as the rope tightened around his abdomen and arms, jerking him off his feet and slamming him down on his back. His handgun tumbled away along the ground.

Aaron pointed. "Somebody lassoed him, just like in the movies." He and Rachel jumped out of the car, brushed shattered glass off their clothes, and ran up to the two men. Rachel covered her ears as the man on the ground yelled obscenities and strained in vain, his arms secured at his side with rope.

His long, dirty blond hair flapping, the second man whipped more rope around his quarry's ankles.

Aaron grinned and raised his hands out in front of him. "Cam Fillmore. It's you. You look different without your guitar."

Cam straightened from his crouch and turned to Aaron. "I couldn't very well throw a lasso with a guitar around my neck."

"I believe that, but I can't believe you're here. You saw my car?"

"Remember, I was watching out for you. My beam blockers warned me today about something bad."

"That's right. Someone is looking for you."

"It wasn't my enemies. They haven't found me yet. I haven't felt their radiation beams."

"So something else worried you today?"

Cam stared down at the man on the ground. "I saw him driving around yesterday. Today, he looked different, and my beam blockers were jiggling like crazy. I figured he had on a disguise."

Cam bent down and ripped a mustache and beard off the man, who screamed more obscenities.

"It's Mick all right," Rachel said.

Cam stood and held up the disguise. "I suspected he was up to no good, and I was right." He looked at Aaron. "I saw him following you."

"Where did you learn to lasso like that?" Rachel said.

"I grew up on a ranch in Montana. I've been good with a lasso since I was a kid. I was one of the best at roping calves."

"It looks like you haven't lost your touch," Aaron said.

Cam smiled. "It sure paid off, didn't it?"

Aaron patted Cam on the shoulder. "Thanks for saving our lives."

Mick yelled more obscenities and scooted on his back a few feet away from them.

Everyone turned as a police car with flashing lights left the road and approached them. Aaron waved the car over.

Aaron leaned toward Cam. "Don't worry. They're not after you. They want him." Aaron pointed to Mick.

"Oh, I know the cops around here aren't out to get me. That's why people can hide here. The cops don't bother you, unless you do something wrong."

A police officer walked up to the group and nodded at Cam.

"Officer, I bagged a varmint for you," Cam said, and then he motioned with his hand. "His gun's on the ground over there."

Aaron and Rachel gave their report, and Cam answered a few questions from the officer.

Rachel whispered to Aaron. "Is that man schizophrenic?"

"Yes, but at least he seems functional on his medication."

Rachel chuckled. "I'm glad he likes you."

"I'm glad, too. I wouldn't want him to lasso me."

After getting the information he needed from the group, the officer, with Cam's help, released the lasso, untied Mick's ankles, and helped him to his feet. Mick put up no resistance as the officer snapped on handcuffs.

Mick scowled at Rachel. "I'll get you. You can count on it." He looked at Aaron. "She squealed on me and got paid for it."

"Come on," the officer said and escorted Mick toward the patrol car. "You have the right to remain silent . . ."

Rachel hugged Aaron and sighed. "It's back to jail for him."

"This time, for good, I hope." Aaron watched as the police car drove off. "He doesn't seem to have any remorse for what he did."

"I heard him mumble once that 'taking back from the government is not really a crime,' " Rachel said.

Cam waved at them and drove away in his truck.

"I wish people would stop trying to kill me," Rachel said. "My hair will turn white."

Aaron felt his pulse. "It's slowing down. Good. You and I have cheated death once again."

"Maybe practice will pay off."

"I hope so. I've got one more test."

"Race."

Aaron walked away a few steps and faced the forest. Cupping his hands to his mouth, he yelled, the words echoing in the trees.

"Race Taggett, where the hell are you?"

Aaron and Rachel returned to the Volvo and swept glass fragments off the seats. Aaron started the engine and headed back to the road.

"What did Mick mean about you squealing on him?" Aaron said.

"That man had me fooled. He was such a handsome gentleman when I first met him. After a while, his true nature came out."

"He was stealing from Medicare, right? Overcharging and getting away with it?"

"Yes, and he was successful at it for a long time. I thought something was not right about all the money he was making, and I asked him once if he have some wealthy patients on the side. He went ballistic and became vicious toward me, and that just made me even more suspicious. He turned into a totally different person, but he didn't scare me away, and I didn't give up. I kept digging and got proof."

"Then you turned him in and got a reward?"

"I reported his crime, and for that, I received a nice reward."

Aaron was quiet for most of the drive back. As he pulled into Rachel's driveway, she turned to him.

"Do you think less of me for what I did?"

Aaron turned off the ignition and met her gaze.

Her eyes were wide. "You hesitated." She turned away.

359

"No, wait a minute. I've just never met anyone that did that," Aaron said.

"You make it sound like . . . like it's dirty or something."

"I'm sorry, I—"

Rachel jumped out of the car and ran to her front door.

Chapter 61

Aaron screeched to a stop in his garage and slammed his fists against the steering wheel. "Aaron, you're a damn idiot."

He called Rachel's number and left a message on her voicemail: "I'm sorry. I didn't mean it. Can I see you again soon?"

He called her three times the next day and three times the day after, leaving voicemails along the way.

Two evenings later after work, he drove to her house in his refurbished Volvo. His last voicemail: "Rachel, I'll be at your house in a few minutes. Please let me in. I have a surprise for you."

Aaron's hand shook as he rang the front doorbell. His other hand held something behind his back.

Rachel cracked the door open. The usual smile was missing from her face.

"Can I come in?" Aaron said.

She crossed her arms and walked away into the front room. Her dogs were quiet.

"I have something, a gift." He thrust out a small wrapped package. Rachel hesitated, then took it to the kitchen table and unwrapped a small black box.

She opened the lid of the box, and her face brightened. "A diamond necklace." She walked to a mirror in the next room and draped the necklace around her neck. Aaron clasped it in the back for her.

"I've thought a lot about this," Aaron said. "What you did took courage."

Rachel snorted and put her hands on her hips.

"The reason I say that is because of your motive. You didn't do it for the money. It's clear to me that you had a noble purpose."

She turned to him, her eyes moist.

"You can be proud," Aaron said. "I'm proud of you."

Rachel embraced him and sobbed on his shoulder. "Thank you."

****

Grant Belkin sat at his kitchen table. One dim light bulb illuminated Grant's figure. He smiled at the empty chair opposite. "You're goin' to need a bigger brush for all that pretty white hair."

He sipped from a glass of water, and propped his face in his hands. "Yes, I am a little worried. The Doc has one final battle."

He nodded. "Right. A whopper of a battle. We've got to support him any way we can."

362

Chapter 62

On his way home from work the next day, Aaron fantasized about pinning Race Taggett in a wrestling match. Just as he had Race immobilized on the mat and down for the count, he slipped into the garage and stepped out of his car.

"No," he shouted as he was knocked to the floor, his breath wheezing out through his nose and mouth. By the time he managed to gasp and inhale twice, his wrists and ankles had been bound with rope.

"Hello, Doc. It's time."

Race hoisted Aaron over his shoulder face down and jogged out of the garage and down the street.

It's happening, Aaron thought.

Soon, Aaron spotted tree trunks whizzing by and he sensed the familiar pine-needle smell of the Big Thicket. At times, he heard birds screeching and small animals bolting away. He strained and twisted his wrists, but the binding wouldn't budge.

It seemed like an hour passed before Race sloshed through another marshy area and then stopped. Aaron's abdomen was sore from bouncing on Race's shoulder.

"Here we are," Race said. He stood Aaron upright. They were at the edge of a large round clearing in the trees. "Welcome to my happy place. You're the only person alive who's seen it."

Two structures stood in the clearing: a log cabin at the perimeter, and in the middle a crisscrossed pile of logs with a horizontal platform at the top. Wind gusts howled in the trees.

Race carried Aaron across the clearing and plopped him down on a wooden chair in the middle of the one-roomed cabin. Two other chairs stood at opposite ends of the room facing Aaron. A skeleton, roped upright, sat in each chair.

Race pointed to the chairs. "Meet my teachers. Before you, they were the only people that were almost as good as me."

So, that's what happened to those two schoolteachers that Preston Benningham told me about. The ones that disappeared shortly after Race left school.

Race nodded. "They're here with me always. They keep me strong."

Aaron studied the skeletons. Each was crowned with a ring of pine needles. Their bones were clean and bright white.

"Kind of like Olympic winners from a long time ago, don't you think?"

Race strolled in a circle around Aaron's chair, then he stopped and leaned toward Aaron's face. "And you'll soon join them." He straightened up and took a deep breath. "I need you here with them, so I can breathe in your strength, too."

Aaron's heart skipped a beat and his chest tightened. *Stay calm. Don't lose it.*

Race strutted to a small desk and opened a drawer. He pulled out a rope and tied Aaron's chest and arms snug to the chair. From the drawer, he raised something else up in his hand. Aaron saw the glint from a huge butcher knife.

Race admired the knife for a few seconds, then his body stiffened and he ran to the cabin door.

I didn't hear anything, Aaron thought.

After Race passed through the door into the clearing, Aaron's body tensed as he glimpsed the silhouettes of two tall figures in the trees. One of them had long, flowing hair.

Is somebody out there? Maybe with the Texas Rangers?

Aaron squinted and searched the trees. The figures were gone.

At times, he heard Race's feet crunching in the underbrush of the forest. After a short while, Race's frowning face appeared at the door. "No one knows about my secret place," he mumbled.

Race stepped inside and grinned at Aaron. "Back to business." He whipped Aaron's chair around to face the rear wall of the room, directly opposite the doorway. He walked over to a crown of pine needles on the floor near the wall. "This will be your special spot, a place of honor in my castle."

Race licked his lips and held the knife high, twisting it, admiring it. "Now, it's time."

Aaron saw the knife closing in until he felt its sharp cold edge against his neck. Then Race bent down so that his eyes were only inches away from Aaron's face.

"Look at me. Look into my eyes," Race said.

I've got to keep my head. It's the only chance I have. Aaron stared through Race's pupil and into the blackness of his eye. He imagined his own vision to be a searing laser beam that could penetrate the deepest recesses of Race's eyes, a beam that could not be extinguished.

Race growled, "You belong here, with me. It's time for you to die."

Aaron stared into the blackness. His body relaxed. *Like a tiger with its prey, Race wants to feed on my fear.*

"Are you ready to die? How about if I cut off your head?"

Sorry, Race. There's no fear in here. Aaron took a deep breath. "If it's my fate, then so be it," Aaron said.

Race threw his head back and laughed. "It's your fate, all right. I'll kill you and burn you on my funeral pyre, then I'll polish your bones spic and span."

An unexpected surge of warmth swelled Aaron's chest.

Race closed in again and their noses almost touched. Aaron narrowed his laser beam vision to burn deeper into the void of Race's eyes.

"If it's my God-given fate, then so be it," Aaron said.

Race's face contorted and his voice echoed around the room. "So, what if it is your God-given fate? All people are cowards compared to me." His nose smashed against Aaron's. "I want to smell your fear. Give it to me."

Aaron didn't blink or vary his probing stare. He imagined how Race's retinas would appear, with their pulsating blood vessels.

"Show me your fear," Race shouted. His face was bright red and swollen, and his breath was hot against Aaron's face and smelled of rotten meat. "I want to taste it."

Aaron didn't flinch, even though the foul, pungent air scorched his face and nose and mouth. He searched inside Race's eyes for a spark of light, a flicker of hope.

Race screamed. "Show me. Show me." His piercing shrieks vibrated Aaron's body.

Aaron took slow, regular breaths and remained still and focused. He spotted a glimmer in Race's eye, like a distant star in the blackness of space.

Race's voice became raspy and his screams weakened, and after one minute or so, Aaron heard a faint moan. Race backed away and began to sob. He fell to his knees and jammed the knife into the dirt floor.

Race sat cross-legged on the floor and wailed. Aaron heard a coyote howling from somewhere in the Big Thicket. Shadows deepened in the room as sunset approached.

Race became quiet and lay back on the floor, staring at the ceiling. Aaron noticed healing wounds on Race's arms and legs.

"Race," Aaron said.

He looked up at Aaron.

"You don't have to do this anymore."

Race leaped up and ran out into the clearing. Aaron managed to twist his body and head around enough to see out the door.

Race shouted at the sky and then dropped to his knees and sobbed, holding his hands out to the trees, rocking back and forth.

It was dark when Race crawled back into the cabin. He kneeled down in front of Aaron.

"What do you want me to do?"

"Come with me. I'll try to help you."

Race gave a slight nod.

"Good. Is the killing over?"

He sighed. "I'm tired."

"Just trust me. Don't fight me."

Aaron stared into Race's pupils. *A life of pain, constant pain*, Aaron thought, then he saw the tiny spark.

Race untied Aaron, and they walked together across the clearing. Race stumbled into the trees and along a dirt path. As Aaron followed, he heard no sound from the Big Thicket.

"Why did you rescue me from the man with the machete?"

Race slowed and dropped his head. "Killing you was for me, not him. It wasn't your time yet."

Aaron pulled out his cell phone. "I'm calling EMS and the police."

Race stopped.

"Remember, you can trust me," Aaron said.

Race sighed and walked ahead.

Aaron noticed that Race struggled to walk in the Big Thicket, and when they approached the back yard of the old Taggett house, Race collapsed onto his knees.

"Let me help you." Aaron hoisted Race across his forearms and marched toward the police officers and Texas Rangers who stood in a semicircle in the yard, their guns drawn and pointed.

"It's okay," Aaron said.

The officers lowered their firearms.

Race's voice broke. "Nobody's ever carried me before."

"Listen to me," Aaron said. "There's always hope, no matter where your life is. Never forget that."

A weak smile appeared on Race's face.

"I'll be checking on you," Aaron said, as he walked toward the red and white flashing lights of a waiting ambulance.

Race gave a slight nod, his eyelids fluttered, and he passed out.

Aaron took a deep breath. *You're right, Race. It isn't my time yet.*

Chapter 63

Word spread around town the next day about Aaron's amazing feat of delivering Race Taggett out of hiding. Congratulatory phone calls and messages and emails poured in. Rachel treated him to a delicious dinner of rainbow trout and stewed okra.

Later that night, Aaron stretched out in bed and thought about his recent adventures. His eyes went to the painting on the wall, and after several minutes, he sat bolt upright.

That's strange. I can't make out the people in the trees anymore.

He walked over to the painting and studied it. His eyes widened. *They've disappeared. Maybe they were hallucinations, too?* His eyes wandered over the trees and sky and winding trail. *I'd like to follow a real trail like that one, in the Big Thicket.*

That night, he slept better than he had in months.

Near noon the day after, Stella and Aaron stood talking in the clinic hallway. She suddenly froze, looking past his shoulder.

Aaron wheeled around. A man in a white shirt walked toward them.

I recognize him, Aaron thought.

"Do you remember me?" the man said. "You wouldn't give me Percocet a couple of weeks ago."

Oh, crap. What now? Aaron clenched his fists. Stella moved next to him.

He stopped in front of Aaron. "I want to thank you." He extended his hand.

Aaron hesitated and then shook hands with him. "Thank me?" *Is this a joke?*

"You told me I might have a problem and that you could help me in other ways. I remember your eyes. I could tell you really meant what you said." He looked down and put his hands in his pockets. "I talked with my wife. It turns out she's been worried about me. I even think my marriage was in trouble. I didn't realize how far gone I was."

He sighed and looked up at Aaron. "I'm trying to turn myself around. I'm in a drug withdrawal program, and I'm getting counseling."

Aaron smiled. "That's terrific."

"I'm going to stick with this program, for the sake of my marriage, and my life."

"You're doing the right thing."

"Thanks again for seeing me for how I really was." He nodded at Aaron, then turned and walked away.

Stella touched Aaron's shoulder. "From the look in his eyes, I think he just might make it."

Aaron took a deep breath and grinned at Stella. "We did good."

"Yes, we did."

"The last time we saw him in the clinic, you mentioned forgiveness. Do you still think about Brad and your son's death?"

"Not really. At least, it's not painful anymore. I'm just glad he and Preston are doing well."

"Preston is still working and off drugs?"

"That's what Myra tells me. She looks happy, and she says father and son are getting to know each other again."

"You talk with Myra? That's good."

Stella smiled. "We have brunch together after church most Sundays."

Later in the afternoon, Aaron spotted someone sitting in a hallway chair.

"Hi, Tucker." *My Cajun bipolar soothsayer.*

Tucker Boudreaux stood and waved as Aaron approached him. "I had a thought about you yesterday, Doc."

"I'm all ears."

"I saw you walking in your yard. You were older. You're going to live in that house for a long time."

Aaron grinned and put his hand on Tucker's shoulder. "I'm glad to hear that."

"But I'm confused about something."

"What's that?"

"I saw you standing by a bunch of cows. Do you have any cattle?"

Aaron lurched back laughing. "No, they're not my cattle. They've been grazing behind my house."

"I've been wracking my brain to figure it out. Why would I have a vision of you with cows?"

Aaron took a deep breath. "Let me put it this way. They're unusual cattle, and those cows and their owner have been an important part of my life recently."

Tucker clapped his hands. "Well then, that explains it. *Merci beaucoup*. Thanks."

"You were right about Rachel. Someone did try to hurt her, and I appreciate your warning me about that. Feel free to let me know your thoughts and visions anytime."

"I will. It makes me feel better to talk about them."

"I imagine your visions are usually accurate?"

Tucker raised his hand. "No, not usually accurate. I'm always accurate. I don't think I've ever been wrong."

Aaron smiled as Tucker strutted out of the clinic.

After work, Aaron pulled into Rachel's driveway in his new candy-apple red 1948 Ford F-1 pickup truck. He escorted her to the truck and spread his arms.

"What do you think? I just picked it up," Aaron said.

"It's old."

"Sure, it is. It's a classic. The one I told you about."

He had a broad smile on his face as they puttered away.

"Where are we going?" she said.

"Let's decide on dinner later. I want to make another stop first."

"You sound mighty mysterious. Is this a surprise?"

"I need to find out something about myself."

Aaron drove for a while along Big Thicket roads and stopped in front of the entrance sign to Ghost Road.

Rachel leaned forward. "Would you believe it? I've never been here before."

"I have once, and it scared the bejeebers out of me." He recounted to Rachel the stories of decapitated ghosts and strange wandering lights along the road.

Aaron turned onto the road and crept along until he reached the halfway point.

"Let's get out." They were alone on the road.

Rachel shivered. "Are you sure about this? Should we even be here in the dark?"

He touched her shoulder. "We can do this. For me now, I feel like it's kind of a rite of passage. That's why I came."

They stepped out onto the road and crept along the grassy shoulder hand in hand. Aaron strained his ears. "The Big Thicket is quiet tonight."

"It smells kind of nice out here, like fresh pine needles," Rachel said.

Aaron smiled at her. "You've stopped shivering. Good."

"It's warm and comfortable."

Aaron stopped. "Do you believe in angels?"

Rachel cocked her head. "I guess so. Why do you ask?"

"I may never know for sure, but since I moved here, I feel like I've been helped by angels. Is that just my crazy brain acting up again?"

Rachel squeezed his hand. "You're not crazy, and I believe you have been helped. We all need help sometimes."

Aaron laughed and lifted a hand to the sky. "Well, in that case, bring on the angels." Images of Marley Brighton and Grant Belkin floated across his vision.

He peered into Rachel's eyes. "You're not a real angel, are you?"

"What if I was?"

"I know. You probably wouldn't tell me if you were, but how about if I keep thinking you're an angel?"

She hugged him. "I'd like that. I'll try to live up to it."

They strolled for about an hour up and down both sides of the road.

As they approached Aaron's truck, a soothing breeze ruffled their hair.

Aaron stopped. "I haven't seen any freaky visions, and the air out here feels really good in my lungs." He smiled at Rachel. "I think we're accepted."

"What do you mean? Who's accepting us?"

"The Big Thicket." Aaron cupped his hands around his mouth. "Thank you, Big Thicket," he yelled. He ran in circles around his truck, pumping his arms in the air.

Rachel laughed. "I've never seen anybody so ecstatic about a bunch of trees."

Aaron stopped and put his hands on her shoulders.

"It's more than that. I know for sure now. This is my home."

An hour later, Aaron and Rachel sat in their favorite Tex-Mex restaurant, munching on burritos and guacamole.

"You don't like my truck much, do you?" Aaron said. "It's okay if you don't."

She touched his hand. "I'm getting used to it. It reminds me of one of my grandfather's old trucks. I have fond memories of that truck."

"Then I'll keep it for a while."

"Good." She took a sip of her margarita. "What will happen to Race Taggett?"

"He's with his mother, Wanda, in the state psychiatric facility." Aaron smiled. "I don't think he'll hurt anybody else."

"I guess the insanity defense was tailor-made for those two."

Aaron nodded. "I'm sure that will be his defense. Besides, I don't think you could execute that guy anyway. He truly has nine lives."

"At least he's out of our lives now."

"Speaking of the Taggetts, I heard something funny recently. Sid Taggett won a lot of money gambling in Las Vegas, and he told his friends here that Wanda's voodoo charms may have helped him hit the jackpot."

Rachel grinned. "I hear some gamblers keep voodoo dolls with them to bring luck."

"Let's go to New Orleans and check into that," Aaron said.

Rachel snorted. "I'll go to New Orleans with you, but I don't know about the voodoo part."

"All right, no voodoo." Aaron snapped his fingers. "I've been meaning to tell you something. One reason I left Connecticut was that there were some complaints about my clinical competence. Well, I got a letter recently from a doctor friend. I've been exonerated of any wrongdoing at my old hospital."

"I find it hard to believe someone would charge you with that."

Aaron blushed and smiled. "Thanks. Turns out it was all bogus anyway. A doctor lied about me, and she and the asshole chief of staff have been sanctioned."

Rachel slapped the table. "Good."

"And get this. The medical staff wants me to come back to my old job."

Rachel frowned. "Are you considering that?"

"Hell, no. I'd never go back there. Besides, you told me that this is your home." He squeezed her hand. "And I want to be where you are."

Rachel smiled, and her dimples deepened.

A song popped into Aaron's head.

"What are you humming?" Rachel said.

" 'Mayberry,' by Rascal Flatts." He laughed. "I guess it's not exactly the Garden of Eden around here, but with you, my new town seems more like mythical Mayberry now."

After dinner, they stood by his car and embraced for several minutes.

"I want to take something back," Aaron said.

"What?"

"I had it backwards. It's more than Mayberry. You do make this place seem more like the Garden of Eden to me." Aaron stared into her eyes. "I feel like this is the beginning of a wonderful relationship, ours I mean."

"I feel the same way."

She planted her dimples on his lips.

Late the next afternoon, Aaron waved at Marley and Cristal walking their dog along the road. He stopped in his driveway to check his mailbox and wait for them.

"I heard you bought a classic truck," Marley said.

Aaron nodded. "I drove it around town yesterday. Let me show you." He opened the garage door and they walked over to his restored 1948 Ford F-1 truck. "What do you think?"

"It's a beauty."

"It's a bit slow and bouncy, but I like it."

Cristal ran her hand along the side of the truck. "It's smooth. I like red."

Aaron grinned. "Red is my favorite color."

"Dale McCorkindale ordered it for you, didn't he?" Marley said.

"Yes, and to his credit, he got me a good one, for a decent price."

"I think he's going to jail."

Aaron's jaw dropped. "Jail? For what?"

"The police think he was embezzling money from his car business."

Aaron shook his head. "I had a feeling that something fishy was going on with him." *I'll bet he blew all that money on his wild investment schemes.*

"His wife filed for divorce, too."

"Somehow that doesn't surprise me." *She probably found out about his VD and his prostitutes.*

Aaron stepped closer to Marley. "I guess Forrester is moving on with life?"

Marley sighed. "It's a struggle, but he's learning to live with his disability."

"I'm glad to hear that." *You stayed by him, all these years.*

Aaron blushed and held up his hands. "Now, don't laugh at me, but I get this strange impression. Sometimes I think you're an angel. I mean, a real angel. Is that crazy, or what?"

Marley smiled. "What an idea." Her eyes sparkled. "Don't you go spreading that rumor."

Aaron shrugged his shoulders. "No one would believe it anyway."

Marley and Cristal stood facing him, hand in hand.

I'm over her, but I'll never forget her, Aaron thought.

"I wanted you to know. We're moving away," Marley said.

Aaron froze. "What? Why?"

"We'll move close to my parents. They can help me with Forrester and Cristal, and we'll be near a major medical center for Forrester."

"I understand. Can I hug you?" He threw his arms around her in a tight embrace. Cristal hugged his leg.

Marley stepped back. A breeze lifted her hair, and she nodded at him. "You can handle it now. You're in the right place, and you've helped a lot of people in this town. You're a good man, Aaron Rovsing, and a mighty fine doctor."

A warmth surged through his body. *I know that now.*

She put her hand on his shoulder. "I heard you stood your ground with Race. That gave hope to him, and you."

Aaron gazed at the remarkable person before him.

Marley kissed him on the cheek, then she turned and walked with Cristal to the end of the driveway, where she stopped and waved goodbye.

Chapter 64

The next morning, Aaron woke up to cows mooing.

He pulled on some clothes and walked out the back door into the early morning light.

"Mornin'," Grant Belkin said, his voice reverberating around the pasture. He sat on his horse by Aaron's backyard fence and not far from the herd of cattle.

Aaron strolled to the fence, his dog at his side. He raised his voice over the din of the cattle. "Meet my new dog, Red."

"Good-lookin' dog."

Aaron rubbed Red's head. "I think I'm getting used to the Texas heat. I'm not sweating so much."

"It doesn't take long."

Aaron scanned the herd. Many of the cows looked at him and mooed in unison, a bovine choir serenading him.

He turned to Grant. "I've been meaning to ask you about that robbery we had in our neighborhood a few weeks back. Did they hit your house?"

"Nope."

"The dispatcher thought you were the person who called and reported it."

"It was just a lucky guess on my part."

"So, it was you," Aaron said. "You know, you constantly amaze me."

"Now, don't get carried away. I've just been lookin' after the neighborhood."

"Thank goodness."

"You're lookin' good," Grant said. "Finally gettin' enough sleep?"

Aaron smiled. "Now that you mention it, yes. Everything's great with me now." He furrowed his brow at Grant. "How about you? Are you feeling all right?"

"I couldn't be better."

"Someone told me that you'd had a brain tumor."

Grant dismounted his horse and walked up to Aaron. "Ever'one has to walk through the fire, sooner or later."

"You mean, the tumor's gone?"

"You don't have to worry about me."

"That's good to know. Did you get surgery or radiation or chemotherapy?"

"I got what I needed."

"What—"

Grant raised his hand. "It's okay. It's all over."

Aaron sighed. "Well, in that case, I'm glad."

Grant pointed at his cattle. "The whole herd came to visit you this morning."

"They're loud today. Louder than I've ever heard them before," Aaron said.

"Yep. They're all into it. They haven't had much to be happy about lately, until now."

"Why are they so happy now?"

Grant turned to him. "The evil is gone. This is a good place again."

"Ah, yes. I keep thinking of the Garden of Eden."

Grant nodded. "Every Garden of Eden has its serpents."

Aaron studied the cows. They continued to moo at him, a lowing sound.

"I'd swear they're trying to talk to me," Aaron said.

"They are. Maybe they're sayin' that you're where you're supposed to be." He put his hand on Aaron's shoulder and lowered his voice. "You and I are here for a reason."

His eyes are brighter than ever, Aaron thought.

Aaron nodded. "I do feel much better about my move here."

Grant stepped away from the fence and mounted his horse. He turned the horse toward Aaron, and his words boomed out. "You've been good for a lot of folks around here, includin' Race Taggett." His eyes were like searing beams of light. "You showed courage when you were trapped in his hidden world in the Big Thicket."

"Thanks." Aaron cocked his head. *But, how would you know I was trapped? I only told Rachel and Constable Greevy the whole story.*

Grant smiled. "Since you've come, we're all in a better place. There's hope for this town now. So I'm movin' on."

"What do you mean, moving on?" *Everyone is leaving.*

"I could do with a smaller pasture, so I'm takin' my cattle to another ranch."

"Where?"

"Not far from here. Don't worry, I'll never be far away."

Aaron lifted his hand. "Wait. You said I showed courage." He pointed at Grant. "I had some help against Race Taggett, didn't I?"

Grant shook his head. "Nope. We were ready to help, but we didn't have to. It was all you. The courage you needed was right there inside you all along." He took off his hat and tipped it to Aaron. "Adios."

Aaron held his hand up and waved. He squinted as Grant and his horse faded away into the misty dawn.

That was a strange light around his body.

He scratched his cheek.

What did he mean: 'we were ready to help'?

Aaron looked over the treetops to the early morning light. *Geez, why do I get the feeling that some people around here aren't real at all?*

That night, Aaron stood next to his back yard fence before turning in for the evening.

I'll miss those cattle.

He turned toward a fluttering noise. Not six feet away from him, a large owl perched on a fence post.

"So, I finally meet you up close, my guardian owl," Aaron said. "I haven't heard from you in a while."

They stared at each other, unblinking.

Aaron smiled. "I'm okay now."

The owl blinked, spread his wings and flapped away into the trees.

About the Author

Steven Gossington is an emergency room physician (medical school - Baylor College of Medicine; residency - Georgetown University Hospital) with over 30 years of patient care experience. For 11 years, he was an academic professor in emergency medicine at the University of Oklahoma Health Sciences Center in Oklahoma City, and he published 20 book chapters and medical articles of original research. His enjoyment of mystery and suspense fiction and his love of writing led to his first novel *Fractured Eden*, a psychological suspense story in which he draws upon his extensive experience with mentally ill emergency room patients. He can be contacted at www.StevenGossington.com.